BOOK 2:

SHIFTING HORIZONS

BY SJ SHERWOOD

Published by Blue Ned Ltd.
135-137 Station Road, London, E4 6AG.

First published in the United Kingdom in 2019.
Copyright © SJ Sherwood, 2019.

SJ Sherwood has asserted his right under the Copyright, Designs and Patents Act 1988 to be identified as the author of this work.

A CIP catalogue record for this book is available from the British Library.

ISBN 978-1-9997929-3-0

For Sheniz.

For Aline.

Thank you.

1

Two things are happening to me at the same time, neither of which I like or I'm used to.

One is a sense of relief.

The other is the claustrophobic grip of chaos.

Combined they leave me rooted to the spot, giving me a detached sense that I'm more alive than I've ever been in my sixteen years on this planet. I've lived in Urban Worlds with digital credits and corrupt Systems, where embracing *hope* often costs you your life.

It's been one Community Home after another, before I ended up in the Holding Centre, kidnapped to Ilse's Dome. I wish it were different, but since my parents died, standing somewhere that is not surrounded by institutional walls has become a place of my imagination.

Somebody shouts my name.

Ned.

But I don't really hear it.

It's more a distant echo, like an aftershock that I don't have to pay attention to if I don't want to.

And I don't want to as I'm more interested in the warmth from the sun, which heats my skin in a way I had completely forgotten.

I glance left, Spencer is dragging a large smooth boulder across the top of the Hatch, which is being forced hard from underneath by the guards that chased us. He's straining with the weight of the rock as blood leaks across his forearm and runs onto the sand faster than he seems worried about. Diego is struggling to walk the soft sides of the sand dune, which encases us from all sides. His weight and short legs aren't built for this doughy, moving terrain. Kuro and Chantal have made it to the top and are looking down, pleading for me to move, so I guess it's them who are echoing my name, but really they are only adding to this strange emotional charge that is pumping through my veins.

Rasa tugs at my arm, while she shouts some kind of instruction at Spencer.

I want to tell her that I never thought we'd make it out.

So my plan is both a victory but also a defeat.

I'm flat out of ideas and I just want to stand here and enjoy the tangerine sun and warm breeze, which continues to tickle my face.

'NED,' she screams. 'WE HAVE TO MOVE. MOVE!'

Even through her pained face, she looks as beautiful as she did the day I first saw her sitting on the steel bench waiting in line to be hung. She's different from the rest of us. There's a mental strength I recognise and admire, but she's tougher than me in many ways.

And I'm tough.

I've had to be.

I know that much about myself.

'WHAT'S WRONG? COME ON!'

'There's nothing's wrong with me,' I say.

It comes out calm and contained, and it zaps the panic straight out of her.

She nods and I can see she is thinking again.

I look towards Diego and she knows immediately what to do. She ploughs up the side of the sand dune and grabs his arm and begins to drag him forward. I step across to Spencer and help him position the boulder, inspecting his arm before I guide him to the top of the dune.

At first, I think he's been shot, but it looks more that he's ripped open the skin as he careered down the alloy conduit pipe from heart of the Dome into the industrial core below.

Once at the top, I have to count that we're all present.

One.

Two.

Three.

Four.

Five.

Six, which includes myself.

It's stupid, I know, and I'm pointing at each of us as I'm doing it, taking in the new surroundings at the same time.

Rocks and sand dunes in every direction, all under the deepest tangerine glow of the like I've never seen before.

It's beautiful.

And dangerous.

Dangerous, because it's open ground and we have nowhere to hide.

Kuro hears it first, but I'm reading his mind as he cocks his head and looks straight ahead.

'Assault Buggies,' he shouts. 'Lots of them,' he adds.

'Ned,' Chantal says, pointing behind me.

I turn to see the start of a mountain range, which I'd somehow missed through the heat haze of what I think is the dying light. I'm not sure what skills I really possess for this life, especially compared to the others in our Pod, but I do have a knack for calculating distances.

We are two and a quarter kilometres from being out of the open.

Diego has already started to run towards the cover of the rocks, and it triggers us all into a sprint for freedom.

Chantal and Kuro soon overtake him, powering on.

Rasa and Spencer pass him next and although I'm at the rear, I suddenly digest Diego's fear at being last.

Left behind.

To die.

Picked off, as the weakling of the pack – another *Denounced* caught running away; to be hung at the next session.

Nothing could be further from the truth, but struggling to climb out of the sand dune has taken its toll on his strength and he was never built for running. I wasn't either, but Ilse's Military Camp has taught me some new skills and honed all our fitnesses to a different level.

'Concentrate on yourself and don't think about the others or what's behind you,' I say.

'They're close… I can hear them,' Diego pants out.

'Close is still not caught.'

I could run faster, but I match his stride, then up the pace after a couple of seconds.

It works.

Chantal and Kuro are pulling further and further away, but we're now matching Spencer and Rasa's pace.

I have another worry suddenly hit me.

Spencer's trailing blood.

His gash must be deeper than both of us realised and you wouldn't need dogs or special equipment to track us. Anyone could follow this trail, and it wouldn't matter if it were pitch black with a storm howling around them. For some reason it makes me ignore my own advice and I glance back, wishing I hadn't.

Three guards are stood at the top of the sand dune from which we've just run from.

The guard at the front takes aim, but even I know he can't hit us from there with his handgun.

He fires anyway, more out of frustration than hope.

A blue electric arc webs out and dies within seconds, far behind me. What worries me more is they don't appear concerned about making chase. Then I see why. The Assault Buggies we heard have appeared on the horizon.

Six of them in total.

They are the same as the ones that transported us around the Dome, but different, too. Instead of the grey and white camouflage, these are two-toned sand colour with splashes of black. They are bigger, too, and no doubt quicker, and they seem to merge into the background, disappearing at times into the heat haze.

These ones are built for war and that's what Pod Fifteen has just become.

Ilse's Number One enemy.

The frontline of resistance.

We've escaped the *City of Hope*. We weren't supposed to, but we did. We beat them. And the guards who came out of the Hatch aren't chasing, because they know they don't have to. They've worked it out, like I have, that although we are in this vast open space, our chances of making the next kilometres before the Buggies catch us are next to...well...

Zero.

'NED!' Rasa screams.

I realise I've stopped running.

But it's okay, because Diego doesn't know he's just given me an idea.

'GO RIGHT!' I scream at the top of my voice. 'GO RIGHT!'

I start running diagonal to the mountain range. It looks suicidal. Like I've made the Assault Team's job half as easy again. Diego trusts me enough to do the same. Kuro and Chantal have almost reached the start of the mountainous section so they keep going straight, but Rasa pulls Spencer right, and the four of us are running into what looks a certain disaster when it happens.

The drivers of the six Buggies had veered right to cut us off and are now slowed by the soft sand that I recognised from the dune by the silky glow it gives off in this dying light. Their vehicles are designed for this topography, but the soft terrain has taken the sting out of their speed and their wheels are spinning on every third turn.

Sapping energy.

I don't have to tell the others to turn left and head the way we had originally intended.

It's done in an unconscious synchronised movement.

The temporary flood of hope gives Diego another gear and we gain on Spencer and Rasa. Chantal begins to frantically wave at me. She must have spotted another danger, I think. Another Assault Crew on our tail. Maybe an Airborne Crew, as I search the sky around me.

But I'm sure I've just glimpsed a smile on her fear stricken face.

I run on, wondering.

Spencer's dripping blood marking our way.

Diego and I reach the edge of the change in terrain. It's gone from medium soft to hard sand to treacherously sharp rocks in less than four strides. I pause to catch my breath and my bearings. Rasa is pulling Spencer through a rocked path and I can now see what Chantal was pointing at. There's an entrance to a cave. Or more a man-made entrance to what looks like a Mine. Attached to the outside wall is a sign with a giant wave, like we're at a beach and the seaside is close.

It doesn't make sense and Rasa clocks it too and gives me a look to say: *what now?*

The six pursuit Buggies have one driver and four armed soldiers each.

That's five per Buggy.

Thirty highly trained and armed men against six of us.

I glance hard up.

The rocks get bigger and sharper and steeper as my eyes search for a path to the summit. The Buggies can't be driven up a mountain. It means we'd all be on foot, so maybe we'd have a chance, but beyond another half-kilometre it's like we'd need ropes and special shoes and those hooks that professional climbers use. It maybe wouldn't matter even if we had all that equipment, because none of us are trained that way, and Diego is never going to make a sheer rock face with or without special tools.

I won't either.

The Assault Buggies slow and the Teams leap from their seats and fan out in a hard-drilled formation, assault rifles held high across their chests.

We've fallen within shooting range, but they haven't raised their guns.

Yet.

We have nowhere to go and are cornered. But it's more than that, I think. Ilse wants us alive. She knows how we escaped, but she wants to know how we came to the conclusions we did, or more to the point – how I did.

If I can deny her that pleasure for a fraction longer then I'll take whatever the Mine has to offer.

I nod on that we should enter, and we scramble up.

Chantal and Kuro duck inside first.

I'm expecting pitch black beyond the first few metres, but instead a flickering grey light seeps from deep inside.

I help Diego over the last of the rocks and watch Spencer and Rasa duck into the entrance.

I'm about to step inside when I deliberately turn and snatch a glimpse at the setting sun.

I've spent far too much of my short life in grey empty worlds and I'm about to enter another.

I wonder if this one will be my final destination.

2

The temperature changes immediately from hot and sticky to cold and damp.

Kuro and Chantal forge ahead, leading the way.

Rasa lets Diego step in front of her and I'm behind Spencer at the back.

I see that he's losing even more blood and he's starting to struggle with his footing as his energy and focus drain from him. The adrenaline he had is no longer enough.

I don't know what to do or say.

We run on.

The uneven ceiling dips in places with pointed, lethal edges, and myself and Spencer are taller enough for it to be deadly if we're not careful. Thankfully, the floor is even but it's covered in a light silvery dust that is leaving a tell-tale footprint.

We come to another fork in what I'm sensing is a mature Mine with a labyrinth of interconnected tunnels. We'd be lost if it wasn't for the strange light that continually reflects off the right side of the wall face. It's both glossy and wet, and I can't work out where it's coming from, or if it's just a luminous glow within the make-up of the rock itself. It's like nature's perpetual torch and it's guiding our way, which means it is guiding the Assault Guards, too.

And I'm sure they are gaining.

Their footsteps were light and distant only moments ago, but they're becoming heavier and faster. It sounds like all thirty of them have entered the Mine, and I know from experience it's easier and faster to chase than it is to lead.

Plus our footprints are mini ghosts ultimately leading them to us.

I think we should take the risk at the next fork and not follow the rock's natural light when Kuro skids to a sudden halt, Chantal snatching out her hand and pulling him back by the arm, like she's stopped him falling.

Diego slows to a stop and takes a worried look in my direction. I can't see what it is that's stopped them, but the expression on their faces is enough to let me know it's not in our favour.

I sprint past Spencer and catch up with Rasa, crouching under a lower part of the roof and then skidding to a stop next to Kuro in an oval shaped space that is much wider than the tunnel we've run through.

'We're trapped,' Kuro pants out.

He's trying not to sound worried.

But he is and he should be.

The tunnel floor has vanished, collapsed in on itself.

I'm staring into blackness and I can't make out the bottom other than I can hear the heavy gush of rushing water.

The sign outside now makes sense.

So do the damp walls.

I check the jump to the other side. It's five metres, dead. Over sixteen feet in one long leap. Chantal and Kuro could probably make it with a good run, fuelled by the fear and adrenaline which is screaming through their veins. Rasa has that ability to make herself light. So I can see her scissoring through the air and gracefully landing on the other side with space to spare – no sweat.

I've no chance.

Neither has Diego.

We'll fall like bags of stones.

Spencer is close to passing out, but he might give it a go – or then again, he might not. He's been in the System for long enough to believe he can perhaps play the odds. Hope that his charm and good looks get him by. Maybe they will, maybe they won't – his luck, like ours, all dried up.

'What shall we do?' Chantal says, all breathy and scared.

Five pairs of eyes stare back at me.

Wild and glaring.

Expectant and worried.

I wish I had the answer, but what I'm really thinking is have we reached that point when it's each of us for ourselves. I can see Rasa is debating the same thought. She knows we have come to a defining moment when we are all on our own once more. It's like being in Court when you're fending for yourself, but without your Lawyer. Not that the System Lawyers were any good. I almost smile, because this is better than being in Court, because in Court you don't really have a choice, but here we do.

You can jump.

Or you can wait to see what Ilse has in store for you.

The choice is down to us as individuals when I'm hit with a new thought.

I'm no longer Head of Pod Fifteen.

I've retired my post.

I'm Ned 5-7-9-0-1-2-3.

An Orphan.

Alone to make my own decisions.

First and foremost – someone who has to look after himself.

'I'm sorry, Chantal,' I say.

'It's not your fault the floor has vanished,' she says, all innocent.

I don't have the heart to tell her that's not what I meant as five of the Assault Team come to a stop, guns raised in our direction.

It the first time I see Rasa still has her handgun.

I recall Spencer dropping his when he ran out of electronic bullets and scampered up the ladder to the open Hatch that led into the sand dune. Kuro did the same. I dropped mine after I emptied all my bullets into Marcellus and killed him. I don't recall Chantal dropping her gun or even having one, but she must have lost it at some point because she doesn't have one now.

Rasa raises her hand and points the handgun between the Assault Soldiers who have fanned out into the oval space.

They don't look too concerned by her weapon, more interested in how close we are to the edge of the drop. I step across to Rasa and pull her hand down. I'm not sure how many bullets she has left. Half a magazine at most, but being antagonistic in this tight space isn't going to help anyone – especially us.

And there's a dark side to me which thinks she may want to keep one of those bullets for herself.

Or even me.

It's another choice, if I think about it.

Not a great one, but it's still a choice.

Suddenly, the soldiers at the front part and Ilse steps through the middle. She's smiling and looking calm, and she always has that way of appearing immaculate and unhurried no matter where she is. It's probably her skill, like I can judge distances. She's dressed all in black, but she's wearing a desert camouflaged jacket, unzipped, her hands in the pockets. I notice she is wearing a green armband as are the other soldiers.

I'm sure it means something, but I don't know what.

Ilse wasn't in one of the Assault Buggies, but a lot has happened in my mind since we spotted them so perhaps she was, or perhaps there's an Airborne Crew after all and they dropped her off, which is why she looks all at ease.

She takes another step forward.

It has the emotional effect of edging us closer to the drop as we match her stride.

She smiles again, her tongue touching the tip of her lips, lizard like.

Red is the colour I hate the most in the world.

More than grey, and I hate the colour grey.

But even I'm smart enough to know she hasn't ordered them to shoot us on *stun*, because she's scared we'll topple into the abyss and she'll lose us forever.

She hates me, I can see it in her eyes; smell it on her breath.

It's mutual.

But she wants us all alive for this crazy experiment that's being carried out at the Dome, one I don't fully understand, or even care to try and work out any more.

I glance behind me and debate the drop. I wish I could see the end point, because I would know how far I was going to fall. But I can hear the water and it's louder than I first imagined, so I'm guessing the stop point is under thirty metres.

A long way.

Or not?

I'm Ned Hunter, not Ned 5-7-9-0-1-2-3.

And I'm innocent of being a *Denounced*.

And I shouldn't be here.

Bad luck at being on the wrong side of a corrupt System is all it is and I don't see why I have to bow to her tune any more.

'Do you remember our conversation, Ned?' Ilse says.

'The *gravitas* one, or the gravity one, I say, looking back at the drop behind me.'

She smiles, cold and reptilian, the tip of her tongue flicking once again between her teeth.

'You're in a unique position, Ned. You can rise above the original purpose we had set for you.'

'Those Hunter Packs were meant to kill us.'

'I always secretly knew you would survive our test and you even exceeded my expectations by escaping. I can help you now – officially. You can be someone, Ned. Someone special in our World. You may even be smart enough to rise to the very top. Be the cream of the cream. The top one percent of the one percent. It's for those privileged few who have what you have – true gravitas. It's a gift, Ned that you shouldn't overlook. Join our World and choose to be someone. Remember, your World called you a *Denounced* and wanted to hang you. You have the chance for revenge. Think about that. It's empowering.'

I've heard her speech before, but the others haven't.

Confusion creases their faces.

Am I with them, or against them?

Ilse takes another step forward.

It's subtle, more a shuffle, but it brings the soldiers with her.

Another one of those and they might be able to rush us, but I'm not thinking of that any more, or the fact that I was always innocent of being a *Denounced*, because my concentration has switched to Diego. He struggled the most with being in the Training Camp and I know he'd rather die than go back. He's staring into the dark pit and listening to the water below with an intensity I've never seen before, and he might as well have Rasa's gun pointed to his head, because he's going to pull the trigger by the look in his eyes.

And deep, deep inside of me there's something which I admire about what he's thinking, because he's making a decision for himself.

It might not be everyone's choice – but it's his choice.

Then I see it coming

And he jumps.

Chantal screams, 'DIEGOOO.'

Time and space fold-in on themselves in a vacuum of panic.

Kuro leaps next, followed by Rasa.

Spencer does what Spencer does and walks forward hands up, ready to take his chances and I don't know why I do it, but I grab the back of his collar and yank him into the hole.

The look of sheer shock on his face as he passes me and falls backwards into the darkness is comical.

'I can't swim,' Chantal screams as soldiers rush us.

I grab her in a bear-hug as a solider clutches at my shirt, but it's not enough to make a difference.

Then we're falling, together.

Backwards.

Chantal is screaming.

And I'm wondering if we'll hit the water first or the rocks.

Or does it really matter?

I doubt any of us will survive the drop, anyway.

3

We're falling.

Falling.

Spiralling backwards.

Chantal's screams cannon off the cavernous walls.

Air rushes past us.

It's all part of the chaos and I can feel the hangman's rope grip my throat as I'm waiting to hit the bottom.

Then ice cold water envelopes me and Chantal's screams stop in an instant.

The shock grips at my heart and I'm decelerating, but being pulled downwards at the same time. It's then the current yanks me sideways. I'm being sucked to another place I don't want to go and it's all black, and I haven't got long before I'll need to breathe. And I don't think Chantal is dead either, because she's gripping me harder than belies her size and she's suddenly kicking against the current. I shift my arms, hooking one tighter around her back, as I free the other and swim and kick up.

She does the same and we break the surface, the pair of us gasping for air.

'I can't swim… I can't swim… don't let me go,' she screams. 'I can't swim.'

I pull her tighter towards me, but it's too dark to even see the terror in her face. Not that I want my own fears reflected back.

'Rasa… Anyone…' I call out.

My voice echoes off the walls and dies into the gush of water that swirls around us.

We're picking up speed again.

'Ned…' bounces back at me.

I think it's Kuro, but I'm not sure over the escalating roar of the water.

I go to call out but I'm yanked under the surface, and I'm lucky to catch a lung full of breath in time. It's like my feet have been grabbed by a giant and his tug is vindictive. Chantal pulls herself closer, like she's trying to climb inside of me. We're moving at speed, but we're not being sucked down any more, more across. I lift my arm and my instinct is right. We've been sucked into a tunnel and the roof is above us. Our danger now is not the water, but a sharp rock piercing our skulls.

We continue to be swirled along and I'm pushing at the tunnel roof in intermittent slots so I don't get knocked unconscious.

It's then I know this is our end.

If this tunnel is hundreds of metres long, we are going to drown.

There's nothing myself or Chantal can do. We're going to die in a dark place and float in the depths of this mountain for an eternity.

Forever, thought of as a *Denounced*.

The ache in the top of my lungs starts to burn and it will soon force me to breathe. I know enough to understand that my reflexive need for air is the thing that will kill me.

As I breathe my lungs will fill with water.

Chantal has started to fight against my grip. Not at me directly, but against her desire to breathe.

Her lungs are smaller than mine, so her need has arrived.

Our pains are building.

Building.

I'm bursting and I know it's all over as I put my hand up expecting more hard rock, but it breaks the surface, so I kick and push and my lungs open and air instead of water floods through my body.

Chantal screams and pants, and her hot breath is all that I can feel until my eyes slowly adjust to the grey shimmering light that still reflects off the right side of the rock wall.

Luminous.

I look up and can't see the roof. The walls are sheer on all four sides and there's no way out, and we're picking up speed again, the current determining our lives.

Chantal's grip is locked on and if we die, we're going to die in each other's arms.

My eyes adjust some more and I can make out Diego and Spencer, and I think Kuro is holding Rasa afloat.

If I'm right, then she's badly hurt or dead already.

The first of us to go.

I always thought she'd be the last or survive us all.

'Ned… Ned…' Chantal splutters out.

I can see what she's trying to articulate. Ahead, the water is being sucked at speed into another tunnel. The funnelling action is giving us a turbo boost we don't need or want.

We have a problem.

Same scenario.

If the tunnel is a few metres long we'll be okay, but if it's hundreds or more.

We're dead.

And where does it end?

And how many tunnels can we take?

'Ned… there… there… look,' Chantal says.

There's a small ledge that water is washing over and running off. It's not much, but it's better than the unknown of what's ahead. I'm not sure I have the strength to swim across, or not with Chantal attached to me.

The water is gaining speed by the second.

Chantal's panic is vibrating through me and taking what strength I have left. She knows if we stay locked together we both could die and if she lets me go then I have a chance.

And I know I have this thing in me to let her go.

Survival.

That instinct to simply pull her off and let her work it out for herself.

We all have, I think.

The System made us like that.

And if I was a Taylor or a Suki type, I would have done it by now, but I don't want to be like them. It's not that I'm a hero, it's just I'm different that way. I didn't want to kill Marcellus either, but I did. I had to.

To survive.

But this is a different choice, like jumping into the hole of water, and not killing the Hunter Pack.

We're trapped in the pit.

It's all choice.

You pick your life.

So, I kick and paddle with my free arm and Chantal uses her arms to try and propel us forward and it's working, or some. I keep kicking and water fills my lungs as I bob under the surface, and it's then I get it.

'Hold your breath,' I shout at Chantal.

She does.

And we dive down, or more let the water do its thing.

I catch the current and then push out towards where I think the ledge will be. We surface and it's partly done what I had hoped and taken us wider of the pending entrance. We paddle and kick, and it's Diego's hand that grabs Chantal's and he pulls us forward. I smash my knee into a hidden rock. Pain crashes through me and makes me see white, but there're enough rough edges of the ledge for me to hold on to and let the moment pass.

Chantal scrambles up and out of the water.

Diego leans across and helps me sit on the rocky ledge.

Spencer is already out and sat against the rocks, blood still seeping from his arm. He's looking at Rasa lying on her back, water running across her legs.

Kuro looks half dead from exhaustion.

I shuffle across to Rasa.

She's not breathing.

'The first tunnel was too long for her,' Kuro says.

I start to push at the top of her chest. A string of water leaks from the corner of her mouth. I push harder. Willing her to breathe, and I'm sure I'm shouting *Come on Rasa... Come on Rasa,* but the noise of the water is drowning out my thoughts.

'You need to give her mouth-to-mouth,' Spencer shouts.

It takes a beat for me to understand what he means, but he's right. I've never done it before, but I've seen footage of it. So I shuffle round and pry open her mouth with my fingers when she coughs water into my face, twisting to her side, spewing more fluid from her lungs.

'If anyone gives me mouth-to-mouth, it'll be the last thing they ever do,' she coughs out.

'You've got no chance from me,' Diego says.

Spencer starts to laugh, followed by Diego.

It's the first joke I think he's ever cracked. And it's more funny coming from him, because he and Rasa have never really repaired their relationship, and I sit back and smile to myself as I check on Chantal.

We're all here.

Breathing and bruised and cut – but alive.

Pod Fifteen as one.

'You nearly killed me,' Rasa barks at Kuro, as she sits up.

'What do you mean, I tried to pull you up.'

'You nearly drowned me, pushing up to get air. I should throw you back in.'

'I pulled you through the tunnel,' Kuro says.

His voice is all high pitched and defensive.

'Always ungrateful,' Diego says. He turns to Kuro. 'Maybe, you should have let her drown,' he continues, the playfulness suddenly gone from his voice.

'We've got bigger things to worry about,' I say, standing, inspecting my swelling knee, before looking at the shimmering wall between us and what I think is another tunnel above.

'It's tough, but it's doable,' Spencer says, following my thoughts.

'Doable or not, it's the only choice,' Kuro adds. 'Unless we want to play the holding our breath game.'

Chantal is helping Rasa to her feet and Kuro has moved to the other side of Diego – I guess, for protection.

I realise, I still have the goggles I took from the Hunter Pack around my neck. I pull them off and remove the strap, tipping the water from the glass. The strap is made of thick strong elasticated material. I step across to Spencer and use the strap as a torque. It was a technique we learnt in the Training Camp.

I pull it tight across his arm.

He whinges, but the blood finally stops.

Spencer doesn't thank me.

Not that I thought he would.

I pulled him down here, after all.

'Can you do it?' I ask Diego, but really I'm asking myself, because I'm not sure I can. Swollen knee or not.

'I'm never going back to that place, Ned. Ever!'

I smile.

My father used to say that you could never defeat someone who won't give up and that's really our only weapon.

We keep going, or we die.

'The first part is easy,' I say. 'But I don't know how we manage the last third. And the wall is wet, so it's going to be slippery. If we fall, we should hit the water so that's a good thing, but then there's the current. Any other ideas?'

'We should swim to that point there and then climb up,' Chantal says.

I see what she's saying as Kuro cuts in front of me to take a better look. The ledge we're on juts out enough to stop the current for two or three metres, and then the tunnel wall beyond has more natural foot holds and protruding rocks to use for our ascent. I've been slow to see that the darker the rock, the dryer it is and, therefore, easier to climb.

'She's right,' Kuro says. 'If we start at that small ridge and work straight up keeping to the right side of that seam formation, we could do it. The only issue is the water this side isn't deep so if one of us falls we'll smash into the rocks below the water line. This side is more slippery but if we do fall we won't hit the rocks, just catch the current. Which risk do we want, Ned?'

I glance across at Spencer.

'How's the arm?'

He shrugs, not looking at me.

'We take our chance on the drier side. Who wants to go first?'

'I will,' Rasa says.

I watch her wade out on the ledge of rocks, which means Chantal doesn't have to worry about swimming to that point. Rasa looks up and gathers her concentration, before reaching up to start her ascent.

'Memorise her path,' I say, sitting down as I watch her carefully make her route.

'Ned,' Diego says, pointing into the water.

I turn and see the soldier who tried to grab me from falling float by face down. Behind him is another member of the Assault Team. We watch them drift by and then get sucked into the tunnel at speed. Nobody says anything and I'm not sure Rasa even noticed. I glance back at Spencer and I can see he's gone from relieved at being alive to being resentful at being pulled into this tunnel.

I don't know whether I like it or not, but keeping Spencer from surrendering means that I'm still the Head of Pod Fifteen.

For now, anyway.

4

I'm climbing the rock-face when I hear Chantal say.

'We deserve some luck.'

I'm not so sure I believe in luck any more – that's if I ever did. And, anyway, if it were true, then I figure as a Pod, we've used all ours up by escaping not once, but twice, so she should shut up and not risk cursing us any more than we already have been.

Diego lowers his hand, which I grab, and he heaves me the last metre, over the top ledge.

I'm the last up and his core strength never fails to amaze me.

I shake out the muscle ache from my legs as I get the sign we saw outside the entrance. We'd run into a disused Mine with a complex structure of tunnels. Maybe it's been mined too much and there are too many hollowed-out seams, or it's the water or the make-up of the rocks, or a combination of all three, but the structures have started to collapse in on themselves. Dangerous and lethal, but today our best friend, so I get what Chantal is saying, although she shouldn't voice it like she is. For all the dangers, the climb up the rock-face was easy, really. All we had to do was to take our time and feel our way to the top.

Since I've been Head of Pod Fifteen, I always worry about something and this time it's Spencer. He looks both lost in physical pain and angry at the situation he finds himself in.

I sure he's blaming me.

But he shouldn't.

What if I saved him and what if he's better off with us than with Ilse?

I don't care, I decide, rolling the tension from my neck as I stare at the silvery light from the Mine-face, which shimmers its way to another opening up ahead.

A way out.

Or that's what it looks like.

Whilst I've been lost in my thoughts, I suddenly realise the others have been waiting for me to move. Embarrassed, I lead the way, careful not to crack my head on the over jagged ceiling within this section. I bend through the opening and the silvery glow changes to a deep tangerine orange, tinged with a fiery red.

I look up and behind me to check what I already know.

It's a replica of the rock-face we entered, but on the opposite side.

We've been flushed through the mountain and we've come out slightly higher, because of our climb, but not by much. And as with the other side it would be impossible to climb to the summit without the ropes and the skills of a climber, so our only way is down.

In front of us is nothing but rolling sand dunes.

If we track left or right we will be hugging the foot of this mountain range.

My gut feeling is if we turn right it will weave us back to Ilse's Dome.

If we turn left, it's anyone's guess as to where it will lead.

My anxiety swells about what to do next, but we have a more pressing problem. The three-day survival kits we were issued to complete the *City of Hope* are all gone. I see now they were joke and not designed to help us survive. But they did have some tools we could use now. We've got no food, weapons, sleeping bags, first-aid kits, rope, not even a piece of flint to start a fire.

We have nothing but ourselves.

I see that Rasa has still managed to keep hold of her handgun and her utility belt, but these were taken from the Hunter Packs and were not our issue.

I almost smile.

Even half-dead and drowning, her instinct to fight to the end has stayed with her.

Myself, Spencer and Diego removed our belts so we could fit down the conduit pipe for our initial escape. Those belts were good quality and might have proved useful here. It's another small mistake, but it's easy to be smart after the problem. And for all the heat of the sun, I can feel a chill brewing in the air, which isn't helped by my wet clothes.

Rasa, Diego, Spencer and myself are still dressed in the grey camouflaged uniforms of the Hunter Pack we tricked into the pit. Kuro is wearing the brown uniform of the Workers and he's the most camouflaged of us all out in this new environment. Chantal is dressed all in Black as one of Ilse's Dome Guards and looks the most out of place. The uniform is too big for her and the material is heavy and not designed for this terrain.

'It's going to get dark and then cold,' Kuro says, all matter of fact.

He has this fake authoritative tone when his nerves come out.

I notice for the first time that he's lost his glasses in the madness of the escape and his vision isn't the best.

Another problem to add to our growing list.

The only positive is we are wearing the boots we were given before entering the *City of Hope*, and they are better quality than they look.

And comfortable.

They helped us climb the rock-face of the tunnel and if walking is what's next – which it's going to be – then it's another stroke of luck, as Chantal would say.

'Which way?' Rasa asks.

It was a question I was thinking of asking her, but I can see she doesn't want the responsibility of the answer.

I don't either.

'We should stay and rest,' Spencer chips in.

'We've made a big head start on Ilse,' Diego says. 'She might even think we're dead. We should keep going if we can. Time is with us and it's not always been that way.'

He's right, but so is Spencer. It'll be dark soon, and with the dark there will be other dangers, the most pressing of which will be the cold.

'Thank you, Ned,' Chantal says, catching me off guard. 'For not letting me drown.'

I shrug and smile.

'I'm going to teach you to swim at the first opportunity I get. But it might not be for a while,' I say, nodding out toward the barren desert.

'I'd like that,' she says, staring at me and ignoring my attempt at humour.

Her openness catches me off guard and I warm with the heat of a flush.

I turn from her and step across to Diego.

'Tell me what you're thinking?'

'That I'm not going back, ever.'

'That's not what I asked,' I say, irritated.

'They'll search the Mine before they do anything else, and even if they do find where we've come out it might take them a day, even two. If you want to rest I can't stop you, but I'm not sure I can wait.'

I know he's right and we should be looking to make good on any advantages we have.

'What about Spencer? He's injured and we can't leave him.'

'He's not that injured, and he'll do what we all do,' Diego says, looking away from me and back out into the vastness of the sand dunes.

I'm undecided, I think, as I turn towards the others.

In the Old World, I'm from New York City; Rasa, St Petersburg; Chantal, Paris and Spencer, London. Four urban kids as you're ever going to meet. Diego's from a farming community outside of Mexico, a place called Tula, that borders onto the desert, so this is almost home from home for him. Kuro has scratched a living in a *Doubter's Camp* on the outskirts of Tokyo, so he's more an outdoor type then urban, and I noticed even back at the Dome he never ate as much as the rest of us and never suffered from a lack of energy. He can go hungry is what I'm thinking.

I call him over and he stumbles on a rock and nearly trips as he walks across.

We both ignore it, like it didn't happen.

'What do you think – stay or go?'

'Diego's right in that we have a solid head start and we should use it. The question is more – which way. If we go right it might creep us back to the Dome. We can't go straight out. It's a wasteland. So it has to be left and at least it gives us cover. We should also be able to find water. It's certainly here,' he says, attempting a smile, as he lifts up his wet sleeve.

'You've lived in this kind of environment before,' I say to Diego. 'If we go straight out, can we do it? Survive, I mean?'

'You'd be killing us!' Kuro gasps out.

'Diego?' I say again, ignoring Kuro.

'This is the best time, right now. It's cool, but not cold, but if it's anything like home then it'll get cold, like cold. And during the day it will get hot, like you can't imagine and we don't have hats or water or food. It could be suicide. But Ilse will never look for us out there, or not for a long, long time. She won't believe you're that stupid to make us walk that way,' he says, turning to face me.

I glance back at the others.

Spencer has closed his eyes.

He's not asleep, more protesting or demonstrating what he wants.

Rasa and Chantal are chatting.

I can't make out what they are saying, but I'm sure it's along the same lines I've been discussing with Diego and Kuro.

I stare back at the desert.

In its own way, it's one of the most mesmeric things I've ever seen.

An ocean, but without the water.

Shifting heatwaves that make the horizon impossible to see.

Rasa walks over to me.

'What are we doing?'

'We should keep going. But out. Across the sands.'

I'm expecting all sorts of push backs, but she nods and shrugs, like she doesn't care.

But she does.

'It's the last place they'll look,' she adds.

I nod.

'What about water?'

I shrug, because I don't have an answer.

'And food?'

I shrug again.

Same reason.

'How many electronic bullets do you have left?'

She unclips the magazine in the handgun and counts three. Not great, but it's better than two. I turn to Diego.

'Is there anything out there we can survive on?'

'If there're cactus we can drink the water in the plant. It's sticky and bitter, but it won't kill you. My brothers used to make a drink from it that would get you drunk. If we tear some material from the inside of our uniforms we can use them as hats for tomorrow's heat.'

'Food?'

'Rasa has the gun so we may be able to kill something to eat. We still have to cook it, but let's see if we can find it to kill it first. If we can find a cactus then we can find desert foxes, because they live nearby. They don't taste great, but we can eat them. The cold is going to be our problem.'

I nod, thinking that doesn't change whether we stay, go left or right, or head straight out.

'We can hug together,' Chantal adds with a half smile. 'You know… body heat. It was in one of our classes in the Camp.'

She's right, it was.

I walk over to Spencer and kick the sole of his boot. Not hard, but still more aggressive than I should.

It's my turn to be angry at him.

He nonchalantly opens his eyes and gives me a: *what's your problem look!*

I don't take the bait.

'Get up. We're moving out and I'm not dragging you anywhere this time.'

5

We trek out in a straight line.

That's it.

The grand sum of my plan.

I'm tempted to lie to myself that it's more complex and I'm somehow smarter than that, but I'm not.

We decided – no – I decided, that turning left or right was a mistake.

But based on what, I think?

My instinct?

Like that has done me a whole lot of favours in the past, and now five others are part of something I can't really articulate, other than to say: *keep the mountain range to our backs*.

I know that we're together and it makes us look strong, but I'm not so sure we are together any more – emotionally, or even that strong.

I trek on.

Leading the way.

And it's cold, but it's hot.

And it's light, but dark at the same time.

My clothes have started to dry and I can feel the warmth from the sand permeating up through my boots. There's a fresh chill in the air, which has started to bite at the corners of my face, and the sun is dropping from the sky leaving a residue trail of red. It makes the sand look the colour of clay and it is softer under foot than I would like. I'm sinking in on each step, not much, but enough to drain my energy at twice the normal speed, so it must be draining the others in the same way as well.

I turn back to check on the rest of the Pod.

They've spread out.

Individuals.

Nobody is talking or looking at each other.

Each lost to their own thoughts. A fear locked into their faces of the kind I've not seen before. I wonder what Worlds they are in. I hope it isn't anything like mine – dark and grey and full of corridors. It's like their hopes are resting on my shoulders. It's weighing me down and I want to be rid of it. I don't want their responsibility. I never did. Ilse handed me a job I didn't want, didn't ask for. Her stupid accusations of *gravitas* and being *special* are haunting me more than ever being a *Denounced* has.

I wade on and reach the top of another dune, panting slightly from the effort of getting to its peak.

Spread out in front of me is more of the same soft clay-coloured banks of sand.

Easy to stumble down.

Exhausting to climb up.

And where do they stop?

I glance back at the mountain range we've left behind. The fear of being caught has trekked us out further than I thought, but we could still make it back before night finally entombs us. It's going to be cold, but the rocks we've left behind will give us some protection at least. I find myself checking the sky for an Airborne Crew or the sands behind me for a Search Team, but Diego is right. Ilse's Assault Teams will either believe we're drowned or at best are still hiding in the labyrinth of tunnels that make up the Mine.

'No,' I hear Diego snap at me from under his breath.

'No,' he growls again, staring me out for a second, before marching on.

Nobody else heard him, or I don't think they did, but he's read my thoughts about heading back to a kind of safety.

I watch him struggle on.

He's taking long hard strides and he looks like he's wading out to sea, which in a way, he is. I know he's not going back because he's told me three times already, so why am I caring that I see this as a challenge to my authority?

I push the thought out of my mind as I walk across the peak of the dune and reach out to help Kuro the final few strides to the top. I then do the same for Spencer, but he ignores my hand, walking past me like I'm not there. Chantal gives me *a don't worry* smile and Rasa walks towards me and stops at my side, panting softly.

'I'm getting cold,' she says. 'We should think about finding a spot to rest for the night.'

I scan the middle distance and see nothing but an ocean of soft sand.

'I know,' she says. 'But it's going to get dark soon.'

'Diego,' I shout.

He keeps walking.

Ignoring me.

'DIEGO!'

I'm not sure where the aggression comes from but my voice booms out, snapping everyone's attention, including his. He stops and turns to look at me. A frown growling above his eyes.

'We need to find somewhere to stop. We have our head start. We rest. We re-group our energies. Ilse taught us that much and it's good training.'

It takes him a few seconds to assimilate what I said, but he nods his agreement and the tension in the group slips away with larger troubles to fret on.

He waits for us to catch him up and we climb another sand dune as a Pod. At the top, we see more of the same in every direction, but off to our right there's a small section of rocks and the sand looks firmer, easier to walk on. I don't have to say anything and we move in unison towards the spot, the sand dune thankfully flattening a fraction. We seem to be in some sort of dip, like a mini valley.

It's either protecting us from the wind or the chilled breeze has eased off.

Either way, it's like a temporary victory.

We sit and look at each other.

We have no water, food or conversation.

Chantal moves first and snuggles into me. I'm not sure what to do and I find my arm is stuck up in the air, suspended, unsure whether it should stay up or down. She reaches up and tugs at my sleeve, pulling my arm down as she gently pulls Rasa towards her. Kuro snuggles into my left side, Spencer next to him and Diego turns his back to the desert, facing into the group and closing off the circle.

The small set of rocks sit to my back and there's still a residue of warmth coming up through the sand, like underground heating. If we had food and something to drink it would almost be friendly. I think of the food in the Canteen at the Camp. Probably the best meals I've ever eaten. They say your mother's cooking is something you never forget, but I don't remember mine. According to my sister, my mum would make a pineapple upside-down cake, where the sugar would melt to the top, because the cake was baked upside down. I don't have a memory of it or I can't even remember the taste. But apparently we loved it as a family and I ate so much once I was sick for a day. If I get out of this place, I might try and find one and see if it triggers any memories from home. If nothing else, I'm sure I'll enjoy the sugar.

I'll add it to my list, like surfing and living by the sea and dating Rasa, which I'm beginning to think is one of the most stupid thoughts I've ever had in my entire life.

Or the second stupidest.

Trekking out here is the first.

'Were you tempted?' Kuro asks.

I wonder what he means for a second, and who his question is aimed at when I see the others looking at me, so I know it's been discussed, or gossiped.

'At what?' I say.

'Don't give me that,' Spencer growls. 'To join, Ilse. She said you could be someone special in their World. She said you have gravitas and that you were smarter than us.'

I don't like his tone and it's another challenge to my authority from another member of the Pod. An authority, I don't want, but it's like I'm in the Holding Centre or one of the Community Homes and if you back down your life is ruined because you become their whipping boy.

'I jumped didn't I, and I pulled you after me – there's your answer.'

'I can look after myself,' Spencer says.

'Says who?'

I say it in the same way, I kicked the bottom of his boot.

He either has to let it go or escalate it, which means I'll escalate it some more, and so on until one of us loses.

Him.

It's a stupid game, but I don't have a choice. Even out here, with nothing, I still have to behave like I'm stuck in the System watching every move.

Fighting for my life.

Which, I guess, I am, but it shouldn't be against Spencer or Diego, or any of them for that matter.

'We're in the Non-Secular World, aren't we?' Chantal asks.

Kuro nods.

Spencer lets out a sigh of disgust.

Diego's stare sinks to the sand and his internal depressions flash across his face.

'You recognised that man in the back of the Buggy, didn't you?' Rasa says to me.

'His name was Andreas Lee. He was the Warden in my last Community Home. He was always nice to me, but he could be cruel to the others. He made me take this test, telling me it was psychometric pre-test to leaving the Community Homes System and getting my digital credits organised, so I could go to college. It was a year too early and I knew somehow it was wrong. A week later, I was accused of being a *Denounced,* so I was tested to be taken to the Dome, like we all were. I'm no different from any one of us.'

I feel this surge of rage at Spencer for accusing me of wanting to join Ilse, but I know my rage isn't actually at him.

It's at Andreas Lee.

I wish I'd shot and killed him and not Marcellus.

I flood with guilt at my murderous thought.

But it's Andreas's fault I'm here, stuck in the desert, on the run, with no food or water.

Or hope.

'Why did they do that? And why are we here?' Chantal asks.

Confusion laces her voice.

'What did we really do at the Dome?' Rasa asks.

'They trained us for the military,' Chantal says.

'And watched us, too,' Kuro adds.

'But why?' Chantal says, more confusion laces her voice.

It's a good question, and I say. 'They wanted to know how we react to situations and how we train.'

'But why?' Chantal asks.

I don't know why exactly, but I wish I did, even though I'm not sure it helps us if we know the answer.

'The way Ilse said she always knew you'd survive the *City of Hope* scares me,' Kuro says. 'Do you think anyone else made it out?' he adds.

I think of Taylor's Pod and Suki, and Arianne's. If any of the others escaped, I would bet on them. And if they did, maybe they were captured straight away, or maybe the Hunter Packs killed them as was supposed to happen, and it's just us who were the lucky ones and escaped.

Not that I would call this luck as I close my eyes and do my best to ignore the growing cold.

And the killer thirst that has started to rage through me.

6

Hunger and thirst wake me.

I blink open dry, sore eyes caused by the desert air. I swallow and focus and see that we're all covered up to our waists in sand, Chantal nearly to her chest. It's built up so much overnight that Diego is supported on his left side, like he's leaning against a post.

I struggle to push myself out of the tiny grains that are in danger of swallowing me whole.

My body is slow to react, stiff from the hammering it took in the Mine, and not helped by falling asleep in a sitting position.

Standing, I lean into my aches, wishing I had some of those pain-killers the doctor at the Dome gave me, but wishing more that I had a drink of water to flush them down.

I remember the strange headscarves that were part of the uniform we took from the Hunter Packs. I know the *City of Hope* was just another extension of the Dome and our test and nothing else. And its name is a sick joke by Ilse or whoever designed the Dome – there's no *hope*. No-one is supposed to get out alive. But the headscarves are designed to cover their head, neck and face in one. I thought it was just camouflage to hide facial features and help them to merge into the City of Hope's landscape. But I see now they were designed for this desert terrain. It stops the sand getting into your eyes and mouth and keeps the sun's heat off your head. They wore them because this is the Hunter Pack's true home and them coming to the Dome was just a job.

I can't recall losing the one I stole or maybe I tore it off in the last moments of the escape.

It was long and distracted me, and I don't like tight things around my neck for obvious reasons.

Rasa, Spencer and Diego had them too, but they've either lost theirs in the escape, or dumped them for the same reasons I did.

It's the same with the goggles.

I thought they were to protect the eyes from the glare of the Dome, and they were, but they were also designed for out here – Ilse's Assault Teams had them hanging around their necks.

I should have kept mine and not tossed them away after I used the strap to torque Spencer's arm.

More mistakes in my growing list and I wonder how many more I will add before the day is out.

I wade up three big strides to the top of the dune and more despair trips through me.

I've made some poor decisions in my short life, but this has to be the worst-of-the-worst.

It's like we've been picked up in our sleep and transported to another location.

I don't know which way we walked and which way we should walk.

The mountain range that was my unofficial compass has gone.

Disappeared.

And, I'm hungry.

But I'm more thirsty than I am hungry.

And the cold has been replaced with a warmth, that even in the few minutes I've been awake is warmer than it was when I opened my sore eyes.

I turn back and see the others start to wake and take in the shock of being buried in sand. I watch them pull tired bodies to their feet as the same fears start to show.

We're lost in the desert.

No food.

No water.

No tools for survival.

Kuro heads for where I'm standing, and my growing concerns are replaced with the hollowness of shame that makes it hard for me to face him.

I wish he would turn back and leave me to my thoughts.

'The sun rises in the East and sets in the West, so I guess that way is North and behind us is South,' he says, in that teacher way he has about him.

I'm not sure it helps us, but his words have a calming effect, giving me an unexpected sense of where I am.

I've seen pictures of the Great Desert at school – the land the Terrorist Wars were fought and lost and won, and lost again, eventually coming to a stalemate. In a time before I was born. A time when they divided our planet into the Eight Quadrants that they are today – four in the Secular World and four in the Non-Secular World. I'm from Quadrant 1 in the Secular World, and I've never been to another Quadrant in the whole of my life, except for now, but I was kidnapped, which I'm not sure really counts.

The four Quadrants of my Secular World have their own Laws and Rules, although many are similar. Then each Quadrant is ruled by an overriding Constitution known as the Authority. The Authority is made up of groups of men and women who are governed by one man: our Secular Head. I don't understand how he becomes elected and why it's always a man, but the election is every ten years and there's only been one in my lifetime. People say it doesn't really matter who is the Secular Head, because he doesn't really have a say in what happens.

He's a puppet.

It's the men and women of the Authority that call all the shots.

It is them who make the System.

So I guess it's them who are the corrupt ones and make all the corrupt rules, and were ultimately responsible for what happened to me in Court.

I don't know how it works in the World of the Great Desert, but it's the land where they say they pray to Gods. I've never seen anyone do such a thing and I can't imagine what it must look like, and I wonder if this person they call God is the same as the Head of our Authority?

The thought alone can get you hanged in my Quadrant and I wonder if this God can see me now as I glimpse up into the crystal blue sky.

No… I decide.

Because he or she would be telling Ilse where we are and nobody is coming to find us out here, of that I'm sure.

I think of my parents.

Or more my father.

As each day passes in my life, my memories of him become more ragged and I wonder what is true or not, any more. The one thing I do know is that he liked to make decisions. He used to say it was nothing more than developing the habit, and I have to make another decision now whether I like it or not, or if I even have the habit or not.

And it's to go back to the mountains.

We have no choice.

There's nothing out here but pending death. Even Diego must realise that. I want to ask him if he's okay with us turning around, as he steps next to me. His lips are pale and look ready to crack, so he's as thirsty as me.

As all of us.

But I don't ask for his approval. Instead, I look at the rising sun and decide to head North for no other reason than I think it's where the mountain range will be. If nothing else it will have water. Once we get a land mark then the others can decide what they want to do. It feels deceptive on my part, like I should explain my thinking, but there's no point arguing.

It will only waste time.

And energy.

All of which we don't have.

'That way,' I say.

Nobody objects and we trek out.

The terrain defines our path and how we walk. The peaks of the sand dunes are the easiest to navigate. The sand is still soft, but the up and down is too tiring, so we need to stay high as much as possible to reserve our energy. The peaks aren't wide enough to walk in unison, so we string out and zigzag our way North.

Or that's what I hope as we could be walking South or East or just in circles.

And it's hot.

Hot like I can't believe.

And getting hotter.

And I can't see anything but the same golden sands in every direction.

'Ned,' Spencer shouts.

I look back to see he's at the rear. He's pointing off to his right. I squint into the heat haze and sure enough I see what he's pointing at. Maybe three or four kilometres the sand dunes flatten out to resemble the hard ground that surrounded the mountain range, but then it turns into a valley with crop of trees.

'Cactus,' Diego says.

The relief in his voice is plain to hear.

'Where?' Kuro asks.

Chantal shouts at Kuro to turn a half circle to his right so he's at least facing the right direction. He nods all agreeing, although I doubt he can see that far, but he's picked up on the rush of excitement the find has created.

The best way across is to go back on ourselves and then veer left after five sand dunes. I was at the front, but now I'm at the back as Spencer leads the way across the peaks we need to navigate to reach the harder ground.

I find myself staring at our new destination.

It seems to be moving away and I'm concerned it's not three or four kilometres but closer to eight or nine.

I know your imagination can play tricks. In the heat they're called mirages. I don't know why I know that but I do. Your mind wants to see the things that it needs. The more desperate you become the more real the mirages are. I wonder if that's like *Hope*. The more you want something the more you ignore the truth to follow your *Hope*?

I stare into the heat haze and don't see the cactus any more, but in their place there's a hangman's gallows, and Ilse and the Holding Centre, but most of all I see Andreas Lee smiling down at me and telling me how much he likes me – how clever I am, and how I'm going to do all these wonderful things. Then I take their Psychometric Test and I end up in Court then a Box and now the Desert. My life doesn't make sense any more – that's if it ever did.

And we walk on.

Nobody speaking, the pace quicker because we have an end destination, unless our minds are playing with us.

Then the sand dunes flatten and the walking becomes easier, and I see that my fear isn't founded and this is not one of those mirages I've heard about.

Diego looks back at me and smiles – it's proud and defiant.

We reach our spot and I'm right that we have entered some sort of dry valley. Maybe one that once had a river running through it as it looks like we're stood in a river bed, banks either side.

Rasa has walked over to a small pool of water. It's dark brown and I can smell its poisonous fumes from where I am. Diego has run over to the first of four cactus trees that are three times the size of me with treacherously long spike-like-needles. He picks up a rock and smashes it down onto one of the flat like protruding arms. It breaks off with a crunch sound, and a thick yellowy syrup oozes from the open sore. Flies buzz around the fetid water. They are the first living things I've seen since we escaped from the Dome and they give me a strange emotional lift.

Hope.

Rasa has broken off another arm of the cactus and is copying Diego who has started to knock off the dangerous needles. He's careful to pick them up from their base and then toss them to one side. He then scores the plant arm with the rock and I watch as more thick syrup starts to slowly seep through the wound.

'Don't drink that?' Kuro shouts.

I turn to see Spencer crouched on his hands and knees by the small pool of dirty water. He looks like a dog about to lap it up from a bowl.

'What are you doing?' I say, walking towards him.

'I'm just checking it,' he shouts back, all defensive. 'It might be better than that sludge from the plant.'

'You can smell it's bad,' I say.

'Don't be stupid,' Rasa shouts at Spencer, looking up from her work.

Spencer ignores us as he dips his finger into the water and touches it against his tongue. I run over and pull him back by the shoulder. My force is enough to spin him round and flip him on his back. He springs to his feet and takes a wild swing at me.

I duck under it.

I could easily punch him back, but I don't.

'I didn't mean it,' I say, holding up my hands to show him I don't want to fight. 'I don't think you should drink it is all. Look at its colour. It's bad.'

'You never mean it. That's your problem.'

He runs at me and I duck right then a quick left, sticking my foot out, tripping him to the floor. I turn to pounce on him when he lets out a loud yelp and grabs at his neck, distracted.

Then I see it.

It's a black creature, like a small lobster, with claws and six legs and this tail that has a spike at the end. It's the size of a big mouse, and it's scurried away under a rock, but not before it's stung Spencer. He's looks stunned and his neck is swelling like a rapidly inflated balloon and he's wanting to speak, but he can't and his face is going red.

'I'm sorry,' I hear myself say. 'I just didn't want you to drink the water.'

He's trying to speak but he can't and his eyes are full of hate and fear, but more fear than hate.

'NED.' I hear Rasa say.

I spin round to see a bank of sand heading for us. It's rising like a wave and it moving at speed.

Before I have time to react it blocks the light and starts to wash over me, tiny grains of sand cutting at my skin.

I reach out to hold on to someone, anyone, but all I grab is more sand moving at speed.

Then I can't see anything.

Then I have to close my eyes to protect them – the sheer force of the wind and the sand forcing me to kneel.

Then I bury my head into my hands as the sand continues to build speed and slice into me, and it's then I realise we are to be buried alive and it's probably their God doing this because we're *Denounced*.

7

I don't know why but the weight of the sand from my back and the noise of the winds have gone.

If I'm buried alive then it's not what I expect, because I'm lying in a bed. I think it's a bed, as there are sheets and lots of cushions, but no mattress that I recognise. The colours are mostly light shades of orange and blues and browns, and I can see Diego and Kuro, but not the girls or Spencer.

My next surprise is that I count four women whom I've not seen before.

One of them is attending to Kuro and he's smiling and eating food, like they've been friends for years. The women are all dressed in long dresses that cover their entire bodies and they each have a scarf wrapped around their heads, which folds and part covers their faces so you can only really see their eyes and perfectly shaped eyebrows.

They are like the headscarves of the Hunter Packs and Assault Teams but different.

Delicate.

And I know that I must be dreaming this strange dream, but it's then that I go to open my eyes and realise they've been open all this time and I'm suddenly distracted by an oily sheen coming from my body. My forearms and hands are chafed raw from what must have been the sands driven at me by the high winds. Even the Hunter Pack uniform couldn't protect me against the onslaught. The hundreds of tiny cuts should be stinging and giving me all sorts of grief, but they don't hurt one bit and the oily sheen is from this sticky, glue like substance that covers my arms and hands.

I sit up and inadvertently cough.

There's a strange pause, as if everyone has frozen, then two of the women rush towards me and I find myself pushing back in the bed, scared of what they might do. They are speaking a language I don't recognise or, not at first, and then it hits me – it's the same language the Trainers and the Workers spoke in the Dome when they were chatting amongst themselves.

The same language I heard Marcellus often speak into his phone.

I'm not in the Training Camp any more, or I don't think that I am, therefore the language must be the language of the Quadrant with the Great Desert, or even the Non-Secular World as a whole.

One of the women reaches out and indicates for me to give her my hand. I'm not sure what to do and I can't see her face, but her eyes look sincere and I'm sure there's a kind smile going on behind the mask because of the way her eyebrows arch up.

I glimpse across at Kuro and he's nodding back that it's okay.

So I lift my hands for the woman to take and she does, gently rubbing at the redness. I expect it to burn like grazes do, but it doesn't, and her touch is soft and my mind floods with memories of my mother and even my sister, Liz, whose touch was never soft.

Holding my hands, the woman kneels in front of me and reaches out to an earthen pot and takes out a wooden like spoon and begins to smear more of the see-through glue across my arms. It's a strange feeling, both cold and warm, and it tingles in a pleasant way. I don't know what it is because it should drip and run and it doesn't.

It's oily yet dry to the touch.

She finishes applying the ointment and looks at me and I realise she's asking if it's okay that she puts some on my neck and face.

I shrug a *Yes*.

And I'm right.

She does exactly what I thought as another woman approaches me holding a plate of food.

Or I think it's food.

It's many small portions of pastes and bits, and it's an array of colours. I'm not sure what to do, but as she offers up the plate for a second time, Kuro says.

'I don't know what the food is, but it tastes good. You use the thin bread to pinch the food between your fingers then you can pick it up. I don't think they have knives and forks, or they're not letting us use them. They would be handing us weapons.'

I look at Kuro then back at the woman and she indicates for a third time that I should take the plate of food, miming what Kuro has just said.

I smile, taking the plate and resting it on my lap as I stare at the triangles of flat bread. It's like someone ran over the loaf with a heavy vehicle. I lower my head and sniff at the little piles of paste. There's a sweetness, like raw honey that comes back at me and my action makes the women giggle, which in turn makes me smile some more. I take a slice of the flat bread, fold it and dip it into a cream, thick like paste, that has a green oil on top. I put the rich paste into my mouth, dripping oil onto my fingers as I do. The texture of the food is soft but the flavours radiate and I unexpectedly smile my approval. I'm hungry and I'm thirsty and it's like the woman serving me has read my mind, because I'm given water in a cup made of metal. I gulp it back and the water is soft and fresh and ice cold, and there's something about the cold that snaps back all my fears.

'Where are the others?' I call out.

Kuro shrugs, like he doesn't care.

Diego does the same.

'How long have you two been awake?'

'An hour before you… I don't know,' Diego says with another embarrassed shrug.

I lift the plate from my knees and place it onto the floor. It's then I see the dozens of rugs that are spread out before me. I take in the rest of my surroundings and if I'm right, I'm in a tent. It's a luxurious type of tent, but still a tent that peaks in the middle and what I thought was a central beam is actually a thick wooden pole that is hinged in the middle and can be spilt in two.

I stand and the two women try to stop me, one of them lifting my plate for me to start eating again. I shake my head and nudge the plate away. I don't mean to, but I push too hard and the plate tips from her hands and food spills across the makeshift bed and rugs.

Standing, I see that I'm dressed in a kind of white robe and I feel naked, but I'm not, and I wonder how I got into these clothes as I look for the Hunter Pack Uniform I was wearing and my precious boots.

I flinch as one of the women touches my arm.

She's trying to get me to sit, but I don't want to sit, and like the plate I push her hand away, firmer than I know is right.

I step between them and head towards Kuro who starts to stand as I approach.

'Have you asked about the others?'

He shakes his head and looks at the floor.

My anger sparks, and before I can stop myself, I've shoved him backward. More petulant than violent, but Kuro's light and he flips back over his bed, falling into the siding of the tent, more food spilling onto the floor. I hear the women talk agitatedly behind me as I step across to Diego.

'What's happened to Spencer?'

'How do I know,' he says all defensive.

'You could've asked.'

'We don't speak their language.'

'You speak it enough to take their food and work out how to eat it without a knife and fork.'

'It's not the same thing,' he mumbles back.

I hear movement and snap round to see one of the women duck under the heavy canvas opening and disappear outside. I catch a glimpse of the desert.

If that's a good thing or not, I don't know, but at least we're not back at the Training Camp.

But it still feels like a prison. And I should know, because I've been in enough. They have their own smell no matter how they might appear. And it doesn't stop there, because I'm in trouble for the plate of food and for pushing the woman's hand. But I was probably in trouble for just being me, because that's been the history of my life since my parents died.

The entrance is pulled back and I want to be shocked and scared, but I'm holding it in. I've somehow returned to the old Ned. The one before I became Head of Pod Fifteen. The one who's going to give problems to the Lawyers and the Court Officials and the Guards in the Holding Centre, and anyone else for that matter who wants my problems, because I've got plenty to share around, and it's better in the long run to take a bit of pain in the now than to suffer in their hands for eternity.

I'm Ned 5-7-9-0-1-2-3.

I'll mix it up with anyone.

In front of me is a man who's wearing the same kind of robe, but with trousers and he has a headscarf on and a sash like belt with a knife tucked into the side, and he's carrying a gun that is strapped across his shoulder. I don't know the model, because I don't know about guns, and I'm not sure I want to, but I do know this one is powerful and is built for War and killing people with ease.

If I had any doubt of where I was – it's gone.

This man looks like a picture from the Great Terrorist Wars.

A time before I was born.

A time before the World was split into Secular and Non-Secular Quadrants.

A time before anyone could be accused of being a *Denounced.*

We stare at each other.

I'm not backing down.

Gun or no gun.

His face is sun-baked and craggy, and his eyes are bright and intelligent, and he's weighing me up, like I'm weighting him up.

Then he smiles.

'We weren't sure who was the leader. You or the one who nearly died. But it's you. Follow me.'

So now I know three things:

    Spencer is still alive.

      This man can speak my language.

        And I'm going to meet his boss – the boss.

I just hope it's not someone who knows Ilse or this person they call God.

8

The man holds the canvas doorway open.

As I step past him, he smiles, but he's really laughing at me, and I don't know why, but I'm sure I'm going to find out.

Instantly, I'm hit by the heat of the day and the white glare of the sun. It stops me in my stride and I squint hard, and as my eyes slowly adjust, I see thirty or more large tents scattered across the golden sands like a makeshift village – which is what it is.

But in the middle of desert.

I'm confused.

There are men, women and children of all ages going about their business. The women are dressed like those who attended us in the tent I've stepped from and most of the men are dressed like my armed guard. I take another step forward but immediately hop back into the shadow of the tent.

The sand is too hot on the soles of my feet.

My guard laughs and leans back into the tent and speaks in his language.

One of the women appears by the door and hands me a pair of leather sandals.

I slip them on.

They are too big, but at least the sand no longer singes the bottom of my feet.

I follow my guard and we weave through the village of tents. Nobody is paying me much attention, which I like, and I sense a relaxed, industrious and happy atmosphere, despite most of the men being armed or at least have close proximity to some kind of automatic weapon.

We walk past another crop of tents and women cooking when I stop and stare in disbelief. In a roped-off pen, I see dozens of large animals with long U-shaped necks, small heads, and a giant hump in the middle of their bodies. The animals are a darker shade of the sand. Without thinking I step away from my guard, fascinated by these creatures that give me a childlike skip in my step. I've seen pictures of them in school, but we were told they were extinct.

All wiped-out during the Great Terrorist Wars.

Exterminated.

Anything that represented the Old World and was seen as a threat was removed.

It was one of the many purges that went on at that time to ensure all our safety.

Camels.

Up close, they are big and ugly, I can see they're mean and aggressive. They have the nature of Ilse and Marcellus mixed into one.

I like dogs and have a memory of riding a horse once with my sister in a forest somewhere, but I don't know how anyone could ride one of these animals. One of them looks at me and snorts, and it makes me jump back. My guard laughs out loud and I feel the heat of embarrassment around the base of my neck, pleased that the other members of the Pod didn't witness me being scared. He steps in front of me and pulls at the harness of the camel that snorted in my direction, lowering its head.

He pats the side of its neck.

'Ships of the Desert,' he says. 'These beasts are thousands of years old and the best way to travel these lands. They are as much of our family as the women and children who you see here. If you kill one of these, it's the same as killing one of our children. Never forget that.'

He encourages me forward.

Apprehensive, I raise my hand and touch the animal's neck. The fur is rough and matted and oily, and I sense the camel doesn't like me. It's picking up my nerves or even my scared smell, but I'm glad when the guard says.

'Come... we can't keep him waiting any more.'

I follow him, looking over my shoulder at the animals, noticing they walk differently. Both legs on the same side rise and fall together, and their feet seem to spread out. It's an evolutionary design so they can walk up soft sand dunes. Much better than the boots I was wearing, I think.

We walk on and what I thought was a random layout of tents isn't. I see there are more armed men on the peripherals and more women in the middle and that I'm heading for a Central section that is the core of this mobile unit. We come to the largest tent of them all and it's the only one with two armed guards outside, who are sitting under the shade of a canvas overhang that forms the entrance.

My body starts to tingle with nerves and my throat begins to tighten.

I always get like this when I sense that I'm about to get into trouble, and I am usually right. Nothing ever good comes from it and I'm scared now, but in a different way that I can't explain.

As I step into the shade of the entrance the guards seem as curious by me as I am by how relaxed and at ease they are in doing their jobs. They say something to my escort in their language, sharing a joke at my expensive.

It has to be about the camel.

The guard who's marched me here removes his gun from his shoulder and hands it to one of the men along with his knife, before opening the canvas door and guiding me through.

The tent is darker inside than the one I left. An aromatic scent, slightly sweet, hangs in the air. The floor is covered in thick rugs that guide my eyes to a stage like area built of cushions. I count nine women and seven men, but none of the men are armed. Light grey smoke wafts from delicate pots that dot the outskirts of the rugs. It's these that give off the fragrant sweet smell. I'm not sure I like the sent, but the smell is calming my nerves.

Like a drug.

In the centre of the cushions is a man dressed in a white, long robe, like the one I'm wearing.

But it is a hundred times better quality.

He's sitting cross-legged with his eyes closed and his back is ram-rod straight. His hands gently rest on top of his crossed knees and his breath is falling in-and-out in the easiest rhythm I've ever seen.

Even sitting, I can see he's a powerfully built man.

I'm tall, but he's taller and wider and it's all explosive muscle power. The kind I've seen in professional fighters on the TV. His skin is the colour of dark sand and his hair is as black as Ilse's.

My guard points to some cushions below the mound and off to the man's right.

They kind of make a chair, but they're on the floor.

I move to them and sit, but I'm not comfortable. There's nothing to support my lower back and I'm not used to crossing my legs for any length of time, never mind sitting on the floor, cushions or not. It's not helped by the injury I'm carrying. The one Marcellus did to me when he threw me onto the floor in our training session.

I do my best to get comfortable as my guard sits amongst the cushions on the opposite side.

Watching me.

I wait, unsure.

The others ignore me, like I'm not here.

Then the man slowly opens his eyes.

They are a deep green colour and as piecing as a hawk's.

He stares at me and I unexpectedly think of Jack at the Holding Centre – the one man who tried to make my last few weeks bearable.

This man looks at me in the exact same way.

It's inquisitive and assessing, with no judgemental tone, and there's nothing aggressive or hidden within it.

I was expecting the Lawyer or Court Official Treatment at best, followed by the vindictiveness of Ilse.

I smile, nervously, then stop myself, because I'm sure it is making me look weak and stupid.

I tell myself, I'm Ned Hunter, not Ned 5-7-9-0-1-2-3, as I tug at the sleeve of my robe to cover my digital number that's been tattooed into the skin of my wrist for the rest of my life.

One of the women walks over and hands me a glass of tea full of leaves. I sniff it and realise the leaves are mint. It's fresh mint tea, something I've never had before. She then serves my escort and finally the main man. For me, their respect is upside down. In my World the people at the top get served first and not last.

He nods for me to drink and I do, all of us sipping at the same time.

The drink is sweet and refreshing, and there's something about the mint that makes me want to drink some more.

And I do.

The man doesn't take his eyes off me, but it's me that speaks first, and I knew I was going to.

'How's Spencer?' I ask him.

Silence.

He just stares at me, sipping his tea.

When he's finished his next sip, the woman who served the drinks glides over and takes his glass handing him a white cloth, which he gently dabs against the corners of his mouth.

He hands it back and thanks her.

'What's your name?' he asks me.

There's a calmness in his voice that I immediately associate with my father. It's both direct and forceful, but non-confrontational, like he's used to having his questions answered after the first request.

'Ned,' I say. 'I'm concerned for my friend and the two girls who were with us – Chantal and Rasa. They are all part of my Group.'

I didn't mean to say *My* but at least I stopped myself from saying *Pod*.

'Ned…' he repeats.

But he doesn't really say it like a question. It's more to himself and it's only then I fully acknowledge he can speak my language as well as his own.

It was the same with Ilse and Marcellus, and everyone else I've met in the Non-Secular World. Nobody in my Quadrant can speak this language, because it would the same as killing yourself if you learnt. It's a crime punishable by death.

So I wonder why they can speak our language and if that makes them smarter than us, because I'm beginning to see that we are so very different in so many ways I hadn't thought of before.

And there's something about these people that I'm supposed to hate.

But I don't.

And I don't know why that is, because I was born and raised to hate anyone who wasn't part of my Secular World.

And the thought that I don't is one of the most uncomfortable thoughts I've ever had in the whole of my life.

'I like that you are concerned about your friends more than you are concerned about yourself. It tells me a lot about you… *Ned*. In our home men and women don't share together unless they are in a union. You were not to know that. I can tell you that your female friends are safe and being taken care of in another part of our camp. The other boy you call *Spencer* is sick. We believe he will live but it's not certain yet. Only things out of our control will determine what happens to him. All we can do is wait and see.' He pauses, looks at me in that inquisitive way of his before continuing. 'You arrive with a certain fascination. No food and no water and out in these lands! You are fortunate that we are even talking to each other. Tell me – where are you from?'

'We were on a Military Training Exercise and became separated from our main group,' I say.

He smiles and repeats my last word.

'Group?'

I say nothing because the best lies are the ones you don't expand on – Community Homes and cruel Wardens taught me that.

He nods to one of the women who walks over and places a large basket on the floor.

Folded neatly on top are four Hunter Pack uniforms.

One Worker's uniform.

And one Guard's uniform.

All from the Dome.

'Tell me about the Black uniform? It interests me the most,' he says in that calm authoritative voice of his.

9

His question about the Black uniform fizzes through me faster than I can think and I desperately start to concoct all sorts of excuses in my mind – some sound good to me, but most don't.

I go to rub my eye with my finger but manage to put the breaks on and stop myself in time. Another *Denounced* I met in Court once told me it is a sign of lying if you do and that the Judges are trained to watch out for it. It must be true, I think, because it's exactly what I want to do now.

It's like my pending lies want to bleed out from me and reveal their truth.

I don't know how but I manage to keep it all under control and stare into this man's hawk-like eyes. I'm not sure what I see behind them, but it's not the usual cruelty or malice I'm used to from people in a position of power, and I'm proud of myself that I'm not reacting to the lies building inside of me.

I have to protect our Pod, I think.

'Anyone dressed in *Black* were the enemy. And anyone dressed in *Brown* were the Marshals of the Exercise.'

I say it as matter-of-fact as I can.

He nods, like he's expecting me to say more.

I don't.

'Interesting,' he continues. 'One could easily mistake them as the same colour if you were in a hurry?'

I swallow, but say nothing.

And I won't, because when I went to Court, I had the worst Lawyer you could ever have. She only cared about her nails and her hair and getting away early for the weekends so she would miss the traffic and do whatever it is stupid Lawyers do in their spare time. But I learnt one valuable lesson from being in the Court and the Holding Centre and even the Community Homes I've stayed in – especially the cruel ones – silence is your best friend.

Your only friend, sometimes.

I learnt that people like to fill in the gaps, especially my stupid Lawyer who couldn't stop talking. Even the Judge told her to shut-up once. Jack could talk excessively, too. I liked it in him. He was a good man, but he was like everyone else in that he couldn't bear the silence.

I can.

So I wait.

And the silence continues.

Then the man stands and his movement prompts everyone else who is sitting to stand as well.

I do the same, unsure what is going to happen next. It's then I see the string of beads entwined between the fingers of his right hand. They are the same kind and colour that I saw our Driver use when he took me through the Wall of Fog back at the Dome. The same type I asked Kuro to use when he became our Driver when we first escaped. Seeing them makes my heart thump harder than it already is as the man steps from his mound of cushions and stands in front of me, a small ripe smile, creeping up from his lips.

'My name is Omar. This is my home. These are my people. We are the Tribe of the Nomads and there are many like us. This desert is our Ancestral Home and you have my blessings to travel through it. You are free to walk amongst us as you please and you are free to leave at your leisure. Please take your belongings. Your own clothes will fit you better than ours.'

The woman holding the basket of clothes presents them to me.

I stare at them uncertain, half expecting a trick.

It doesn't come and I thank her, taking the basket.

It's light, but it's also the heaviest load I've ever carried.

'Please,' he says, indicating that I should lead the way.

I step forward carrying the basket and he steps in line. There's an ease to his walk that I've never seen in anyone before. The guards outside seem to know we are coming. They are stood to attention as the canvas entrance is pulled back. The guard who escorted me here now steps to the front and leads the way. The heat outside is something I've never experienced before and had we not been rescued, Pod Fifteen would be dead now, of that I'm certain had we not made it back to the mountains.

I notice that everyone nods and acknowledges Omar as he walks past. There's a genuine reverence in people's attitude and it's a kind of power I've never seen before.

I guess the word I'm looking for is *respect*.

It's not something I'm used to seeing, or not this type.

Omar stops at an open kitchen and one of the women cooking offers him a sample of food to taste. He uses his fingers to take the offering as another woman hands him a cloth to wipe his hands. He thanks them both as a small boy runs up to greet him. Omar kneels and speaks with the lad, like the little-man is the most important person in their Tribe. I don't understand what is being said, but I do know I'm unexpectedly upset, even jealous. There's something giving and supportive that I can't recall happening that much in my life once my parents were dead. There's Jack, of course, and there was Andreas Lee at the beginning, but look what he did to me with his fake words and acts of kindness – I'm a *Denounced* because of him.

I block that painful thought as we walk on, a dog running between us, barking excitedly. I occasionally glimpse at the contents of the basket I'm holding. I'm being punished. Omar knows I lied, which I did. I feel guilty, but I don't at the same time. There's nobody looking after me, but me. And whether I like it or not, I'm still watching out for our Pod, because when we are in harmony, we are as good as this Tribe of the Nomads, even though for now we've fallen back into our dysfunctional individual selves.

I wonder if that is my fault?

I don't know.

I hope not as we turn right and duck through the canvas opening of another tent.

Inside are three women and they stand immediately and give a short bow towards Omar. It's more a slight nod of the head, which you could miss. They part and behind them, Spencer is lying across a bed of cushions. His skin is sweaty and pale, and he's twitching like he's in a bad dream and I guess he is.

'He was stung by a Scorpion,' Omar says. 'Their venom shocks and stuns the body. It is designed to paralyse its prey so the Scorpion can then eat at its own desire. Mean, but effective. We should all perhaps operate like Scorpions for a successful life – quick, deadly and leisurely. What do you think?'

'Will he live?'

'The poison is still in his body and many would have died at this point. There is fight in his Soul.'

I flinch at his use of the word *Soul*. It's banned in our Quadrant. It can get you fast-tracked to the hangman. I remember when Ilse told me we could use the word, but I'm not sure how to use it and I'm not sure what it means because everyone seems to have a different understanding.

In the Holding Centre we would chant the word at the Prison Guards after lights-out as a way to abuse them.

Soul.

Soul.

Soul.

A rhythmic chant that usually ended with a reduced food rationing and a beating for some. Not that we cared, because only the *Denounced* would chant it as they were dead already.

The canvas entrance is pulled back and a member of the Tribe hurries in and speaks with Omar. It's the first time I see Omar frown, but if that represented a loss of composure it is over in the split second it appeared.

He says something to the Guard who has escorted me here and I'm told to sit in the far corner. I do, but as Omar steps out of the tent I glimpse two of the Assault Buggies, which chased us into the Mine, parked in the sand in the near distance.

That's eight solider and two drivers.

Ten highly skilled and armed men.

I stare at the basket of clothes I'm holding, touching the Black uniform, before looking across at Spencer. I don't know why but I want to say sorry to him. Sorry to Diego, too, and to the others for all separate reasons, most of which I can't explain.

Now we're all going back.

Ilse will look to force me to be part of whatever it is she's doing if her talk in the Mine is anything to go by. The others are *Denounced,* their outcomes likely sealed. This Pod are the only friends I've ever had; my new-found family and, I'm about to lose them.

That's the loss of two families in one short life.

The canvas entrance opens and I stand, waiting for the Assault Teams or even Ilse to enter behind Omar.

He looks at me and I let my eyes drop to the rugged floor. My heart aches in a way I can't explain. The heaviness in my stomach makes it hard to stand. I have nothing to say and even if I did I wouldn't give him the pleasure of hearing my fears and pains and disappointments.

I'm Ned Hunter and I won't piss my pants as the other *Denounced* did before they were hung.

'Ned we have guests.'

I nod, looking up.

But I only see Omar, and then his smile.

He continues. 'As someone who is new to our lands you won't know that our sandstorms come on three consecutive nights. The last night is always the worst and tonight is day three. We prepare by lowering our tents to a quarter of their height and then we eat before the storm arrives. We will start to lower the tents shortly. Afterwards, I would be honoured if you would join me as my guest at my table?'

'Me?'

'Yes, Ned... *you*. Our guests in the Buggies have their own homes to go to.'

10

I stand-by and watch the men, women and children of the Tribe of the Nomads work to lower the tents to less than half their normal height.

There's an intensity in their work and everyone appears to know exactly what is needed and what their individual job entails, no matter how small or seemingly insignificant. I miss being part of this type of collective energy and it triggers vague memories of the days before I became an orphan. I have the urge to help, join in and do my part, but I know I would be more a hinderance than anything else – and by the darkening of the sky the time is short before the final storm arrives.

My guard leads me on and we hurry past the camels, which continue to fascinate me. I'd never seen one before today and I'd been told they were extinct – which they're not. They've all kneeled in a circle, heads tucked down, facing inwards, eyes closed under thick long lashes. It's like they know the storm is coming and if I ever needed a barometer about imminent sandstorms then I have the perfect gauge right in front of me. I'm sure the safest place tonight is in the centre of these large and strange looking beasts.

I'm guided to a tent that has already been prepared for the storm and my guard flips back the canvas entrance. I stoop so low that I'm almost crawling on my hands and knees to get inside. It's warm and lit with low lights coming from a kind of electronic lantern I've not seen before. I know he's not going to follow me and he doesn't. What I don't expect is him to start hammering long pegs into the sand, securing the canvas entrance shut.

I tense.

Is it to keep the pending storm out?

Or is it to keep me secured in?

I want it to be the former, but I'm sure it's the latter.

My sight adjusts to the new light and the tent could easily house twenty or more. I declined Omar's invitation to eat with him, because I care more about our Pod than being a guest of someone I don't know. Plus the idea of being centre of attention at a large meal would kill my appetite dead.

I don't know or even care if Omar was insulted or not, but I had to follow my heart, and he's been true to his promise. In the middle of this tent is a circle of cushions, creating the home. Inside is sat Rasa, Chantal, Kuro and Diego. We're all here except Spencer. Even though it's been strained between us since we escaped Ilse, I feel his loss even more with the others present. There's always an odd balance between us when we're one down, and I'm sure at times like this we're at our most vulnerable – maybe more from each other than the outside world. As a six we're balanced.

In the centre of the cushioned ring there're dishes of food and plates for us to use.

It smells good and I'm hungry.

But nobody eats and they stare back at me like I'm the enemy. I'm filled with more pounding of guilt. I don't understand why Omar didn't invite them to his tent for supper, either. We could all be his Guest of Honour, I think.

I crawl towards them and it reminds me of the time I was first taken to Ilse after we started the fight in the Dome to get the First-Aid box so they wouldn't know it was our Pod who had tried to escape. When I came back to the dormitory that night, they'd convinced themselves, with the help of

Marcellus, that I'd made a deal to hand one of them over to save myself from being whipped. I'm sensing the same belief now – like I've struck some secret deal – but I didn't then, and I haven't now, and the truth is I don't know why Omar wanted me to go for dinner with him and exclude the others. I don't know why Omar didn't hand us in. It doesn't make sense, so I can't explain something I don't understand.

It hits me that I am more happy to see them than they are to see me.

A pang of rejection rolls through me.

There are times I wish I could express myself like Chantal would, but I'm sure it would make me look weak and I'd lose their respect, so I'm never going to be that vulnerable.

I scramble over the cushioned mound as one side of the tent billows, like a sail on a ship. It momentarily distracts everyone and I'm pleased to have their eyes off me. I use the moment to sit between Diego and Kuro, and face Rasa and Chantal. I reach out and place some of the meats and pastes onto a plate. We don't have knifes or forks but the flat breads do the job and my eating makes the others reach for plates and food, a hint of camaraderie returns.

'Do you think it'll hold?' Chantal asks, as another gust shakes the side of the tent, the lights within the lanterns flickering and dimming.

'They know what they're doing,' Diego says. 'They've lived in this place all their lives. We'd occasionally get sandstorms in Tula. Not as bad as this, but still storms of sand. It reminds me of home, but I couldn't be further from home if I tried.' His stare follows his voice and drops into a vagueness that I associate with a low kind of depression Diego suffers.

I watch his fist involuntarily clench and open, and then clench again – his knuckles stretching his skin to breaking point with each repetition. Chantal reaches out to him, but he shrugs her hand away. Rasa is about to saying something, but I nudge her foot with mine and shake my head for her to ignore it.

She catches her internal anger and sits back, blowing out her breath.

'Where did they take you?' Kuro asks.

'To see Spencer. He was stung by a thing called a Scorpion. Their venom paralyses you. He's still sick, but Omar is sure he'll make it. He's getting good care from what I can tell.'

'Who's Omar?' Rasa asks.

Her voice is laced with suspicion and I don't blame her.

My tone was friendly and I made it seem like I'd bonded with our new Warden, which I haven't – not even close.

'They are called the Tribe of the Nomads and he's their Head.'

'O… mar… O… mar.' Diego says.

Sarcasm and anger and resentment smash into our cushioned space.

The tent billows again and sand starts to rasp the canvas walls. It sounds like rain, but if you listen hard you can hear the cutting sharpness. I glance at my arms, which are still sliced from getting caught outside in last night's storm. The pegged entrance hasn't moved and I think of the place we escaped.

The food was the best I'd ever eaten.

The facilities were clean and safe.

But it was still a prison, and the Trainers were some of the cruellest people I've ever encountered.

I wonder what the difference is now?

The food I've eaten so far is different, but as good as in Ilse's Camp. These tents are as luxurious a place as I've ever stayed. But the men are armed and they are watching us, and we don't need enclosed walls and barbed wire to keep us in, because hundreds of miles of sand dunes does that job adequately enough.

So Omar's words that we can go at any time are as hollow as Ilse's smile.

And what if Omar is just another Ilse template?

He's all charm, but underneath he's an evil person waiting to use us for his own agenda.

It's all possible.

I've seen it all before – we all have.

'What's going to happen to us, Ned?' Diego says, his tone changing, the sadness returning.

'I don't know, but I do know I lied to Omar and he knows that I did.'

Chantal folds her arms as her eyes dart between us.

'What did you say to him?' Rasa asks.

'He had the clothes we escaped in. They were all cleaned and pressed and folded into a basket that he made me carry. I know this was stupid thing to say, but I said we'd been on a Cadet Training Session and had become separated from the main Group due to the storm.'

There's a pause and I can see them thinking about what I've said as the sides of the tent flap some more. Sand skids across the roof, making us all glance up.

'That's okay,' Rasa, finally says. 'There's no reason why he shouldn't believe it. I haven't said anything to anyone about how we got here. Has anyone else?' she says, looking at the others.

They shrug and shake their heads, looking back at me.

'There's something else. Two of the Assault Buggies turned up with full armed crews. I'm not sure if they had the authority to search the camp or not, but they didn't stay.'

'Didn't stay or were sent away?' Rasa asks.

I feel the tension crease my face as I stare at Rasa.

'I can't be sure, but I think Omar had more authority than them so he sent them away, which means he didn't tell them about finding us in the Desert.'

'So he lied to Ilse's men?' Kuro asks.

I shrug.

It's the question I've been asking myself.

Chantal gasps, putting her hands to her mouth.

It's Kuro's turn to fold his arms and look at everyone for their reaction, worry darting through his eyes.

'Why did he do that?' Diego says.

'Yeah, why did he do that?' Rasa repeats.

Diego sounded nervous.

Rasa's was all mistrust.

I shrug.

'Why didn't you ask him?' she says.

I shrug again.

'I don't know. I didn't want to go there,' I say.

I recall all my hatred toward her when we first met and how it's changed into a mixture of confusion and respect and feelings I don't understand. I don't even know what I feel about her right now. She's a complicated person whom I'm not sure I can trust. Maybe I never could and I've been kidding myself all along because she's the most beautiful person I've ever seen.

Which is a stupid reason to trust someone.

'What if he's setting you up?' she adds.

'For what... he said we're free to go. He could have handed us all in and he didn't,' I say, all defensive.

'What do you think the Assault Team said?'

'What do you mean?'

'They must have asked about us?'

'Maybe, maybe not. It could have been a routine stop, looking for water or supplies?'

Rasa scoffs a spiteful laugh.

'Those Assault Teams don't need supplies. Omar didn't hand us in because we're his prisoners now and not Ilse's.'

'And why would we be his prisoners?'

'We escaped. We're valuable. There's a price on our heads and an even bigger one on yours, and he's going to collect. That means we're not going back to Ilse. We're going somewhere else. Somewhere worse.'

11

I open my eyes to see the centre of the tent is being lifted back to its original height.

I can't see by whom, but I can hear men grunting and the wheels of pulleys churning through the gears from outside the tent.

As I continue to blink awake, unsure when I fell asleep or if I even dreamt, the guard who's been my constant companion since we've been guests – or is it prisoners of Omar – steps in.

Behind him, two women enter carrying a tray each of what I now know will be fresh mint tea.

I stand and to my surprise I don't ache or feel stiff. The cushions appear to have had a magical effect of supporting me and are comfortable at the same time. The painful niggle I've been carrying in my lower back since Marcellus threw me to the floor is still there, but it's slightly better and if I do have to run again today my movements should be freer.

The women pour the mint tea into tall glasses, steam wafting from the centre like smoke from a chimney.

We take one each.

The tea is hot and sweet and refreshing, and it's a drink I could grow to like.

When we finish, we return our empty glasses and my guard invites us outside, indicating that I should go first. It seems odd, like he's being subservient towards me, and I don't trust it. Even Kuro throws me an unsure shrug. I do as I've been instructed and as I reach the canvas entrance it's pulled back from outside like they know I'm coming.

Hesitant, I step into a ruby red sunlight. The golden sands that roll out before me look on fire and the storm has shifted the terrain.

Everything is banked high on the right side and it reminds me of the Dome and the *City of Hope* with the ever-moving landscape that was designed to confuse us, but this is natural and Ilse's Dome World wasn't, and I'm once again grateful for being in the open air.

I let fresh warm air fill my lungs.

I see too that the camp is twice the size I thought it was and that we are in a separate annex away from the main hubbub. It's like we're in the village and the main town is off to our right. I look for the camels and I see them standing, eating from a sack pouch, which has been placed over their mouths and held in place by a rope that loops around the top of their heads.

'Look!' Chantal says.

Her voice is all whisper and urgency and it makes me tense even more than I already am.

The fight-or-flight is unable to leave my body and let me relax.

It's been like that for years.

I turn and then gasp inwardly, seeing something I've never witnessed before.

Men and women are kneeled on rugs and look to be praying toward the ruby-red sky.

I once saw a photograph of the same scene in the Holding Centre.

Smuggled in and passed around as a commodity to be traded for chocolate or anything sweet.

It's the single most banned image in our Secular Quadrants, and owning the photograph can get you shot on the spot – no stupid Lawyers, Court Officials or Judges required.

And here it is alive in front of me, like it's okay to do it.

'Are the Tribe of the Nomads *Denounced*?' Chantal asks. 'It could be why they helped us?' she adds.

Rasa, Diego and Kuro all crowd around me and we stare into the throng of bowed men and women.

I don't think they're *Denounced* and I don't know what they are other than praying seems to be accepted, like talking about the Soul.

'They could be,' I say, as I'm distracted by Spencer heading towards us.

The others rush towards him, forgetting what they've seen.

I hear Diego call him *Spence* rather than *Spencer*, and their friendship seems immediately re-instated.

Spencer is groggy and looks unsure about where he is and what has happened to him, and I can see he's struggling to smile and gain his focus. Chantal hugs him and Diego gives him a gently thump on the arm, as Kuro inspects the spot on Spencer's neck where he was stung, nodding like he's a doctor. Rasa stands on the peripheral to them all, but she's smiling and extending her emotional warmth in a way I haven't witnessed before.

I'm jealous.

I'm also the odd one out having not moved, and Spencer glances over at me, annoyed that I've not joined the rest of our Pod for his reunion.

I reluctantly move, slower than I should, finally extending my hand in a gesture of warmth and welcome.

He looks at my open hand, struggling to hide his disgust, but feeling the tension from the others, he reaches out to shake it.

'You okay?' I ask.

'Looks like I got stung by a *scorpion*, whatever that is. What is this place... is it freak show Number Two now we've left the confines of Dome?' he says, giving me a half smile and trying to sound all cool.

I give him the quick version of what's happened, but I know that's not his real question.

Because he wants to ask if this is really the Non-Secular World, which it is, of course.

And will we live or will we die?

Like all of us, I don't know any of the answers.

He nods and tells me he can't remember anything other than running from the Dome. I don't believe him. Much has happened from when we stepped out of the Hatch to him being stung. But he's been in the System for long enough to understand that having a poor memory is as good a defence as silence.

It's then he spots the men praying and looks at us both concerned and surprised; wanting someone to answer.

Nobody does, because we're all too scared of what we once thought was true of our lives no longer exists.

My guard indicates it's time to move and he asks me to follow him as another man starts to herd the rest of the Pod towards another tent. We're being split again and apart from the worry that dashes across the faces of the others there's also a sprinkling of suspicion that I'm being treated differently to them.

I am.

Ilse did the same and it's making my life harder than it already is.

I never asked for this treatment, as I never asked to be Head of Pod Fifteen, and once again I'm forced to fight my annoyance as we split and go our different ways.

I don't have it in me to turn back and face the rest of them, which I'm sure is a mistake.

A sign that I don't care.

It's not true, I just can't face them.

I walk on, following my ever-present guard who continues to be over polite. The sky is changing as snippets of blue push the ruby red to one side and the growing heat of the day sucks at my skin, and I see now how this robe I'm wearing cools me yet keeps me warm.

We start to veer left and I immediately recognise the tent we're heading for.

It's Omar's.

Its shape is different. Hexagon while the others are round or square. It's bigger, too, but then he is the Tribal Leader so some things never change for those at the top.

We move to the front and the same two guards are outside, looking relaxed, drinking mint tea and chatting idly in a language I don't understand.

I step through to see Omar sat on his mound of cushions. There's a low table in front of him with food for two. Omar points to the cushions opposite and invites me to sit, as one of the many women that always seem to be in his attendance, guides me to the spot. I lower myself into position and another woman approaches with a bowl of water. She reaches out to my hands and I flinch, pulling away. Omar smiles and indicates it's okay. So I relax and let the woman take my hands and she starts to bathe them in the warm water that smells of lavender and honey.

I'm not sure how I feel about this, but there's a side of me that likes her touch and I think of my mother… but I think of Rasa more.

It's confusing and exciting at the same time, and I'm glad when the woman stops and Rasa leaves my mind.

'How did you sleep, my friend?' Omar asks, as he points to a dish I should try first.

'I didn't hear the storm once so I must have slept well,' I say.

'You have a bad back, if I'm not mistaken?'

I nod, surprised.

He beckons one of the women over.

She carries a small glass of liquid on top of a silver coloured tray.

'Drink it,' Omar says.

I hesitate, momentarily scared, but I take the drink. It's sweet and tastes of oranges and makes my tongue tingle. I feel the warmth grip my stomach and a few seconds later the remaining stiffness in my back eases, and the constant niggle of pain I've carried for weeks evaporates.

Omar smiles, like he knows what is happening inside of my body.

As I put the glass down, my wrist exposes itself from under the robe.

5-7-9-0-1-2-3, burns brighter than the sun outside.

I'm suddenly conscious of it in a way that I've never been before.

Back in our Secular Quadrant they say some numbers are unlucky and when they get recycled that bad-luck gets recycled with them. I've never wanted to believe it. I never wanted to be defined by my number. I'm Ned Hunter not Ned 5-7-9-0-1-2-3, but maybe what they say about the numbers is true. A bad number equals bad luck and there's nothing you can do about it.

'Tell me about your tattoo and why they glow?' Omar asks, staring at my wrist.

I jam the sleeve down, hiding the fluorescent glow and instead reach for the food he indicated I should take, ignoring his question, like the moment didn't happen.

He doesn't push me on it and we eat in silence.

I continue to stare at my plate, avoiding eye contact.

'You're amongst friends, there's no need to be shy, Ned.'

Anger bolts through me.

'You don't know me, so I'm not your friend. And what if I don't want to be your friend? My friends are out there and I want to go back to them.'

He looks at me in that way he does:

Assessing.

Evaluating.

I don't like it and I don't like him.

Judging me like I'm an animal in a cage.

More anger courses through me and for some reason I'm not scared of him anymore. I should be, but he's the same as the rest of them, and he can do what he likes, but I'm not going to pretend to be his friend or play this stupid game.

I won't be isolated any more.

Forced away from the few people I trust.

Made an enemy within my own Pod by the actions of someone else.

It's not fair.

I stand.

'Sit down,' he says.

The calmness in his tone isn't as calm, so I know I've got under his skin.

I'm good at that.

'You said I was free to go. So I'm going, unless I'm a prisoner?'

'You are correct, Ned. You are a prisoner.'

Rasa was right and I was wrong.

We're nothing but a prize to be bought and sold at his pleasure.

He continues. 'But the bars and chains that restrain you are the hardest to break, because they are all in your mind.'

I stare at him, unsure what he means.

He continues, his calmness returning. 'If you want to be truly free then somebody has to teach you how, otherwise you'll be a prisoner your whole life. A prisoner of your past experiences, which will haunt you in your present life. You can never escape them and most people get trapped for ever.'

'Yeah… I've heard people like you bang on about this stuff before and you're all the same. You're using me.'

He slowly wipes his mouth and hands, and then stands, towering over me.

He could kill me with his bare hands, but I'm going to fight him to the end if that's what it takes.

I'm scared, but I'm not.

I've always known this moment would come in my life.

And I'm ready for it.

I was ready from when I was seven years old and they gave me that red trunk.

'You remind me of someone. The same passion. The same stubbornness. That person is dead now. But you are not. If you truly want freedom in this life then it starts in here.' He points to side of his head, his mind. 'But you need someone to teach you. To help you understand and point you in the right direction. There's a reason why you can't do it on your own, because right now you are blind. The blind can't lead the blind. It's impossible. But if you want and if you can trust then I can show you how to think differently. How to break the inner chains that hold you back.'

'And what do you want in return – my blood?'

'No, my friend. That belongs to you, and you should never give it up cheaply.'

'What then?'

'All I ask is that you listen with an open mind.'

'Is that it? It sounds easy.'

'No, Ned. It's far harder than you think and for some people, it is impossible.'

12

The silence is one of the longest I can ever remember as Omar continues to stare at me.

It's not aggression, but something else.

Understanding.

I'm trying to work him out and he's doing the same to me, but in a different way and his eyes are smiling – laughing at me, maybe.

Like his guard did when the camel scared me.

Then he points for me to sit on the cushions, but it's not in a commanding way, more a request, and the way he does it makes me feel better about the situation and myself.

But I don't sit.

In my mind, I'm still in the Holding Centre.

And he's my Court Official.

And I'm going to be difficult.

Why not, I think.

'You're like a boisterous puppy, Ned. You want to fight everyone and everything, which in some ways is good. It means you'll never be a slave. But you can't fight the World, because at some point, you will lose. It's bigger than you, remember that. You need understand how to negotiate and then that way you never lose.'

He sits and reaches for his food and starts to eat. I suddenly feel foolish stood on my own. I look through the spacious tent with its many cushions and rugs which divide the space and realise I'm in both his home and his office – no, *throne* – all combined in one.

The women stare back at me, like they know what I'm going to do.

I sit.

'Eat,' Omar says. 'Your brain needs more fuel than your body, and it's time to start using that muscle more than you already have.'

I reach for a meat ball. I don't know what the meat is but it's spicy and it burns the inside of my lips as I chew. I like the sensation so I take another bite and then another.

'Protein and fats are the right fuels for your mind. Always make sure you get enough of them.'

I'll eat what I want, I think.

'Why can you speak two languages?' I ask.

'Who says I can only speak two? I can speak many languages, my friend – and we are friends?'

I shrug at his last point and say. 'You know what I mean.'

'I do know what you mean, yes. I am older than I look, Ned. I've seen many things and done many things. But more importantly, I've had time to *think* about many things. The number of languages I speak is unimportant. What's important is the words you use in your mind and how you think about the problems you encounter. The story you tell yourself, about yourself, is where it all starts.'

I nod, but I'm not sure what he means. The story I tell myself is clear – I've been a prisoner all my life and I want my freedom, and as each day passes, I want it more and this man isn't going to stop me if I have my way.

'Where am I?'

'You know where you are?'

'I don't know which Quadrant?'

'Quadrant?'

'Yeah, Quadrant. I'm from Secular World Quadrant 1, North East, Section Two-C or in the Old World – New York City. So what Quadrant is this?'

He shrugs and smiles. 'We're in the Great Desert. A place that has never changed since our planet was made and has been the home of our people long before Quadrants came into existence. But if it matters, I believe this is Quadrant 7.'

Quadrant 7.

Emotions ricochet through me as my darkest fears are confirmed.

'I'm in the Non-Secular World?'

'But you knew that all along? It can't come as a surprise? Why don't you trust what you feel?'

'You're talking to me like I'm a fool.'

He smiles at me before looking over to one of the women. She approaches with a bowl of warm water. He cleans his hands and then dries them on a white cloth, never taking his eyes from me.

'Tell me about your Tribe?'

'I don't have one,' I say.

'Now you are being a fool to yourself. Those five others who are with you are your Tribe. Your family, no?'

I think about what he's just said for a beat, because I've never thought about myself being in a tribe, before.

Family yes, but not a tribe.

I nod.

'Good. Tell me about them? Tell me about the one who nearly died? He's strong inside. I like that. But he doesn't like you? Maybe, he wants to be you, but he can't. He hasn't got what you have within him. How are you going to deal with that? Are you going to keep fighting him?'

'We haven't fought,' I say all defensive.

'But you will. It's only a matter of time. If you listen to yourself then you know what I am saying will come to pass.'

A woman appears and takes my food, while another comes to wash my hands. I'm not sure I could ever get used to this. My sister, Liz, would never wash my hands. Watch over me, maybe, and shout at me if I did it wrong or missed some dirt around my nails, but never wash them – no chance.

Omar continues. 'I'm intrigued about this man that wants to fight you. Tell me about him?'

'His name is Spencer. He's an orphan, like me, and he's been in the System, for ever. He's capable, but lazy.'

'And you don't like him for that?'

'When we need him the most, he doesn't deliver. I want to trust him, but I'm not sure that I can. He lets people down.'

'Or is it that he just lets you down?'

I don't like that question and I'm not sure.

Silence.

Omar nods and then smiles. 'And the strong one who looks like a wild bull?'

'Diego is from Secular World Quadrant 2, Central, Section 1-A or in the Old World – a place called Tula in Mexico. He's solid and I trust him, but he gets depressed and it messes with his mind.'

'So he makes bad choices?'

I nod.

Omar continues. 'He's not an Orphan, though. I can tell.'

It's my turn to smile. 'He must have told you that?'

'I will speak with the others in time, but as a Leader it's important I talk with other Leaders first. And you are their Leader?'

I'm Head of Pod Fifteen, I think, which for now is the same thing.

I nod and he continues.

'We want the same things. We have the same desires. But we are going to come at them from different ways.'

'I don't understand.'

'Of course you don't, but you will in time – if you listen, that is. I'm curious about the other three. The thin boy who bumps into his environment. Can you trust him?'

I nod. 'His name is Kuro. He's from Secular World Quadrant 4, South Central, Section 17-E or in the Old World – Tokyo, Japan. He's clever. Smarter than he knows, but he's a worrier and he's easily bullied so he needs to be protected. But we owe him much. We've survived because of him. He has problems with his eyes and he lost his glasses, which is why he bumps into things.'

'I like that you've assessed him well. I can see he can be trusted.'

'Why are you helping me?'

Omar stares at me – his eyes smiling, his face stern.

'Tell me about the two women in your Tribe. They intrigue me. One is very beautiful. Her light hair and blue eyes are rare in these parts. She will get noticed. That could be a problem for you if you're not careful. But tell me about the smaller one, first?'

'Chantal is from Secular World Quadrant 3, North West, Section 10-S or in the Old World – Paris, France. She's kind. Too kind for what's happened to her. My parents died, but hers sold her out, especially her mother. She doesn't talk about it much, or not to me, anyway. Rasa probably knows more of the truth.'

He nods. 'This Chantal holds it well. She doesn't appear the bitter type. You should use that in her. She's stronger in the mind than she looks, which is true strength. You can learn something from her. Remember that. And the one with the magical eyes?'

I'm not sure why, but I don't like how refers to Rasa's eyes.

It bothers me and I hesitate before I start.

'Rasa is from Secular World Quadrant 3, East Central, Section 4-B or in the Old World – St. Petersburg, Russia. She likes trouble, but she can handle trouble, so I guess it balances out. She's her own person and she's going to do what she wants. I don't have a problem with that. I shouldn't have but it has helped us.'

'I think you do have a problem with it.'

'I told you I didn't,' I snap back.

The smile in his eyes broadens.

'Do you love her, Ned?'

His words catch me off guard and I retreat into myself at double speed, eventually throwing him a half-shrug.

'I don't know,' I add.

'And do you trust her?'

'For now,' I say.

'So you are going to trust someone who is going to do exactly what they want for themselves – is that wise?'

I don't have the answer or one that I like. Rasa has always reminded me of me, and I have that thing within when I could cut lose and leave them all if I had to. I nearly did it in the Mine. I think we'd both let the others die to save ourselves. Kuro, Chantal, Diego and even Spencer wouldn't. I hate myself that I can have those thoughts, but it's true and I can smell the same disease on Rasa. I never asked to be Head of Pod Fifteen, I tell myself.

'I'm not sure,' I say.

He nods and I'm sure he knows I'm holding out with my final answer.

'Do you know what being a Leader means?'

I shrug, not sure that I care.

'It's about making decisions, and sometimes making tough decisions, decisions you don't like yourself. Some people have it in them. Some don't.'

'If you say so.'

'Think about what I said.'

I shrug.

He continues. 'I find it interesting that you mentioned the Old World when I asked you where your tribe were from, like you miss it?'

I scoff out a laugh.

'How can I miss it? It was hundreds of years before I was born.'

He gives me his holding smile again and then says something to one of the women in his language.

She bows and hurries outside.

I watch her go and turn to see Omar standing.

He beckons me up.

'They say that previous lives can get carried within us, and that they get passed from one generation to the next. Maybe that is what is happening with you. Maybe that is why you talk about the Old World. Come, my friend.'

Omar leads me out of his tent. Outside, I'm greeted by twenty of his soldiers waiting for us. One of them hands Omar an automatic rifle which he slings across his front, and then a knife that he tucks into the sash of his belt. We walk on with the soldiers as an entourage behind us.

I keep looking over my shoulder towards them.

Unsure.

Nervous.

Apprehensive of where we are going, and perhaps more apprehensive of what is behind me.

'They are your friends so remember their faces. Each and every one of them will die for you if I ask them to.'

I almost laugh at what he's said as I take another look at the soldiers.

'They shouldn't because I'm not going to die for them, or you.'

He smiles.

'Come, Ned. I need to show you something'

13

Omar leads me out of his tent and through his camp.

There's a purpose in his stride that keeps people away and his entourage of soldiers stay a respectful distance to our rear.

I wonder where we are going, but I'm wondering more about the word *Ordained.*

I didn't like the way he said it and I don't know what it means, but I do know he used the same tone as Ilse did when she told me I had *gravitas,* and look at the problems that's given me since.

We stride past another row of tents and ahead I see a group of camels have been carved out from the rest of the herd.

I gulp.

These ones have saddles mounted across their central humps and they've been made to kneel. Their legs stick out at the back, like they belong to giant grasshoppers.

I do a quick mental count, I can see there's enough for Omar and his soldiers and two spare.

My palms go sticky.

I'm going to have ride one of these beasts, and I'm not sure I can or even want to. I do another mental count, hoping that I'm wrong and there's no spare rides when I see Rasa being led this way by a woman and two soldiers guarding her rear. She's changed into a long white robe with a sash belt and a headdress, which covers her head and neck with enough to wrap around her face and across her shoulders.

She looks elegant dressed in their attire, like she's one of them.

A natural.

A warrior of the desert.

A leader of the Tribe of the Nomads.

I'm suddenly distracted by a woman who presents me with a headscarf and sash belt, which have been neatly folded onto a tray with a knife on top of the items, holding them down. I'm unsure what to do next when the man who's been my guard steps across. He places the sash around my waist, inserting the scabbard into the side and then attaches the head scarf to my head, wrapping and folding it in a way that holds it in place. It's similar to the ones we took from the Hunter Packs, but lighter and more comfortable, and because it's folded correctly a perfect fit.

The guard steps back to admire his work, before nodding to himself. He ushers me forward. I hesitate, both scared and ashamed that I'm terrified of these beasts of the desert. They are big and aggressive and I'm not good with animals, even small dogs. We don't connect, like they sense my independence.

I glance across to check on Rasa, but she's been distracted by Omar who has personally walked over to introduce himself. He gently nods and offers his hand as he guides her the last few steps towards the kneeled camel she's expected to ride. She glares at him, resistant to his charm and I'm pleased that she does, but he continues to smile and wait, like he has all the time in the world – and maybe he does.

I watch on, jealousy forging through me.

With everything that has happened and all the pain we've endured, I've forgotten how beautiful Rasa is. Watching Omar present his charms reminds me of the first time I laid eyes on her as she was sat in the queue to be hung. Her beauty made me trip on the step and Omar in his own way is tripping now. I want to tell him that she stabbed her Warden because he repeatedly put his hand on her leg. It's how she became a *Denounced*. Some of the Trainers in the Dome looked at her too in the way Omar is looking at her now, and it's weird, because none of us can help how we look when we are born, and in many ways what should have helped her has become her over-riding problem.

A man holding a short stick guides me the last few steps toward one of the kneeled beasts. The animal stares at me and grunts. It can sense my nervousness. I glance quickly through the other camels and apart from Omar's, I'm sure mine is the largest. The man points at me to climb onto the saddle. I do, gripping what appears to be a handlebar at the front.

As I settle into the hard seat, the camel lurches forward and I'm thrown backwards and in the same instant the camel's back legs spring up and I'm shot forward as I'm suddenly flipped back again.

My knuckles go white as I grip the handlebar of the saddle.

All I can hear is the laughter of the other soldiers.

I keep my balance, just, and look around to see Omar smiling as Rasa appears queenlike and lofty sat upon her camel, as if she was born to ride these magnificent animals.

I sit upright, like I've done this hundreds of times before, doing my best to ignore the hilarity I've caused.

The man holding my camel's reins hands me the short stick, struggling to hide his grin, as he motions that I should hit the side of the camel's neck. I get what he's telling me. The quicker I tap, the faster the camel will move. The other riders are still smirking in my direction as Omar taps his camel's neck with his stick and the animal moves to the front of the group. The rest of the camels instinctively seem to know what to do and I'm jerked to my right and then suddenly I'm toppling to my left, having to grip the handle on the saddle, like a little boy in a toy go-cart.

It generates more laughter and Omar takes a quick look over his shoulder, joining in the banter at my expense.

I glare back at some of the soldiers, all defensive, determined not to fall.

Omar turns back to face the front and it takes me a few more strides to get used to the camel's movements.

I remember how it strides all on one side first, before switching to the next. This helps me and I have to force myself to relax into the motion, and it's like being on a boat at sea than being on a walking animal. We move on out and I continue to struggle to find a comfortable spot. I'm tempted to jump off and walk when I see Omar has now been flanked by several of his soldiers, and more have moved into position to flank myself and Rasa, as we're hemmed into the centre with the rest of the mounted troop pulling up the rear.

Then the pace is upped.

I don't have to tap my camel's neck with the stick as it takes the pace of the others.

I'm not sure how I'm managing to stay onboard. It's like I should be going up in the saddle, but I'm going down instead, and when I should be going down, I'm going up. The saddle is banging on the inside of my thighs and I'm sure I'm about to fall when the pace slows to a fast walk and I eventually find a rhythm.

We walk on and I grow a little less scared, finally able to concentrate beyond the camel.

The dunes in front of us have opened up and it's impossible to get any point of reference as everything looks the same. This soft sand is nothing to these beasts and their long, relaxed strides mean we traverse the peaks of the dunes with ease.

'Where do you think they are taking us?' Rasa whispers as our camels fall in line, side-by-side.

'Finally, she speaks,' I say, all sarcastic, refusing to look at her.

'You could have spoken to me,' she snaps back.

She tugs on the reins of her camel so it slows a stride.

I know she's right and I'm annoyed at myself for letting my jealousy peak and getting the better of me. She's here because I told Omar I trusted her the most out of our Pod and not because he cares about her beauty – or that's what I hope.

I tug on my camel's reins and slow so we are once again riding side-by-side.

'I don't know where he's taking us,' I snap out.

'So what's he been discussing with you then?'

I flinch internally at the question, uncomfortable with the brewing answer.

'He said he'll talk to everyone.'

'But why you and not all of us together?'

More internal heat courses through me.

'He said he only talks to the Leaders at the beginning.'

Rasa scoffs a laugh, which I ignore.

'I was annoyed at you when you said we are as much his prisoner as we were Ilse's,' I say.

'It's okay. Anyway, so far, it's better here than at the Dome… it feels different.'

For now, I think, as Omar slows his camel, allowing ours to come alongside his. His soldiers part so myself and Rasa can ride as a line of three.

'The Tribe Leaders finally engage,' he says, that smirk in his eyes returning. 'The Secular World has a strange way to communicate. We do it differently. Better, from what I can see, but perhaps there's a hidden secret in the way you go about it that could work for us. One day, you'll have to help me understand your ways.'

'Where are we going?'

'Tell me, Ned – what do you see before you?'

I look out and see nothing but golden sands and heat hazes all under a white-hot sun. That it isn't what he's asked, but I don't know what he means either, so I shrug.

'You see Freedom. And with Freedom, comes Peace. But freedom starts in the mind, and when you have freedom in the mind, you have peace in your lands.'

I look at Rasa and she looks as confused as I feel.

'Where are we going?' I ask again.

'If you were a mouse who would be your predator?'

I steal another glance at Rasa before looking back at Omar.

Omar continues to smile at me, waiting for my answer. It's a loose smile, soft lips and inquisitive eyes. But there's something behind it that I can't name. It's like he's waiting for me to understand something that I'm not getting.

'I don't know… a cat?'

'That's right – a cat. And who is the predator of the cat?'

I laugh, embarrassed. 'A dog?'

'And the predator of the dog?'

'Man, I guess.'

'And who is the predator of Man?'

'No-one.'

'Man is the predator of Man. And we are the worst predators of all. Where the dog will surrender when one of his kind proves its dominance, Man will kill to make his point. That is the true reason behind the Great Terrorist Wars. Some men didn't have peace in their minds so they had to get it by taking it from others. To negotiate you have to listen and if you listen you will begin to see people's true motivations. That's leadership, Ned.'

In the distance, I hear low flying aircraft and within seconds two Airborne Assault planes, the colour of the desert, slow and hover above our heads, blasting the sand around us like a flash storm.

My heart pounds with a new fear.

We all wrap our headscarves tighter across our faces to protect us from the cutting grains, myself and Rasa keeping our heads and eyes firmly down. The camels grunt their displeasure, but they don't bolt at the noise. It's more an inconvenience.

I imagine Ilse and her Assault Teams and even the Trainers from the Dome, looking down, scanning for us. I'm worried to my core, but I can see the soldiers around me aren't when there's an intense roar above our heads as the aircrafts bank left and power off, continuing their search of this vast open space.

Searching for *Denounced*.

Searching for me.

We ride on, Omar turning to look back towards me.

He's not smiling any more and there's a seriousness in his eyes, which I haven't seen before.

'He wants you to trust him,' Rasa whispers. 'And you're a fool if you do.'

14

We ride on.

Separated more as a group, but still keeping the basic formation – Omar at the front, Rasa and myself in the centre with Omar's soldiers flanking us from all sides.

A seriousness and silence has fallen upon us since the Assault Planes left and our journey has an endless feel to it.

I've long given up wondering what's in store for myself and Rasa at our final destination and I allow my mind to drift, forgetting about the heat and the desert and my ever-nagging thirst. Mostly, I dwell on my sister, Liz. I'm not sure why I think of her the most. Maybe it's because she's the only living relative I have left. Or maybe it's because she's the one person I can still tangibly remember from my family, and if we were to ever speak again she'd be the true connection to my dead parents. As she's older than me, she's sure to remember them better than I, having had a longer, more established relationship. So I hope she can pass on more of their wisdom, especially my father's, which I'm convinced he was saving for me until I became older.

I allow myself a momentary warmth of joy.

I forget she must have a different view of each of them to me and I'd be curious to get her reality of who my parents were as individuals. It's a conversation we've touched upon, but it was more her telling me about them than me inquiring in the way I would like to now. It would be like getting a new set of memories. A fresh input on a familiar theme. I smile to myself and I don't know why but it makes me think of Chantal. I often feel that she's the hardest done by of us all, even Rasa, who's spent most of her life fighting off an unwanted attention from men, which I'm just beginning to understand. Chantal was given up by her mother who wanted to save herself. Sold out by her one remaining parent who couldn't handle the responsibility of having a child. I can't imagine what that must do to you as a person or what kind of cruel self-absorbed parent would do it. My sister let me slip into the System, too, but she was young herself and she thought it was for the best and never dreamt I'd become a *Denounced*. She believed the Community Homes System would do a better job of making me into a responsible adult. Liz had just turned eighteen herself and her life was starting so she wasn't to know the corrupt world she was placing me into.

How could she?

If we ever meet again – which I hope we do – I will tell her that I have finally forgiven her for what she did.

I wonder if Liz regrets her actions now or thinks they were justified because I ended up a *Denounced*?

I wonder if Chantal's mother regrets it, too?

I think I would like to ask Chantal, but I won't. She has enough problems surviving like the rest of us so it's not fair to make her think of painful memories.

People are strange and I guess you never know what's really going on behind their eyes. That's why their behaviour is everything. It's the closest you'll ever get to know who they really are and what is really going on in their minds.

I learnt that the hard way.

In the System.

So has Chantal.

Jack helped me make sense of it, but ultimately what somebody does is what they are no matter what words spill from their mouth.

That's a fact.

I know it as the one truth I can hold onto no matter which Quadrant I end up living in.

I look at Rasa then back to Omar who suddenly points to his right. Our caravan of camels turns and we trek across another sand-dune before we pull to a stop.

In front of me, the sand drops and then flattens out into a half-moon, before gently banking high and curving out to our left. It looks like a semi-buried spoon. And it's the same golden glow as everywhere else but here it is heavily dotted with bleached white stones.

But they're not.

My skin goose-bumps as I steal a glance at Rasa who has her hands covering her mouth.

Tears welling in those penetrating eyes.

We're both thinking the same.

This is going to be our final resting place.

This is where it all comes to an end.

Omar sides his camel next to mine.

'What do you see, Ned?'

I can barely get the words past my scorched lips.

'Death.'

'The unburied Dead is what you see. Hundreds, maybe thousands. And they're all young bones. Bones like yours, of people who still had a future to live and enjoy. A future that has been robbed from them.'

I stare out into the mass grave, which seems to expand before my eyes as I understand what each bleached peak really means.

'Is this where my journey ends?'

'If you had stayed in the Dome, then maybe. But you misunderstand me, my friend. This is where your journey begins.'

'Who are they?'

'They are young people like you. These are not the bones of men or women. We have seen many of these graveyards on our travels across our Desert. The winds will die down over the next few days and in time these will vanish, but for now the desert has decided to reveal its darker secrets.'

I stare at a skull, which is beckoning me on.

Wanting my attention.

I look into its hollow eyes and I know that I've numbed my feelings, scared of what they might reveal about myself.

'Tell me about the Dome, Ned?'

His question sends a shockwave through me, but you wouldn't know it if you were looking on. I've spent years teaching myself to hold my emotions inside. I've locked them away from the world where nobody can see them.

Safe inside.

Safe from the pain of disappointment and rejection.

'I can only tell you what I know.'

'That's more than enough, my friend. And we are friends?'

I look at Rasa and then back at Omar, and nod that we are.

'We were all psychometrically tested in the Secular World to see if we were eligible for the Dome. It was to get us out of the System and they did it by accusing us of being Denounced.'

'And once you're a Denounced, nobody cares about you?'

I nod. 'It's a death sentence. The System is cleansing itself of non-believers. Myself, Spencer, Rasa were all in the Community Homes System so we were easy to test and then accuse. Chantal was sold-out by her Mother. The police told her she had to fill out a form but it was really the Test. Diego had been arrested for causing trouble along with a group from his village. The police did the same to him as they did to Chantal. Kuro had lived in a Doubter's Camp all his life so he's always had the shadow of being a *Denounced* hanging over him. The System tricked him into taking the Test, telling him he could leave the Doubter's Camp and go to school and get his digital credits when he became eighteen if he passed. But he was never going to pass, or not in the way he believed. There is something about us that made us special for the Dome.'

Omar nods, thoughtful.

I can see his mind churning what I've said.

'And what happened to you once you got to the Dome?' he asks.

'There were originally ninety of us. I didn't know anyone and I don't think anyone knew anybody else, either. Some of them I had seen in Court, and the Holding Centre, but that's it. Rasa and Spencer had the same Lawyer, but again they didn't really know each other. We were split into fifteen Pods – six within each Pod. We were Pod Fifteen and I was told to be the Head. It wasn't my choice. I see now that each Pod had its own strengths and weaknesses. That must have been deliberate. I don't know how long we were in the Dome for, it felt like months but each day was basically the same but getting more intense. It was fitness and then military training. They fed us well and housed us in warm dormitories. We lived as our Pod, but they were watching us all the time, spying on us. We were scored, too, for everything we did and it was like an internal competition between the Pods. I'm not sure, but it looks like the bottom three Pods were executed for not being good enough. I guess they are out there somewhere, now.'

I pause at my own words, looking across the sands.

Rasa wipes at her eyes.

More bleached bones catching my sight.

'Go on, my friend.'

'The final part of the training was for us to survive a place called the *City of Hope*. It was a fake City built within the confines of the Dome. The final test consisted of the top Pods being dropped at a Start Point and we had to find one of the special Exit Points. We were told that if we made it to one of the Exit Points then we were free to go, but we had to avoid specially trained Hunter Packs who were sent to track us down. It wasn't until then we understood it was a kill or be killed policy. We were given food for three days and three nights, so I think that's how long they thought we'd survive.'

'There were never any Exit Points,' Rasa adds. 'We were trained to be soldiers. They wanted to see how we would fight and react, and what we would do to survive. But really, we were trained to be hunted like animals. You people are sick.'

'They are not my people. But you escaped?' Omar says to me, acknowledging Rasa's statement with a nod of his head.

'We escaped by doubling back. We only spent one day and night in the fake City.'

'And now they hate us,' Rasa adds.

'No, they don't hate you. They admire you. You have something they want. Come, walk with me.'

'We don't want to,' I say.

'It's part of what you need to see. It will teach you something and it's growth, and growth is always painful.'

He looks at me and I can see something in his eyes that I'm not used to seeing.

Friendship.

Or a respect of some sorts that I can't define.

A soldier walks to the front of my camel and pulls on the rein as he taps the animal's neck with his stick. My camel grunts and then drops forward. But I'm ready this time and

I instinctively lean back to compensate the animal's move, before leaning forward as his hind legs drop.

I climb out of the saddle.

My legs wobble like they belong to someone else, but the familiar feeling soon returns.

Omar starts to walk and I follow him along with two of his soldiers. Rasa behind me. We step carefully, avoiding parts of ribs and legs and more skulls as we head to the middle of the golden graveyard.

No… this isn't a graveyard, I think.

It's a Murder Pit.

'What does all this tell us, Ned?'

'That we should all look after ourselves.'

'A statement from an angry young man who has much to learn. The Great Terrorist Wars nearly destroyed our Earth. The men of that time found a solution by dividing our World into the eight Quadrants that we all know today – the four Secular and the four Non-Secular. I don't know about your Quadrants, but within our four there has been much debate amongst the Elders of the Deserts since those days about whether our Ancestors were right or wrong in their decision to divide the World as they did. Nothing is perfect and I am not one to answer that question, but I do know there's been great peace since the Day-of-Division. A peace that may not last. Things are changing, Ned, and you are the proof we have all been waiting for.'

'How?'

'There are many Tribes who roam these lands. It is our custom to meet and share our news; to discuss what is happening in our four Quadrants. We have seen more graves like this and have heard of experiments being carried out on those in the Secular World. Many of the other graves have adult bones, not young men and women like you see here.

Maybe that shows us that the experiments are both deep and wide, but wars are fought by the young, and often the young can offer more insights than the old. Their minds are fresher, less exposed to the complexities that come to us all over time. Young people, like you and your Pod, see the world differently. You see it with clean eyes. That is powerful knowledge, especially to Ilse's employers. Not only did you escape, but you proved something else to the Powers-that-Be.'

'What did I prove?'

'That they can lose the war?'

I glance at Rasa.

'What war?'

'The Unification War. The unification of the eight Quadrants.'

15

The Murder Pit has left its own poisonous cloud over us as we head back, the setting sun starting to mark our return.

Omar slows his camel and it slips between myself and Rasa's, the three of us riding in unison.

'I need your help with something, Ned?'

I shrug and nod at the same time.

'You said that each Pod had its own strengths and weaknesses. I wanted to know what were yours?'

I think for a moment, glancing at Rasa.

I'm sure she's reading my mind and I'm even more sure she'll agree with what I'm about to say.

'We're not scared to fight, but we don't always get on, which can be weird at times. But I'm sure we all trust each other or we do now,' I add.

Rasa nods.

Omar smiles.

'Why do you want to know?' I ask.

'That makes you extremely valuable to the Powers-that-Be. You're prepared to fight and you're prepared to trust each other. We were taught that in your Quadrants everyone only looks after themselves. Only cares about their own needs and these things you called Digital Credits.'

'Who are the Powers-that-Be?' I ask. 'Ilse, who was in charge of us at the Dome, talked about them.'

'I wish I knew. Although we have four Quadrants that makes up our World everyone sees them as one. The Desert People, like me, are the oldest in our World. Nothing much has changed for us and in many ways we have more influence than we will ever use. But after the Day-of-the-Division it was not all peace in our lands. There are many religions and it took a time for all of them to live as one. The Powers-that-Be are a collective of those many Religions. There is no one leader. Directives are issued from a central Temple that it is said to consider all Quadrants and Religions and People. They are a powerful force and of late there has been a change in direction. It's been subtle but nevertheless a change and one which concerns many of us. Not only the Desert People, but others who do not want change. It is said that the Powers-that-Be have lost contact with the people they lead and have become a danger, even an evil force. These are worrying times for everyone.'

'I have only lived in Quadrant 1 and from what I've seen it is corrupt.'

'It is hard for people in power to not fall victim to their own positions. It is their challenge and most fail.'

I nod, I've seen that with my own eyes. Omar continues. 'You saw my men pray this morning?'

I glance at Rasa.

'Yes, I did.'

'Did it scare you?'

'I guess it did… a bit.'

'It shouldn't.'

'Who were they talking to?'

'I don't know. You should ask them. They will tell you.'

'You're lying to me.'

'And what do I gain by that?'

He waits for my answer, but I don't give him one, because I don't have one.

'We have many Gods in our four Quadrants and they mean different things to different people. I have my own and he is personal to me. Some say you are not really praying to anyone just giving yourself advice, mental nourishment. All that is important is what you say and what you believe. The words you use in your mind and the story you tell yourself about who you are is the most important thing you have in life. It is not for me or for you, or for anyone, to interfere in another man's prayers or beliefs about himself. We are all in our own ways talking about our Souls. A great man once said that the thoughts you have colour your Soul. He was right.'

'I'm not sure I will ever pray.'

'That is up to you, Ned, but you should live in a World that lets you make the choice. And from what I can see, you do not. But you will always have a choice about what you say and think about yourself.'

'Do you have choice?'

'I have more freedom than you and my choice at the moment is that I don't want to fight a war.'

'One of those skulls out there should have been me. I can never trust the Non-Secular Quadrants.'

'I'm not asking you to, but you can't trust your own Quadrants either, so what do you do?'

'I hide.'

'For ever?'

'What else can I do?'

'I told you once of someone you reminded me of. Someone proud and stubborn.'

I nod.

'He was my son.'

Omar's words momentarily fade as his mind goes somewhere else. I feel embarrassed, like I shouldn't be here. Like I shouldn't be privy to what this great man is feeling.

His eyes turn alert and come back into focus.

'I lost him, Ned. Not out here. He wasn't strong, like you. He was born physical weak and I knew he would never get to be the man and the father I wanted him to be.'

Omar holds my stare and I'm not sure what I should say, if anything at all. I know about loss. I wonder if I understand his pain more than he understands mine.

He continues. 'I've been blessed with many things and with many daughters from many good wives. Some of my daughters are now married and they have given me strong grandsons, but they will not be my sons. But my life is more than that. My life is guiding my people. It is not to be a predator of Man. It is to help keep what we have because that is better for the greater good.'

I nod because I'm not sure what to say, but I also want him to continue. His voice calms me and I find myself hanging onto his every word.

He smiles. It is full of a sadness that I'm not used to seeing in him.

'You have given the Powers-that-Be a problem: in one way they need you. You were kidnapped for their observations of your World and you and your Pod have beaten them so that makes you valuable. But you've also escaped their clutches and, as you can see, not everyone in the Non-Secular Quadrants wants a Unification War. The rumours are now real and you are proof of that. It will be the same in your Secular Quadrants. Those who live in a Doubter's Camp, as you call it, might want a War because it suits them, but is that true for everyone else? I doubt it.'

'But the people in my Quadrants sent me here.'

'Is that true, Ned. I ask you to consider who sent you here? Was it the Authorities who devised your System or was it the Sympathisers of the Powers-that-Be who have infiltrated your Quadrants?'

I glance across at Rasa for support.

She says. 'If what he says is right then it wasn't the System that sent us here, it was the Powers-that-Be.'

'But our System is still corrupt. *Denounced* get hung every day.'

'That is down to your Authorities who are corrupt. The Powers-that-Be with the help of its Sympathisers have been clever. They have used that structure of your System to work against itself. You have been a victim of the *Sympathisers* and not the System.'

I let these thoughts roll through my mind.

Sympathisers.

Corruption.

The Authorities.

Everything not quite right in our Quadrants, the door left open for a war to start.

A Unification War.

We enter the Camp and a man immediately hurries towards Omar, glancing at me in a way I don't like. Their language is so alien to my ears I couldn't even begin to translate, but I know one thing as clearly as I can see the sun leaving the sky. This man is talking about Pod Fifteen.

Omar nods and then says something to the man, before heading towards me.

The grip of panic tightens the already over-wound knot in the pit of my stomach.

'You need to follow me, Ned.'

I fall in line, Rasa scurrying behind me. We march on and I sense people's furtive, but worried looks. It's the first time I've seen Omar come close to rushing and the speed of his march has me almost trotting in his wake.

We cut left and ahead is a tent with two soldiers outside. As we approach, I can hear the noise of congregated people coming from inside. The taller of the two soldiers, reaches out and pulls the canvas entrance back and we all duck inside.

I hear myself gulp the minute I stand straight.

The tent is full, like it's about to burst at the seams. It takes me a few moments to get my bearings as the heat of worry creeps up my spine. Spencer and Diego are camped between four soldiers with their hands bound in front of them. Spencer throws me a guilty glance before letting his stare fall to the rugs by his feet. Diego looks defiant and I'm sure he has a cut above his right eye like he's been in a fight.

They both look guilty, like *Denounced.*

I hate myself for that sudden thought.

Off to their right is Kuro and Chantal. Relief lights their faces at seeing myself and Rasa. Chantal moves towards me but she is stopped by one of the soldiers. Her eyes are puffed from crying. Close to Chantal and Kuro is another group of men and women and children – all members of the Tribe of the Nomads. I look amongst them trying to fathom the connection when it hits me that what appears to be a haphazard crowd isn't. They are a family group and standing next to a young dark-haired girl with hazel eyes and olive skin is a man.

It's her father.

Father and daughter.

I look back at Spencer.

Then the father.

Then the dark-haired girl.

She is beautiful.

Not in the striking way that Rasa is but in a pure way like she's lived in a protected shell her whole life and somehow life hasn't scarred her like it has myself and the other members of our Pod.

Spencer is handsome.

And he knows it.

I gulp again as Omar turns to face me.

'This is a matter of grave concern to the ways of our Tribe, Ned.'

I don't answer but instead stare back into the crowd and see something in my mind's eye I never thought I'd ever see again. I'm back in the Holding Centre and Jack is walking me to the Waiting Room where I'll meet my stupid Lawyer who will then go through a routine, which I never understood, before being handcuffed and taken to the Court Room.

And that's what this is.

A Court.

Of the Tribe of the Nomads.

And Omar is not only their Leader but their Judge, Jury and ultimately the Executioner.

And I have this deep bad feeling that I've suddenly going to become Spencer and Diego's Lawyer.

The one job that is worse than being Head of Pod Fifteen.

I'm ushered forward and the two camps part – Spencer and Diego on one side; the family on the other. In front of me is a raised section and Omar takes a seat on one of the central cushions. He indicates that I should sit next to him, which I think means I've just been promoted from Lawyer to Judge.

I sit and look at Diego.

I know whatever they've done, Diego's been dragged into it by Spencer. I wonder if he's still calling him 'Spence' in his mind – I doubt it somehow.

The soldiers make them step in front us, stood off to the right.

The man and what I'm sure is his daughter stand to our left.

Omar starts to talk to the father in their language. I don't know what they're saying but I look at the girl and then at Spencer and my palms go hot. Spencer ended up being a *Denounced* because he got into the wrong crowd and broke into someone's home and smoked a joint. But that's Spencer. It's not what he does, it's what he doesn't do. He goes with the crowd. He goes with the easy option. He has zero willpower.

He doesn't know how to say – *no*.

He's good looking and he's lazy and he's institutionalised, and it makes him think of only the now. Jack told me that most of the boys and girls in the Holding Centre suffered from the same mental-disorder.

Jack called it: *discounting your future.*

I was never sure what he meant, but I think I get it now.

I stand up.

I hear Omar tell me to sit down but I'm not going to.

I'm Head of Pod Fifteen, whether I like it or not. And if I have this *gravitas* thing then I'm going to try and use it.

I step down from the cushions and walk up to Spencer and stand so close I can feel his worried breath on my face.

'What happened?'

'I didn't mean it.'

'That wasn't my question?'

'I'm sorry.'

'What happened?' I repeat through a clenched whisper.

'She's the one that's been looking after me. She came to put that ointment on my arms for the sand burns. And I was just making conversation.'

'Did she understand what you were saying?'

'I don't know. Some of these people can speak our language. She was smiling and she laughed.'

'Did she speak with you?'

He shakes his head and I feel my anger begin to rise.

'Then what?'

'She came back with some food and that sweet mint tea they give us. I spilt some and when she went to wipe it up… I… I'm sorry, Ned.'

'You what?'

But I know the answer to my question.

It's why over two-hundred people from the Tribe of the Nomads are crammed in a tent.

It's why this is a Court and not a party.

'You what?' I snap.

'I kissed her, Ned. It's was only on the cheek and I didn't mean anything by it.'

I glare into his eyes until he looks away. I want to punch and punch and punch him. I turn to Diego. 'How did you get that cut?'

'Some of the soldiers came in and started on Spencer. I had no choice.'

I turn back to Spencer.

'Say sorry.'

'I did, already.'

'No you didn't. Not in the way you're supposed. Now. Loud and clear in front of everyone. Apologise to the man and then his daughter.'

'I said sorry.'

'This isn't the Holding Centre or a Community Home where you lose face if you say sorry. Say it or there will be nothing I can do to help you.'

I see another type of panic wash through his eyes and he nods, sniffling like he's about to cry. I step away, climb up the two steps and sit next to Omar, staring at Spencer. He turns to the man's daughter.

'Sir, I apologise to you for my actions towards your daughter. I wasn't thinking. I ask you to forgive me?'

'Now to the girl,' I shout.

Spencer snatches a glance at me and then nods, looking back at the man's daughter.'

'I would like to apologise for my poor behaviour when you were only trying to help me. I'm sorry. I hope you can forgive me.'

Omar slowly turns to face me.

His face is stern.

His eyes are dark.

'This man and his daughter have been dishonoured. That wrong needs to be put right. You are the only one who can fix it.'

I want to ask Omar what he means, but I know what he means, because I've just been promoted again.

This time from Judge to Executioner.

16

Omar sent me to a tent on my own.

To think, he said.

To contemplate their Laws.

But why, I think.

I've seen enough to know Spencer's outcome was fixed before the proceedings had even begun. It was like I was in my Community Homes and the Holding Centre and Ilse's Dome all over again. I've always struggled to understand any Law. It's a language that speaks in riddles, and it's the same in the Courts that has another language all to itself, so I have no chance of learning the ways of the Tribe of the Nomads in less than a few hours.

This is history coming full circle to do what it's always done.

To lie to me, and then to let me down.

I sigh long and loud.

I don't understand so many things, but most of all why this is happening to me, and what I'm supposed to do.

I know the man's dignity was taken by Spencer, which is a terrible thing for Spencer to have done. He should have known better, because as an orphan you only have your dignity and if you lose that you sink to nowhere.

Spencer did a wrong.

I know that and he knows it too.

He needs to be punished and I know it can be hard to forgive without some form of retribution, which is what the man with the daughter said.

I understand all this.

I'm old enough to get it.

And even Rasa is angry at Spencer, because I think she loves him, even if she doesn't know it herself, and he kissed another girl, so she wants him punished too.

But I don't understand why Spencer is going to have to die.

It's the law of the Nomads, as Omar keeps telling me.

But Spencer didn't mean it, and we should all be given a second chance.

And Omar looks so relaxed, like this is just a normal day to him.

And he wants to discuss it more today and tomorrow if we have to, and even the next day if we must. He talks, like we're going to discuss the weather or some food we might have eaten, or a ride on one of his camels.

I don't understand Omar or his Tribe or this place, and my eyes are wet, and it's the closest I've been to crying since they dropped me off at the Community Home and I had to drag my red trunk into the dormitory, knowing my parents were gone forever.

I'm glad the rest of the Pod aren't here.

I'm glad I'm on my own, because I only have to think about myself. Decisions are simple to execute, less painful in every way.

Another long painful sigh falls from my lungs as I sit up.

Spencer was always our weakest link. I thought it might be Chantal or Kuro, or even Diego, especially when his moods get the better of him. But, no... it was going to be Spencer, because he takes the easiest routes and the easiest routes always end up being the hardest ones.

I don't know why that is, but it's how life works.

I dry wash my face with my hands, wishing Jack was here, wondering what advice he'd give me?

I wonder what my father's advice would be?

Not that it matters, because all that really matters is what I say and do.

I jump back, hearing a ripping sound behind me.

I look to the noise and see a knife slice down through the canvas of the tent.

The sound is as crisp as the knife is sharp.

Then the slit is pulled open and a soldier pokes his head through the gap. I recognise him as one of the men on the trek to the Murder Pit.

He smiles a worried smile and urges me out through the escape route he's cut.

My instinct is it's a trap, because every time someone has helped me in the past that's what has happened – our rescue from the gallows being the biggest trap of them all.

But I can't stay here and I can't keep looking at the roof of this tent, lost in these painful and confusing thoughts, so I stand and hurry towards my slice of freedom.

Outside is dark and cold, and I've never seen so many stars in the sky as I do now.

Millions of tiny twinkles light our way.

The soldier moves quick and quiet, and all the Military Training we had in the Dome kicks in.

We soon reach the far end of the camp and to my surprise the rest of the Pod are mounted on camels with two more camels kneeling, saddled and ready to go – one for me, and one for the soldier who has guided me here.

Rasa, Spencer and Diego have their wrists bound in front of them and Rasa is gagged. She'd never be one to go quietly if she didn't want to do something. Chantal has been crying and Kuro looks as worried and scared as I've ever seen him. Six more soldiers are mounted and ready to move.

Their body language indicates they are concerned about time and are keen to go.

I recognise them all from today's ride.

My so-called friends.

I mount my camel with a surprised ease and then we trot out of the camp. Nobody talks and once we clear the outer edges, we fall into a single line, traversing the top of the dunes in a steady pace that only these camels can do.

Even in the dark I can see tears have welled in Rasa's eyes.

Like me, she's seen what's out here and maybe that's where we are all heading.

Another Murder Pit for Pod Fifteen.

A special one, just for us.

We trek on.

The soft sound of hooves on grainy sand.

Spencer hasn't looked up once and Diego has retreated to one of his dark moods that have a habit of exploding onto us all.

Ahead, six more riders appear out of the shadows of the dunes. The rider at the front is Omar. He sits with a straight back and I'm sure he's the closest I'll ever come to meeting a King.

He gallops forward to greet us, stopping next to me, my camel facing one way, his the other.

If I'm going to die, I hope it's painless. I deserve that if nothing else – I've suffered enough, I think.

His men ride up and surround the rest of the Pod.

They unsheathe their knives.

The steel glints in the dark of the night.

I'm calmer than I should be and I know I'm going to fight, I just don't know at what point I'll start.

I watch Omar's knife.

Waiting.

Preparing.

When he suddenly twists it in his hand and presents the handle for me to take.

'For you,' he says. 'It's a sacred knife and a gift to my son.'

His voice is light and calm, but always forceful in the thin air of the night.

I stare his knife for a long moment, letting his words sink in as I watch three of his men cut Rasa, Spencer and Diego free. Another one reaches across and unties Rasa's gag.

She spits and coughs, fresh gasps of air filling her lungs.

Omar takes a bag that is hooked across the front handle of his saddle and hands it across.

'Inside is food and a map. There's enough to eat for four days. You dismount here and then walk with the Moon on your right shoulder, always at two-o'clock. You will come to the foot of the Valleys by the morning. You then need to find a place to rest. Stay out of the sun and watch for snakes. It will take you two days to cross the Land of the Valleys. Always move at night and use the stars as your light. On the third day you will come to a road that leads to a town called Anbus. The road will be deserted, but as the morning rises you will see a crowd gather. When the moment is right you join and walk with them. Keep your heads covered and stay in the centre. It will be Market Day and most of these people will be sellers or buyers of goods. As you approach the main gate of Anbus is where your danger will be the most acute. Anbus is a strategic town in these parts and the Powers-that-Be always deploy their Elites on Market Day. They will look like the Assault Teams you know, but the Elites wear green armbands, which is how you know who they are.'

I flinch, realising I saw these Guards in the Mine when we escaped the Dome.

I clocked their armbands.

The Elites came after us.

Omar continues. 'Not everyone will go into Anbus so you stay with those that don't. Once you clear the town, you need to walk for another day and you will come to the City of Delf, which is on the coast. Again, it will be full of Assault Teams, both normal and Elites, but the City of Delf is large and busy and if you are smart it's a place you can merge into the crowd. The people there are only interested in themselves. You will need to find the Port and then Dock Thirty-Four. From there you will know what to do. Goodbye, Ned. You were the son I never had. I wish we'd had more time together, but what we shared will stay with me for ever.'

I look at the others who have dismounted and are waiting expectant.

'Why?'

Is all I can think to say.

'My people are good people, but they follow the Powers-that-Be, which I respect, because so do I, even in these troubling times of change. Your presence scares them. They would have listened to me, but when Spencer broke our Laws your Pod lost their trust. If I defend you any more, I will lose their trust as well. It is how it works and you will understand one day when many more follow you. My people think you have been taken to be killed and it is better for all of us, including them, that they believe that. Because we have met, I can talk to the other Elders and we can wage our own internal war to stop the Unification War. That is our battle. Yours lies in your own World. You have to warn them that the Unification War is coming. The Powers-that Be want total control and total control always corrupts. If our Quadrants know they have lost their element of surprise they will think again before they attack the Secular World.'

'They will never believe me. I'm a Denounced!'

'You have to make them believe. You maybe still a teenager but there is a good man in that Soul, and one that can make a difference. You have to find a way to make them listen. You are very special Ned to have escaped the Dome. Never forget that. I can get you to the door of your home, but the rest is down to you.'

'How will I know what to do at the City of Delf and then the Port?'

'You have to trust yourself in a way that you have never done before and then you will find the path you need.'

I'm not sure what to say and I sense a deep apprehension has infected our Pod since the trial of Spencer.

It's like I don't know who they are any more.

Something has fractured.

Broken us apart.

I turn to Omar and go to speak, but he stops me.

'I'm doing this for the people of our four Quadrants and you must do the same for yours. This is bigger than you and I.'

My camel folds to the floor, followed by Omar's.

We dismount together.

He steps forward and embraces me in a hug that squeezes the breath from my lungs.

I choke back my emotions.

I have wanted a mentor for a long time only to have him snatched from me by the actions of Spencer.

'You need to stay in these clothes and keep your faces hidden behind these headscarves, especially the beautiful one. Her blonde hair and eyes will be your downfall, if you're not careful. There is one more thing. I have met enough men to know that Spencer will turn on you. Use this walk to prepare yourself to kill him, so when the time arrives you will be comfortable with the decision.'

I glance across at Spencer who looks at me, smiling weakly.

I turn back to Omar who has already mounted his camel.

'Remember, my son, the Moon always on your right shoulder at two-o'clock.'

17

I watch Omar and his men gallop into the night.

They fade into the blackness of the desert and the loneliness that has haunted me for most of my life returns to the pit of my stomach.

I turn to face the rest of the Pod, secretly pleased that it's dark and we can't see each other's expressions.

We are stood like the last remaining pieces on a chess board waiting for the opponent to make the next move. Which is going to be me. We are more disjointed and disconnected than ever before. At least when we were first forced together, we didn't know each other and everything about us was new – even our flaws. But now, our personalities and angers and resentments bounce across the desert sands and not just at me – but between us all.

Kuro breaks the silence, which he nearly always does.

'You have a map, no?'

I nod.

He continues. 'We're supposed to keep the Moon on our right shoulder, always at two-o'clock. If that's correct, we should walk straight along that set of dunes,' he says pointing straight in front of me.

I know Kuro needs order to make him feel safe. He hates the chaos and the uncertainty that we have been forced to live in, and having a focus eases his ever-present worry.

To a degree, I like the chaos and the mess, or maybe I'm just used to it.

It's hard to tell any more.

I unhook the bag from my shoulder Omar handed to me and toss it across the sands to Kuro. I don't care about the map or even the contents, and he's a better map reader than me, anyway.

'It's good to have you back,' Chantal says.

'I never went anywhere,' I say with a bark in my voice.

I don't need to see her face to know she's upset at my tone, because she likes to talk for the same reason Kuro likes order, and one sentence isn't going to give her the remedy she needs.

'She's right,' Spencer says.

'Right about what?' I snap back.

'You've had special privileges since we got here. The Nomads like you better than the rest of us and it's gone to your head.'

'Maybe there's a reason they treat me different. What if they are right?'

I regret my arrogant statement the second it leaves my mouth.

It was a stupid thing to say.

It's not me.

And it's not what I think.

'What if those specialist privileges saved you?' I say with a defensive tone.

'I only kissed her on the cheek. It was just a bit of fun,' he says, snatching a glance in Rasa's direction.

I hear her scoff as I take two steps forward then stop myself, Omar's words screaming through my mind about preparing myself to kill Spencer. Omar's knife close to hand. The idea that I might even be capable of it makes me want to be sick.

'Why dump us out here? It doesn't make sense,' Diego asks.

Kuro has found a small torch in my bag. He switches it on and it takes all our attention. It looks bright in the blackness of the desert, but the undulating terrain of the sand dunes will protect us from being seen. I think of the Assault Teams, but decide it's okay, for now. Omar wouldn't have dropped us in a danger zone or even given us a small torch if he thought it would work against us.

Rasa walks across to Kuro and takes one side of the map and studies it with him.

I stare at Spencer who stares back.

I can't see his eyes, but his anger continues to scratch at my skin.

'The map only starts at the Land of the Valleys,' Kuro says. 'They have marked out a path for us that will take us across to the other side. The town he talked about – Anbus – is marked and so is the road to Delf. So basically, once we are the other side of the Valleys we are out of the Desert and heading towards the coast. Then what?'

'No more sand dunes,' Diego says with a sigh.

'Then we have to find the Port in Delf and Dock Thirty-Four…'

'Why?' Spencer says before I can finish my sentence.

'From there we will be able to find a way home. Back to our Quadrant. Our World. Out of this place and away from Ilse.'

'Yes…' Diego shouts, pumping the air with his fist.

'They'll hang us the minute we step on our home shore,' Spencer says. 'Do you want that?' He says, addressing the rest of the Pod.

The wind picks up.

I hear sand brush across the top of my boots and I'm sure what sounds like a man's whisper.

I tense, wondering if we're alone or not.

'He has a point,' Kuro says, switching the small torch light off as he folds the map back into my bag. 'What's there for us once we get home, other than the hangman's noose?'

'Then why did we escape?' I say.

'We had no choice but to run from the Dome,' Rasa says. 'We were all going to die in there anyway.'

'Agreed, but what's here for us in this Quadrant? Ilse and her Assault Teams? Another Dome?' I say.

'I'll take my chances in our Quadrant,' Diego says. 'I want to go home. This place isn't for me. I'm done here.'

'You have a family that'll protect you. The rest of us have nothing,' Spencer says. 'Whether you like it or not we are safer here, except Diego, maybe?'

'You can all stay with my family if we make it back. There's room for us all.'

'They won't take us,' Rasa says. 'They can hide you and they will, because you're one of them. We'll generate too much attention and someone will hand us in to protect you and the group. I've seen it happen before.'

Rasa's right and it makes me think of her again in a different way. I wonder if she's escaped once before, from somewhere else, and she knows what it's like to be on the run.

'You heard Omar, there's going to be another War,' I say. 'A Unification War. We should warn our Quadrants and do what we can to stop it.'

It's Spencer's turn to scoff, which turns into a snigger that slowly grows into a spiteful laugh.

Even through the dark I see Rasa and Diego start to smile.

Kuro and Chantal say nothing.

'Tell me... Great Leader,' Spencer says between his now forced laughter. 'Why should we help our Quadrants after all the things they've done to us?'

I stare at him through the darkness, wondering what he can see in me.

It's how I felt when first Omar told me.

And there's a part of me that still feels that way.

'This isn't our home. And it never will be,' I say.

'And neither is the place we left,' Spencer says. 'They don't want us. They tried to kill us, remember.'

I can feel, even smell his aggressive confidence towards me growing.

Omar's words ringing through my mind.

'Spencer has a point,' Rasa says. I can hear the reluctance in her voice. She continues. 'The Authorities aren't going to believe us and what if we are better off staying here and trying to make a new life. Omar protected us. What if others will?'

'It could be like living in a Doubter's Camp?' Kuro adds. 'One of Omar's men told me there are many tribes like theirs and small villages beyond the Valleys. If we are prepared to work hard, even learn the language, who knows… we might be better off. Spencer's got a point.'

'I can't see me ever learning the language,' I say.

'It's easy.'

Kuro says a few words.

It catches us all off guard, but it makes us laugh, breaking the tension a little, which I'm pleased for.

'I was asking for some hot mint tea. See, it's not that hard.'

'Not hard for you, maybe, but for me… impossible. I know Diego wants to go home, so that's two of us. Chantal?'

'I don't want to be hung and I don't want to go back to the Dome. I think I could learn the language if I had to and live in a Doubter's Camp in these Quadrants.'

'It wouldn't be a real Doubter's Camp,' Kuro says. 'I was just using it as an example. We're not *Denounced* here and that's the important thing to remember.'

'All we have to do is avoid Ilse and those who have allegiance to the Unification War,' Rasa says. 'It's worth thinking about because we may be able to have a life here. Why should any of us go back and make ourselves *Denounced* when we weren't in the first place?'

'Think about it. We are all innocent, but if we choose to stay here then we become a *Denounced*. If we fight to get home when we didn't have to, it proves our innocence.' I say.

I see Rasa start to shake her head from side-to-side. 'You're just playing with words. We are *Denounced* in the minds of the people back home so why go back?' An anger has returned to her tone. 'Look at all the lies they taught us. The Great Desert had no people. Camels were extinct. Praying poisons the mind. The list is endless. There's more truth here from what I can see then there ever was in our Quadrant.'

I look at Spencer, but I know his answer.

'I'm going to stay,' he says. 'Now I know what these Powers-that-Be really want and why Ilse was training us, why not join them? We escaped. We're special. That's what Ilse was saying to you in the Mine. But we all escaped, Ned. Not just you. I'm sorry she didn't give me the choice before. Why be on the run from her when we could be her friend? She could help us enlist for real and we could fight against our Quadrants; fight against those who wrongly accused us of being *Denounced*. And more importantly, we would belong somewhere. This place would be our home. That's justice, Ned.'

'That's revenge,' I say.

'No, it's not. It's justice. And if we worked for the Powers-that-Be we'd have respect. I don't want to go to a Doubter's Camp or something similar, because I'll always be looking over my shoulder for the rest of my life. I can't live like that any more. I've done it enough. I've had more than my share.'

'And what if our Quadrants win the Unification War and defeats the Non-Secular World. We will be traitors?' Chantal says.

'At least I'll have had a choice,' Spencer says. 'And my choice is to fight against the injustice that was done to me. And if that means a Unifications War then why not.'

Silence.

I wait.

I don't want to speak first.

'What are you going to do, Ned?' Chantal asks.

Her voice is calm, yet full of fear.

The truth is I don't know. I get what Spencer is saying and he's right about our Quadrants, but he's wrong, too. It was the Sympathisers to the Powers-that-Be in our Secular World that wrongly accused us for their own needs and not the Authorities or our System. It's a big difference and Spencer doesn't get it. And I don't have an allegiance to Omar and I'm not going to fight for the Powers-that-Be. If they are anything like Ilse then I'd rather go home to the System. And what if I do get home, who is going to believe me about a Unification War? They'll think I'm mad… more a *Denounced* than ever before. But what I want more than anything else is my freedom. I knew that when I was falling backwards into the Mine unsure what I would hit. In those terrifying seconds, I had something I haven't experienced much in my life.

I was free.

I'd rather be dead than be a prisoner – and I'm a prisoner here and I'm prisoner back home… but I'm more a prisoner here, because the truth is I was set up by the Sympathisers.

I want to go home.

I want to fight for my innocence.

I want our System to change for the better.

The words thump through my mind.

'We can't stay in the Great Desert. Ilse is still looking for us and Omar's camp is a no-go zone because of what Spencer did.'

'Don't you blame this on me.'

'It's true, so shut up,' I say.

He steps forward but Diego steps in front of him and pushes Spencer so hard he crashes to the desert floor, sand splashing like water around him. He roars with an animal anger. Rasa joins Diego to double up, so I don't have to move. He can't fight them both and I'm even more convinced that Rasa is angry at him for kissing that girl.

Omar's prediction isn't going to come true today – his knife still sheathed in my sash belt.

I continue. 'If we don't move soon the night will lift and we'll lose the Moon as our compass. We stay together until we get to the other side of the Valleys and then from there we can go our own ways. Any objections?'

I wait but I know the answer.

Diego offers his hand to help Spencer to his feet.

Spencer slaps Diego's hand away as he stands by his own volition. He glares at me. I still can't see his eyes because of the night light, but I'm sure they are full of hatred, even murder.

'There's one more thing,' I say. 'And I'm making this official. When we clear the Land of the Valleys, I'm no longer Head of Pod Fifteen. I'm just Ned Hunter and I'm going to do what is right for me. You should all do the same.'

Nobody says anything, which is fine by me.

I nod at Kuro.

He turns and leads the way.

The Moon is off to my right shoulder, Spencer is off to my left.

One gives me hope.

The other fills me with dread.

18

The Moon begins to fade in the morning light as the Land of the Valleys starts to loom in the near distance.

Kuro has done a great job of leading us out of the desert, helped by the pair of glasses Omar put in his bag. The lenses are round and inserted in a frame of thin wire that hook around Kuro's ears. It's another small gift for us as a Pod and one more thing I don't have to worry about.

Kuro points to the Valleys, pleased with himself and, no doubt, pleased that he can see them. I know before we'd been thrown together as a Pod, I would never have befriended a personality like his. I would have considered him weak and a danger to be around. I'm ashamed to think that I may have even bullied him if the circumstances had suited me – even though I hate bullies. His intelligence and insights have helped us enormously, and he's taught me to respect different personalities in a way I never did before. If we ever do get to where we are supposed to get to and survive, I hope we remain friends.

I do a quick check on the others.

Diego seems energised with a new lease of life. The scent of his home is strong in his mind.

Chantal has fallen to the back and she's been quiet for her standards and I'm sorry I snapped at her, but I'm also sick of apologising for how I feel.

She needs to get over it.

Rasa and Spencer have been talking between themselves for most of the night, and I see Rasa reach out again and touch Spencer's arm as they share an intimate joke, pointing to the new terrain ahead of us.

My emotions cry out with jealousy.

It also worries me more than I think it should.

Spencer wants to stay and fight against our Quadrant – join Ilse and the Powers-that-Be.

I get it and I get his anger, and he's welcome to make his own choices, but if I'm watching this right he now has an ally in Rasa. If I was Head of the Pod I would be worried about my position, but I'm giving up my responsibilities, so I shouldn't let it bother me.

Forget it.

We're only together now because we can't wander the Great Desert on our own and expect to live for long.

This is just mutually beneficial to everyone.

It's no longer friendship.

Our Pod is broken once and for all.

I take a sip of water from my leather pouch that always seems to keep the water cool no matter if it stays in the sun or not. We are tired and hungry, but I know for sure that once we hit the foot of the Valleys there'll be somewhere safe to hide and rest up. Omar knows this terrain inside out and upside down, and he's laid the path for our safe entry into the City of Delf as best he can. It's now for us not to mess it up or get caught, or lost, or do something equally as stupid.

'Ned?' Chantal says, coming up on my inside.

Her voice is soft and I sense she doesn't want the others to hear what she is about to say.

'Are you mad at me?' she asks.

'No, I'm not. Why would I be?'

'That's good. I don't like it when people are angry at me. It upsets me. I worry about it. Worry what they think and it makes me anxious.'

'Jack used to tell me that if everyone likes you then you're doing something wrong.'

She smiles, but it's full of worry and I get hot with the guilt of snapping at her when she was only trying to be kind. We all snap at people we shouldn't, I think, so I should get off my case about it.

'I like that, but I'm not sure I can ever be that way. Who's Jack – your dad?'

'He was a Guard at the Holding Centre responsible for our Section. He was kind to all the Denounced, because he knew what was going to happen to them. He was a good man in a bad job.'

She nods.

'You never talk about the Holding Centre. Was it tough?'

I shrug. It was more cruel than tough, but maybe they are one and the same thing. I don't know.

'I'm glad I didn't have go to one. I don't think I would have survived.'

'You'd surprise yourself. We can all do things we don't think we can. You survived what your mother did to you. You survived the Dome.'

'We survived the Dome because of you, Ned. That's why Spencer is angry at you. He wants to believe he could have escaped and can do this on his own, but he can't. He's lying to himself and he doesn't like the fact that he needs you.'

'In less than a day he'll be on his own to make his own choices, so he doesn't have to be angry at me any more.'

'He won't survive.'

I look across the sands and watch him share another moment with Rasa. She seems to have forgiven him already for kissing the other girl, which I don't understand. I'm still jealous of them, but not in the way I was before. Not in that way that played with my personal emotions about my feeling towards Rasa. Perhaps Spencer is clearer in his mind about what he wants to do with himself now, and my journey is too tough and complicated, which is why I'm jealous.

I want his journey.

It's easier.

And what if I joined the Powers-that-Be via Ilse?

She wants me too from what she said in the Mine. Omar thinks she does, too. I'd get respect. My life would be simple. All I'd have to do is fight against my four Quadrants and help the four Non-Secular Quadrants win the Unification War.

Could I do it?

Yes, I think.

Would it be that bad a thing to do?

I'm not sure.

'Are you really going to leave us on the other side?'

'I'm going to find Dock Thirty-Four. That's my plan. That's it.'

'Then what? Are you really going to go home and tell them there's a War coming their way? Spencer's right. They'll laugh at you and then hang you. They'll probably make a big announcement of it and show it on TV as a warning to the Doubters.'

'What if they hang us here?'

'What if they don't?'

'But you don't know.'

She nods.

Tears moisten her eyes and I know what she's going to say next.

And, I'm right.

'What's going to happen to me? I won't survive without everyone.'

'Yes you will.'

She nods, but it lacks conviction and my guilt spikes until I get dizzy.

I have nothing against Chantal, but I can't help her.

She has to help herself.

Am I wrong for thinking this?

'Kuro is going to look for a Doubter's Camp or something similar. If you don't want to fight or return home then you can join him. If it's just the two of you then it'll probably work out. Rasa was right about us all hiding as one group. It's too risky. You and Kuro are the two smartest people I've ever met, so you'll be an asset to any new group you join and not a hinderance.'

'No, Ned – you're wrong. You're the smartest person I've ever met. Everyone looks to *you*. Whatever it is *you* decide, you have to make the others do it. Even Spencer.'

'I'm not going to do that.'

Tears start to roll down her cheeks and I have to force myself not to say sorry.

'I hate you,' she says and walks off, sand kicking up from her heels.

I hate myself and have for years, I think, as I see Kuro point to what I realise is the start of a path that will ease us out of the desert and through the beginning of the Valleys.

'Let's find somewhere to rest and sleep,' I shout out.

'What if I want to keep walking,' Spencer yells back at me.

'We only have one map and we need to rest,' Kuro says.

'What if I take the map?' Spencer says.

He's smiling and joking and Rasa nudges him in that way to say – don't be stupid, and he doesn't mean it.

But he does mean it.

He means every word.

And it's another sign of his growing confidence as he throws me a smile that reminds me of Taylor in the Dome.

And now I have another problem.

It's two against one and I need to eat and sleep, and sleeping is probably the most stupid thing I can do right now.

'Kuro. Give Spencer the map,' I say as light-hearted as I can.

Kuro looks all concerned and starts to walk towards Spencer, presenting the map.

Spencer, pushes Kuro's hand away.

'Let's eat and sleep, and we can decide what we want to do when we get to the other side of the Valleys,' he says, like he's now Head of Pod Fifteen.

And maybe he is, I think.

Maybe he is.

19

I watch a squawking eagle fly by before letting my eyes settle on the opposite side of our makeshift camp.

It's not the noises of the animals or gusts of wind that continually wake and scare me. It's the presence of Spencer and Rasa and their potential combined force, which terrifies me the most. I can't shift the idea that they'll attack me while I'm asleep, dreaming of another life, one that I've never had or at least I don't remember.

It's an irrational thought, because we all have to get to the other side of the Valleys to survive, and it's a no brainer that we're better off sticking together.

At least for now.

And I'm sure Diego and Kuro and even Chantal will watch my back, defend me if they have to, more for themselves, if not for me.

But once on the other side, it's going to be a different story, so I should try and sleep while I can.

But I can't.

My body is screaming to stay awake.

To not trust anyone.

I push up softly from the floor and rest against one of the rocks that have protected us from the sun and the heat of the day. Omar must have spent time where we are, because it's like a secret within a secret. The place has a feel that select groups and individuals have slept in this natural cul-du-sac of rocks for protection. The entrance is hidden and we'd have never found it had it not been for Omar's explicit map and Kuro's skill at reading it.

I reach for my water, careful not to make a noise as I don't want to disturb the others.

Diego has slept by the entrance.

He's our natural guard so I'm not surprised, although I don't think we have anything to worry about from outside for now.

All our dangers are within.

Kuro has made his bed in one of the rounded corners and he's as inconspicuous as he can get. That's Kuro all over. Chantal has laid her mat in the middle of the circle and she looks oddly isolated. If I'm being honest with myself, I'm worried for her once we finally leave the World of the desert, but there's nothing I can do.

I let my eyes drift back to Spencer and Rasa.

They have laid their mats as close as they can to each other without making it seem they are now a couple.

Which I think they are or certainly want to be.

My feelings have shifted to something I don't understand, and those thoughts I had that she was once the one for me no longer are true. I'm surprised how quickly our lives change in the Pod and I do my best to push down those unclear emotions of jealousy I hold. It's then I notice where I've laid my mat. If where the others have slept tells me about their personalities then mine must say the same.

I'm at the back, the perpetual outsider.

This Pod was once my Tribe, albeit forced, and it no longer is. I'm a stranger within my makeshift family and I view the rest of them as people I no longer know. I take another drink, deeply scared I will never be part of something with any meaning in my life again. Omar said he wanted to be my Mentor and there was a side to me that wanted to stay with the Nomads and learn from him. I think of his people and their smiles and their kind eyes. They appeared the happiest group I have ever seen and I liked the way they instinctively attended to each other's needs. At times, our Pod has been same, but it's not been consistent and when it does happen it happens when we are most stressed.

I wonder what that says about us?

And if it's a good thing or not, or does it mean we don't really know or care about one another, and we're only working together to survive. So it's really a fear that's keeping us together, like a special bond, which highlights the fact we don't care or know each other very well.

The thought saddens me and makes me think of my age.

I was sixteen when I went to the Holding Centre and my seventeenth birthday was seven months away.

I wasn't supposed to make that day, but everything changed in a split second.

So has seven months passed since we were rescued from the gallows?

Apart from knowing when it's day or night, I've lost track of the time, of what day it is, or even what month we are in.

If it is seven months since I was convicted of being a *Denounced* then it would be November. It feels too hot to be November, but the desert months might work differently and it could be this hot all year round, or this could be the cool months and it gets hotter in the summer – so it might still be August, which means I'm still sixteen?

But if I am seventeen, does that explain all these odd thoughts and feelings that I'm having about myself, because I'm finally becoming a man?

In my old life before I was convicted of being a *Denounced* that would have meant I was a year away from being an adult and being released from the Community Homes System.

Free to do what I liked.

I would have been given a Home and some Digital Credits, enough to have gone to college if I had wanted.

And I wanted to do it.

To be an Engineer.

The weight of sadness and loss hits me hard.

Omar told me freedom was taking responsibility.

I don't think I understand what he meant, because freedom to me is not having someone tell me what to do, and that's what I'm doing now by not being Head of our Pod?

I'm taking responsibility for myself and not them.

Or is not being Head a form of cowardice and I'm abdicating my responsibility, like Chantal's mother did with her.

I look at Chantal and Kuro and I know they are most at risk if they stay in this Quadrant. I want to help them, but I have to let them make their own decisions. I'm going home and I just can't carry them any more.

Or can I?

The question gnaws at my insides and there's a lightness that begins to overtake me, like I'm not a real person and there's no substance to me any more.

I tense, suddenly.

Chantal has her eyes open and has been watching me all this time.

It's like she can hear my thoughts and I flush with guilt and she smiles, unsure.

I'm about to smile back when the eagle returns over our secret resting place and squaws louder, like it's our predetermined alarm.

Sent by Omar.

It wakes everyone else and in watching the bird fly on I notice the sky is turning tangerine orange, which means the sun is setting and it's definitely time for us to move.

Spencer leaps to his feet and the speed of it catches me off guard, and I turn ready to fight him.

Everyone looks at me surprised and I shake off the incident like it didn't happen.

He smirks, helping Rasa to her feet with an outstretched hand.

'How long can we walk and map read without using the torch?' I say to Kuro.

He glances up into the sky.

'Not long, a few hours at most. These help,' he says with a smile, pointing at his lopsided glasses.

'Omar wouldn't have given us the torches and told us to move at night if it wasn't safe for us to use them. We can use them any time and we should. Let's move out.' Spencer says.

Kuro looks at me, like he waiting for another instruction.

Chantal glows with embarrassment.

Rasa stares at me, waiting.

'Is there a problem?' Spencer barks out.

'No,' Kuro says, looking at me for more support.

'Then let's move out. We can eat as we walk. We've rested enough and the sooner we get to the other side the better. You have any issues with that?' Spencer says, turning back to face me.

Omar's warning spins through my mind that the day will come when I will have to kill Spencer, but all I can think about is getting to Dock Thirty-Four and going home. If I can get out of the Land of the Valleys then I'm free.

Kind of.

'Let's walk and eat. It's a good idea, and be careful with the torchlight,' I add.

Spencer stares, like he's waiting for me to be more sarcastic or to challenge him in some way, but I turn from his aggressive posture and pick up my things, taking a dry biscuit from my bag.

I pop it into my mouth and stride towards the entrance.

I'm doing what he said, which is eating and walking, and each new step is a step closer to Delf and hopefully Dock Thirty-Four.

A step closer to getting home.

20

It's a crisp cold morning and it reminds me of a time when I lived back in my home Quadrant.

A time, I have almost forgotten existed.

I step forward, careful to stay in the cover of the rocks as the crowd ahead begins to thicken as it moves towards the town of Anbus. I wonder where all these people have come from, but the scene is exactly as Omar described. A winding, dusty road, which forks at the entrance to the town: one half disappearing behind a fort gate and into the town I will never see or care to visit, while the other spirals towards the coast and the City of Delf with its Port.

I spot what I think are police and small groups of soldiers. They look more like Assault Teams than Elites. It'll soon be time to move and I can't wait to have Anbus behind me. It'll be a strange moment for us all, because nobody has discussed, other than me, what they are going to do next. I will walk on, past Anbus towards Delf. The only thing I know for sure is that Diego will follow me. I glance across at him. As far as travel companions go, it could be a lot worse, and if we do butt into trouble, I know he'll fight to the end.

So is going home my final solution, or my final resting place? I don't know and I won't know until it happens. And I'm struggling to think clearly, because I'm tired and I'm irritable and I'm angry at myself for not getting enough rest.

I check on Spencer, stood off to my right with Rasa, as he looks intensely into the ever-growing crowd. He's hyped, like he's taken a drug and his frenetic energy is seeping across into Rasa.

He's putting us all in danger and Dock Thirty-Four looks further away in my mind than it has ever been.

I find myself drawn to the knife Omar gave me.

I glance at it.

It's inserted into my sash belt.

I'm trying to stop myself, but I can't, and I'm slowly moving my hand towards the handle.

I pause, then I wrap my fingers around it.

It's cold to the touch.

The grip is designed for comfort and it almost seems like the size of the handle was crafted for the size of my hand.

I stroke it once, unsure, hating the thoughts that are churning through my mind and combining with Omar's warning.

I slip the blade clear of the scabbard and let the knife fall by my right side, hidden from Spencer's view.

He's blindsided to my weapon and my intent.

I twist the handle in my hand, ensuring the grip is right and the killing edge of the blade is twisted to the position I want as I gauge the distance between myself and Spencer.

The energy starts to build in my mind, moving through my body, and I'm thinking and wondering and thinking and wondering when Chantal puts her hand on mine. Her touch is delicate and soft and barely startles me, which it should have done.

We look at each other.

Hazel coloured eyes, soft and caring, but knowing, drill deep inside of me.

It's not often I sense somebody else has dared to understand who it is I am.

Perhaps this is what Omar means when he talks about looking into somebody's Soul.

And it's happening to me, I think.

Chantal gives me one of her kind smiles and eases her fingers over mine and gentle guides the blade back into the scabbard.

There's a dull click as it locks back into place.

Nothing more than a harmless tool once again.

The building energy I had reserved dissipates and the moment is gone, shared between myself and Chantal with not a word spoken.

'When do we move?' Kuro asks.

I shrug. Our danger will be leaving this hiding place, because once we merge into the crowd we will become one of them. It's a place and feeling I know well. I survived the Community Home System because of my ability to blend in. But Spencer's hyped state will be like waving a flag to the police and soldiers.

They're trained to pick up on energies that stand out.

'Are you going to join the Powers-that-Be if you get the chance?' I ask Spencer.

My question is aimed at Rasa, too.

He shrugs, which I take as a *Yes*.

'Then you have to let us go first. We need the head start.'

He turns and glares at me. His pupils are dilated and wild and I'm not looking at the Spencer I know and I'm not sure who this wild animal stood in front of me is any more. Diego's natural sense to protect his clan makes him stand next to me, which I wish he hadn't because he's made us gladiatorial – him and me, against Rasa and Spencer, with Kuro and Chantal the reluctant audience.

I step aside to break the confrontational pattern and it works to a point.

'They'll ask you where we are and they'll want to know everything that's happened. That means you're going to have to tell them about Omar and how we got out of the

Mine and then the Great Desert. They're not stupid. They'll know we'll have had help to get this far.'

He continues to stare at me and then the others.

Defiance locked in his face.

Rasa touches his arm and it breaks his spell.

'Ned's right. It's best we give the others the head start they want.'

The pain of betrayal floods into my body and I struggle to see beyond my own selfishness. Rasa's statement tells me she's going to join the Powers-that-Be.

And that she and Spencer are a couple.

A union.

I've never really trusted him, but I thought if nothing else Rasa and I had mutual respect. And there's something else I don't say, because I hadn't thought about it before now, but they both know where I'm headed.

Dock Thirty-Four.

It doesn't matter what they say now because at any point they can give my secret away.

I think again about drawing the knife, but could I really do it?

Kill Spencer for my own needs and in front of the rest of Pod Fifteen?

I don't know and I'm scared of the answer, but I'm thankful of Chantal's intervention.

'What are you going to do?' Spencer asks Kuro.

Kuro flushes with being put on the spot, letting his head fall as he stares at the dusty ground by his feet.

'I'm going back to our Quadrant with Ned. I know how to live in a Doubter's Camp and I'd rather take my chances in a Doubter's Camp in our Quadrant than something similar here.'

'What if there's a war and our Quadrant loses?'

'They might win. But there might not be a war, too,' he says, like he somehow knows the outcome.

'There's going to be a war and the Powers-that-Be are going to win,' Spencer says.

Defiance laces his voice.

'Chantal, what are you doing because I know what the Mexican is all about?'

He says it in a way that disregards Diego. I get why he's angry at me but not the others.

'I'm going to join Kuro. I think I can live in a Doubter's Camp, too. I like Omar and these people, but they are not my people and I might never be accepted in this World. I'll take my chances back in our Quadrant – war or no war.'

Spencer glances back into the gathering crowd.

'I'm going to go into the town and hand myself in,' he says. 'They'll take me to Ilse and I'm going to tell her I want to join the Powers-that-Be. It's a risk, but it's less of a risk than going home. And let's be honest, Ned, Omar let you off the hook because you were going to let him kill me if you had to make the choice. I know you well enough to know you would have done it.'

I hear the gasp of the others as his words stab at my heart.

I glance at Rasa, my mouth as dry as the sands I'm stood on. Her stare drops to the floor, embarrassed. It tells me she's discussed this with him in one of their quiet moments.

I want to shout that it's not true, not a single word. I'm angry at Spencer for cutting my relationship short with Omar, but I would never send him to his death and he'd always come before Omar. We're our own tribe, I think, and I'm struggling to understand his twisted anger towards me when he continues to speak before I can gather my thoughts and say anything. 'That will give you twenty-four hours, which should be enough time to get to Delf and find Dock Thirty-Four if Omar's map is accurate.'

'How do we know you won't tell them about our destination the second you enter Anbus?' Diego asks.

I watch Spencer chew on the thought, sucking on his bottom lip in the process.

'I don't owe Omar anything. He wanted me dead. I will tell Ilse he helped us. I will tell her we split, because I'm going to join her War and you wouldn't.'

Rasa suddenly steps in front of Spencer, her back to me. They whisper in rapid tones and I can't hear them, but I see Spencer nodding and agreeing to something. Rasa steps aside and Spencer walks towards me. I tense, but I can see the anger and hatred in his eyes has subsided enough for me to drop my guard.

To my surprise, he extends his hand for me to shake.

I take it, but he doesn't shake it, rather holds it like he's got the upper hand in a wrestling hold that I can't move from.

'I'm going into Anbus with Rasa. We'll hide out and hand ourselves in the following morning. That gives you the best part of two days to do what you need to do and get on the ship at Dock Thirty-Four. After that we're quits. We survived being *Denounced*, maybe because of you, maybe not. But you only have my loyalty for two more days. If we come across each other in a Unification War, I will see you as the enemy.'

I nod.

I get it.

I want to kill him.

But I won't.

Not today, anyway.

'Let's move out,' I say.

It's the last command I'll ever issue to Pod Fifteen.

We collect our belongings and slip between the rocks. The pathways are deeper than they looked from our vantage point and they offer more than enough protection to get us out into the crowd, only the odd head turning to witness our arrival.

We're dressed like everyone else. I have an old sense of calm return that I'm used to when merging into any crowd. The only thing which is odd about us is our boots, but I'm not sure anybody is ever going to notice.

Up ahead, the crowd is already splitting and some are being searched as they enter Anbus. It doesn't look like a serious investigation, more a cursory check and the few soldiers dotted about look disinterested. I relax some more, checking on everyone else. Diego looks the most worried and I tell him to chill.

It's rookie mistake, because my language has several heads turn and look at me.

The dread of my mistake grips my stomach in a fierce knot.

Rasa throws me a stare and I nod my mistake with my eyes.

We walk on.

The crowd starts to bottleneck into the left turn and I veer more to my right so I can continue on with those who are bypassing Anbus. Rasa gives me nod of goodbye and my only hope is that I believe Spencer will stick to his word because of Rasa's presence.

They can kiss all they like now we've gone.

I nod back.

Goodbye I say in my mind.

 Diego glares at me.

'You should never have trusted him. You made a mistake and it's cost us. I hate you!'

My mind can't comprehend what he's said and why he's said it as he turns and bolts back towards the rocks. I see Spencer run towards me, murder in his eyes. It's Rasa who stops him and points for them to sprint the other way.

'Ned,' Chantal screams.

I can't see what is happening other than the crowd is pulling away and it's not only isolating me but creating the thing I hate the most by making me the centre of attention.

It's then I see why.

Omar is sat on a camel.

Ilse and her Head of Security are in an Assault Buggy by his side.

They're surrounded by heavily armed Elites and some of Omar's loyal guards.

The crowd continues to scatter, like frightened chickens with a fox in the pen.

I watch Spencer and Rasa run toward Anbus hoping to get lost in the crowd, but they are about to be cut off by two of the Assault Teams.

Diego's already been caught and he's fighting like a crazed wolf.

Soldiers are chasing Chantal and Kuro and it's only a matter of seconds before they're back in chains and once again *Denounced*.

I pull the head scarf from my face and expose who I am.

Ilse smiles.

Omar looks on impassive.

I'm Ned Hunter, I think.

And if you want me, you're going to have to come and get me.

Because, I'm not moving for anyone.

21

It's dark and damp, and I'm back in a prison cell and it's all too familiar – an environment I always knew would find me once again.

And it has.

I stare at the stone walls and then the long metal bars, and think it must be a design from another time and another era that I know nothing about. I'm used to solid steel and double doors and concrete blocks impenetrably deep. I'm half expecting Jack to enter my cell and tell me one of his terrible jokes that always made me laugh and feel better about a bad situation.

But he's not coming to make me laugh or even to speak with me.

Ilse is.

And back in the Holding Centre we all knew what time and date we were going to die, and even how it was going to happen. Court Officials make a point of telling you and they do it with a joyful sneer plastered across their faces. You get used to them and it becomes a sick game we all played by shrugging it off and pretending we don't care about death.

We did, of course.

We were all terrified.

Like I am now, and if there is a thing worse than death, I have a feeling it's coming my way.

I look at my purple Denounced Jumpsuit, the cloth rough against my skin, and the white trainers, more scuffed than I remember. The design and colour of the Jumpsuits was to make you stand out from the crowd and to feel the shame of your crime, but compared to what the people wear in this Quadrant, it's a design that stands out tenfold and has taken on another level of vindictiveness I didn't think was possible.

'We should have never listened to you,' Spencer says full of spite. 'You think you know it all, but you're no better than any of us – maybe even worse because your big ego gets in the way. I don't get it why people think they have to bow to you or even follow your every command?'

I push up from my wooden bed and stand at the bars.

Opposite in another cell is Spencer, Diego and Kuro. And in the cell next to them are Rasa and Chantal. Both Rasa and Diego have scratched faces and necks, and I bet they are covered in bruises, because they would have fought hard to the end, and I wouldn't have expected anything less.

'I never asked to be Head of Pod Fifteen.'

'So you keep telling us, but you've loved every second of it. Loved the power it has brought you. You can't see it or don't want to admit it, but it has gone to your head and you strut around like you're the President of all the Quadrants. It was a mistake to have trusted Omar and we did it because of you. This is your fault.'

'You forget you were bitten by a scorpion and the sandstorm nearly killed us. It was Omar who found us and took us in and you abused his trust when you kissed that man's daughter.'

'That girl wanted me to do it. She liked it.'

'No, she didn't. And the fact that you can't see it is why you'll never be Head of anything but your own stupidity.'

I want to comment on his relationship with Rasa, but I hold my tongue. It's not my business. Diego pushes up from his bed and comes and stands by Spencer's side. He carries a dark cloud within – in that thing they call a Soul – and I can see it is raging to come out. He grabs the bars by the cell lock and then places both feet at the base, ether side of the door, and begins to pull. At first, I want to laugh at the foolishness of his actions, but then the bars start to groan and the lock seems to strain under the sudden force.

Spencer joins him and together they begin to pull at the bars, grunting with a guttural effort I'd not thought possible.

Then the joints of the lock start to groan.

Tears stream down Diego's face.

Tears of anger and desperation, and most of all belief.

I've never felt someone's inner pain ride over mine as I do now.

'Stop, Diego,' I say. 'You're going to hurt yourself and there's nowhere to go even if you do get out.'

He stops and stares at me, still gripping the bars.

'Don't listen to him,' Spencer says. 'This lock will give.'

'No it won't,' I say.

Tears continue to pour down Diego's face, and he begins to rattle the bars like he's a two-year old having a temper-tantrum.

'This is your fault. THIS IS YOUR FAULT. We were nearly there. Nearly at Delf. And you walked us right into the trap because you trusted Omar over us. I could be on that boat going home now. This is your fault, Ned...' he says, his voice trailing to a whisper of despair.

I fight the urge to defend myself, instead retreating back into the darkness of my cell.

I sit back on my wooden bed that has no mattress and drop my head into my hands.

I want to cry but I know I won't – or can't.

I've suffered too much in my life and crying never got me anywhere.

I dwell on what Spencer said and if I could have done anything differently?

I don't know the answer to that question other than he's right in that I trusted Omar.

I didn't want to admit it to myself but he reminded me of my father, or certainly of the bits I can remember and liked. My father had patience and would always try and be there and explain things to me in a meaningful way. Omar had the same quality, albeit harsher, stricter. More than anything in my life, I wish I had better memories of my father and that we had got to know each other more. I needed, wanted, someone to tell me what being a man was all about. What is expected of me and what I'm capable of. I'm probably never going to make it to eighteen. Ilse will see to that, but having to work everything out by myself has drained my life, and there have been times when I needed guidance.

Jack knew that.

Not just for me, but for the other boys in the Holding Centre, as well.

It was the root of his kindness.

I look back into Spencer and Diego's cell.

They've disappeared into the blackness, but their angers linger by the bars like ghosts, especially Spencer's.

What if I've been too harsh on Spencer?

Really, who has helped him, other than himself?

He ended up being a *Denounced* because he made a poor choice of friends and ended up in the wrong crowd. If he looked to me for leadership then I did let him down, but I never wanted this job.

Gravitas or not.

But you've got it whether you like it or not?

The voice makes me jerk back, looking through my cell to see if I had company I didn't know I had.

Or is it the ghost of my father come to haunt me?

Or Jack?

'It's okay, Ned – it's me.'

I look out and see Chantal stood by the bars of her cell, staring at me with her forever kind smile. I'm sure I was in my mind and not speaking aloud, but maybe I wasn't. Maybe everyone heard my thoughts and they hate me a fraction more than they already do, and they can't even find the energy to comment any more.

'Go to sleep,' I say. 'You're going to need the rest.'

'I can't sleep until I know you won't leave us?'

I want to laugh at her pointless question.

I'm in a cell in one of the Non-Secular Quadrants, wearing my Denounced Jumpsuit, probably hours away from death and the only place I'm heading is *Nowhere Town*.

'Sure, I won't leave us. Now go to sleep.'

'You have to mean it, Ned. I mean, really mean it, or we are all going to die.'

I'm not looking at her and I don't know why, but I hear something in her voice that I can't quite articulate. It's not a pleading or a request or even a form of calmness.

I stand and move to the front of my cell, gripping the bars and thinking of the strength Diego must have to make this metal creak.

Chantal's smile broadens.

It's like she's happy and I don't understand why, and I always thought of her as our weakest link. She's small and petite, and my ever-lasting impression is of a girl who will cry at every opportunity. She's a talented crier for sure and she's everything I don't understand in a female. Rasa, I get, one hundred per cent – her anger, her fight, her independence and her lack of trust – but not Chantal. Yet there's an inner strength to Chantal that goes beyond my understanding.

Omar told me she had it and he's right. She has a trust about herself and life that I don't get. She seems to see things and connect us as a group in a way that constantly surprises me. I've always gone to Rasa for advice, or to Kuro for his rational analytical explanations, but I think Chantal is maybe the smartest of us all.

She's our Oracle.

Our emotional barometer.

A glue that we would fall apart without.

'I'm sorry, but Pod Fifteen is over. It's no longer about me leaving or staying, or if Spencer wants to fight against our Quadrant or lead the Pod. It's about something else. Omar betrayed us, and we'll never get to Dock Thirty-Four. Ilse has her plan and there's nothing we can do but wait to find out what that is. We're *Denounced* again. Our curse never left us.'

I see her churn this thought through her mind, nodding to herself.

Then her smile returns.

It's warm and kind, and full of something that I think is still hope, which I can't even begin to fathom.

My World is dark.

Chantal's is full of light.

'Promise me, Ned. Just promise me you won't leave us. No matter what Spencer or Diego say. Or what Ilse or Omar do. We need you.' Tears start to stream down her face, but she's smiling, too, her eyes alive with her inner light. 'Promise me, Ned.'

'I promise.'

'You promise what, Ned? What is it that you have to promise?'

'I promise not to abandon Pod Fifteen.'

22

A key rattles in the lock of my cell door and wakes me from a troubled sleep.

I was dreaming that I was stood on the gallows and my sister was about to open the trap door to my death. In her own way, she did, by leaving me in the Community Homes System when she had the chance to be my primary Guardian.

I sit up, hoping it's Jack with some more chocolate pudding.

It's not, of course.

It's one of the Assault Team Soldiers.

He's a big man with a close-cropped beard and a shaved head. He has trained every day to deal with people like me. He's eyeing me in that way that tells me violence is close to the surface and he has permission to use it if he must.

Marcellus was the same.

So I stand and stare him out, because I know something he doesn't realise – if he hurts me before I see Ilse, she'll kill him. At least there are some good things the corrupt System teaches you.

He tosses across a pair of handcuffs for me to put on.

I should catch them, but I don't.

Instead, they fall to the floor and I kick them under the bed, smiling as I do it.

I've won and he sees his mistake.

I wonder what he's going to do, because I can see the flash of dilemma in his eyes when two more Assault Soldiers turn up and save his problem. They're smaller than him, but not by much, and they are younger, too, and clean shaven with tanned faces and short black hair.

They say something in their language.

I don't understand it, but I get the implication – *I'm late for wherever it is I'm meant to be.*

The younger of the three walks in and picks up the handcuffs from under the bed and snaps them on my wrist, shoving me in the back and pushing me towards the cell door. I've continued to stare at the big man with my Court Official mocking sneer. He wants to react but the fear of what Ilse will do is holding him back and it makes me sneer at him even more.

I'm hoping I can push him past his limit, but it seems I can't.

He leads the way forward and I step behind him, the other two penning me in from behind. The rest of Pod Fifteen have come to the front of their cells and are watching. Chantal is crying and I'm sure she whispers, *be careful.* I walk on, an inner numbness I've become accustomed to starts its descent upon me. It's my own way to protect myself of more pain and it works, but I'm not sure if it does me any good or not.

The big man opens another locked door and we walk on.

I think prisons and Holding Centres and even Community Homes must all be the same. Just grey dark corridors with endless numbers of doors and locks and security cameras.

I'm led into another corridor and the surroundings start to open up. I smell mint in the air and up ahead is a large ornate wooden door with two more Assault Team Soliders stood outside.

These ones are wearing green armbands so they are the Special Guards to the Powers-that-Be.

The Elites.

One side of the door is immediately opened as we approach and I'm told to go in.

It's a large room with stone walls and carpets and cushions and long chairs to relax in. Something, I'm not going to do. I count eight arched entrances that lead onto a balcony with a view of the Land of the Valleys and part of the Great Desert. I can hear the noise of a busy town below and the hubbub sounds happy like whatever is happening is good and maybe even fun.

Fun – a word that is no longer part of my life.

I glimpse over my shoulder to see the soldiers have stepped out.

I'm alone, but I don't move because I know someone, somewhere is watching.

'Hello Ned. It's good to see you again. You look well… considering.'

Ilse has appeared, from what I think must have been the balcony. She has that ability to vanish and re-appear, and she's done it once again. She's dressed in a black robe, like the ones Omar gave us, except ours were white. She has her head covered with a matching black scarf that is wrapped in a way that covers her neck and can easily be pulled up across her face so you could only see her eyes.

She looks the same as she always does, but different.

Her red lipstick bright and delicately applied.

'You're a killer, Ned. A stone-cold killer.'

I wonder what she's talking about, but then it hits me, filling me with a dread from the pit of my stomach.

I killed Marcellus.

I shot him as he tried to kill Rasa and then me.

'I was only defending myself,' I say.

'Marcellus was not a careless man and you shot him nine times. It was cold and calculating. You're a killer, Ned. A professional. I like that.'

I'm not a killer, I think. I was defending myself and Rasa, and the rest of the Pod, and I wouldn't have done it had I not been kidnapped into this Quadrant and made to do all the things they have made me do.

'I'm innocent.'

Ilse moves towards a table which has small jug of water and pours herself a glass.

Lemon slices splash from the jug.

She offers me a drink and I shake my head.

'It's a mistake to keep rejecting people,' she says, still holding out the glass for me to take.

I know what she says is true, because it's been said to me before.

And I know, too, that the way she said it was a threat.

I take the glass from her with my handcuffed hands and gulp back the water. It's cool and fresh and I was lying to myself. I was thirsty and I'm hungry and tired.

'Thank you,' I say.

'It's me who should thank you. I've been waiting for a star like you to appear in my life. I know you don't believe me, Ned, but there were Exit Points in the *City of Hope*, which if you had reached we would have completed another assessment to see if we thought you valuable enough to keep alive. Your escape makes me look good. It proves my methods work. All you have to do is say *yes* and I'll remove those handcuffs and give you back your clothes. You can be one of us. You can be free. No longer a *Denounced*. How does that make you feel?'

'But I'm not a *Denounced* and I never was and I don't want any part of your Unification War.'

I twitch with defiance.

She smiles.

'It would appear I will have to revaluate my friendship with Omar. I'm assuming it was him that told you about the Unification War?'

'I worked it out myself.'

'If anyone can it would be you. But there's one thing you can never change. You're a *Denounced* until I say otherwise. That's how it works.'

'What if you don't win the War? What if you lose?'

'Be careful, Ned. It's a mistake to make an enemy of me.'

'It's possible,' I say, ignoring her warning.

'No, it's not possible. We've all worked too hard and too long. We are nearly there. You *Denounced* have taught us how to win against your own that's what the Dome is about. It is our school, not yours. We are the ones in class, not you. But you have a unique quality Ned that we need. You are both empathic and ruthless and you understand our enemy in a way that we do not. You can be a great leader. A great asset to everyone in this Quadrant. The Powers-that-Be will need people like you once we obtain victory and they would bestow great gifts. You'll be one of the first to turn and that would give you tremendous influence in the Unified Creation. You'd be more powerful than me. I would have to listen to you, obey you. You could even have me killed.'

She laughs.

Her words smash through my mind.

'And what would I have to do to get that power?'

'You know what you have to do.'

And she's right. I do.

I would have to fight and kill people in my Quadrants.

I would be a traitor in the Unification War.

I shake the thought from my mind. As much as I hate the System it was the Sympathisers for the Non-Secular Quadrants who used our corrupt System to their advantage to get me kidnapped and not the System itself. Why should I kill my own because of them?

'And what would happen to the rest of my Pod?'

'You have to stop thinking of Pod Fifteen. Those days are gone. Your Training is over. You qualified with full honours. Spencer is useful as he has angers that can be harnessed.'

'The others?'

She smiles and sips at her water and I know her lack of commitment means they'll be hung.

'I want you meet someone.'

She walks to the door I came in and it opens like the soldiers outside knew she was approaching. She steps outside. I'm suddenly alone again and the speed of it unsettles me. A warm desert breeze bounces in from the balcony. I want to look out across Anbus, but I'm scared to move.

Then the door opens and Taylor walks in.

He's strutting and smiling and he's dressed like one of the Assault Team Soldiers.

I stare at his green armband.

Shocked.

But not.

I'd forgotten about his natural brutality and menace, and there's an arrogance in the way he carries himself. The scar that runs from under his left eye and seeps into the edges of his cheek, looks more pronounced than I ever remember. He was always the alpha boy in the Community Homes he's lived in. Omar said I was special to have beaten the Dome and I'm not surprised Taylor beat it and he's now one of the Elites.

He circles me like I'm his prey, and in many ways I am.

He pats me on the side of the right shoulder like we're old friends.

We aren't and the pat is more a warning of his strength and new position than anything to do with friendship or support – two words that mean nothing to him.

'Nice uniform,' I say. 'It suits you.'

There's a smirk on my face and a cutting tone in my voice that I've cultivated for Community Home Bullies like him – because that's all he is to me.

A glorified bully.

If Taylor gets it, he doesn't clock it.

'Did you escape?' I continue.

'Complicated story, but let's say the rest of my Pod weren't as lucky as me.'

He laughs and I know what his *complicated* story really means.

He sacrificed them to get where he is today, a quality Ilse admires.

He's a rat.

And I hate him.

And he was never one of us.

'Were you a *Denounced* – a real one?' I ask.

'You mean back in the Secular World?'

'Yeah… back in our Quadrant?'

'I'm not even sure I know what it means any more. My father beat me so when I got big enough I beat him.' Taylor laughs and then leans in. 'You know, you were the only person to ever beat me in a fight. I've not forgotten that.'

'You should,' I say. 'So *Denounced* or not?'

'After I beat my father they put me in the Community Home System. To be honest, I liked it. I did what I wanted, when I wanted. The Wardens were all scared of me, so yeah, I'm probably a *Denounced* because I probably broke some law I didn't care for or even know existed. But I knew I wasn't going to die on the gallows or even in that Dome. I'm hard to kill. I'm invincible.'

'I wish I had your confidence.'

'You know why I'm here, don't you?'

'To talk me into joining.'

'Look around you and think of the place we came from. Yeah… these people talk weird stuff. Your *Soul* and *Fate* and *Destiny*, like everything is set out before you're born. But who cares if it's true or not? In my mind, the Power-that-Be are like another set of Wardens. People who make up the rules to suit them. But if we play their game we're free. We can do what we like. What have we got back home? It's grey there. They give us digital credits and you buy stuff and watch endless programs and we're told what we can and can't do, but really there's more you can't do than you can. When I was in the Holding Centre they told me I was a prisoner, but everyone's a prisoner in our Quadrant – they're just too stupid to see it. I've seen the light, Ned. We are the *Elites*. We were picked and now we can go back and get our revenge. And when we win we can live free. DO. WHAT. WE. WANT. Imagine, that! They tell me you're smart and you'll make a great leader. But if you can't see that it's better living in these Quadrants than our own then you ain't that smart.'

His eyes are wild with excitement. The scar on his face is glowing somehow. And I'm seeing what I've seen in so many people I've known – in my sister, in the Wardens, in the Judges, in the Court Officials and my Lawyers and Ilse, and even Spencer.

Their minds are already made up.

Their decisions have long been made.

'I'm innocent. I'm Ned Hunter.'

'You're a what?' he says, walking back towards me.

'I'm not Ned 5-7-9-0-1-2-3. Hunter is my real name. What's yours?'

He looks at me confused.

Like his mind is lost.

And there's something about Taylor that will never be right. Giving him a gun and soldier's uniform and sense of power is like telling an evil person it is okay to be evil.

'I hate to lose,' Taylor says to me.

'Then don't fight against your Quadrant.'

He smiles.

Then he headbutts me.

And I crunch to the floor, blood pouring from my nose onto the tunic of my Denounced uniform, and there's this strange pain that seems to hurt on the outside, but at the same time relieve something greater on the inside.

23

I'm dazed and in pain and my Denounced Tunic is covered in blood from Taylor having head butted me.

Not that I care about my clothes or even my nose, and Taylor's nothing more than a thug who had to wait until I was handcuffed to get revenge. So I beat him again, I realise. And Ilse will have lost a notch of belief in him and Taylor won't have worked that out yet, so I can smile to myself for another victory under my belt.

I'm led along a corridor into another room and to my surprise it's bright and airy and not a prison cell.

Not even close.

The Assault Soldiers who led me here, close the door behind me and I hear the lock turn as I take in the space. I'm alone and I see it's more an apartment, but in the style of one of Omar's tents with cushions and rugs and what I think they call tapestries hanging from the walls. I wander over to the largest of them. The pictures within them are all of the Old World, before the Great Terrorist Wars. Pictures of a World that is not too far from what I've experienced in this Quadrant. Only a few months ago they would have filled me with fear, but there's something normal, even comforting about them now, and I gaze on seeing part of the design is men riding camels across a desert.

Whoever prepared the room has left fresh fruit and mint tea on the table.

I take what they call a fig and pour myself some tea. It's hot and sweet and refreshing. I wonder if this is what my life would be like had I made it out of the Community Homes

System and been given my digital credits and allowed to start my next cycle as an adult?

My own place.

But without someone locking the door behind me.

Not a prison, but a place I could call home.

I finish my tea and walk into the bedroom and see clean clothes have been laid on the bed. Off to my right is a large bathroom with the widest shower I've ever seen. I strip off and head in. As I step past the glass the water fires on automatically. I step out and it turns off. I step back in and play this stupid game with myself a couple of times, smiling as I do – almost forgetting where I am and why I'm here. I wash the desert and the smell of the cell from my body, and the ache in my nose turns into a deep throb. I touch the top of my bridge and hear myself go *Ouch*.

It's not broken as I first thought, but it should be, and it's going to hurt for days.

I step from the shower and dry myself with the biggest and softest towel I've ever used. Then I change into the clean clothes, which is a version of what Omar would wear.

I pour myself another glass of mint tea and head out unto the balcony and freeze.

Ilse is sat in a chair, drinking mint tea.

'Sit, Ned… enjoy the beautiful view of your new Homeland.'

She smiles at me, but I know she's really laughing at me. Her red lipstick highlighting her smirk, the kind I so often give Court Officials and Wardens when I'm in one of my defiant moods.

'How does it feel to be free?' she continues.

I want to point out that I'm not. That the door is locked and there are soldiers outside and I don't know how to get out of Anbus to Dock Thirty-Four but I know what she's implying. She's saying I could have a place like this and I can come and go as I please, if I do what she says, and it's a feeling that I don't dislike and one I could get used to. I don't tell her something I know deep down inside of me and that is I would still be her prisoner, no matter what she says, so I'm never going to be free as long as I stay in these Quadrants.

Ever.

'I'm not used to it,' I say. 'It feels, odd.'

'You're going to make a great diplomat one day.'

I have no idea what she means, but I sit and I look out across the balcony. We are high up and I'm in some sort of tower. There's nowhere for me to go, but like that's a surprise. Below the Market has come to an end and the hubbub I heard earlier has died to a joyful hum. There's a strange mix of people dressed like me and then soldiers and police and camels and Assault Buggies and Hover Planes and Special Guards with arm bands. In the near distance are The Land of the Valleys and beyond the faint outline of the Mountain Range where the mine must be. It is all under a setting sun and everything is turning into an orange glow that will be my lasting memory of this place.

I wonder about Rasa, Diego, Spencer, Kuro and Chantal and how they are being treated.

They are still in their cells, I'm sure.

I hope they've had food and water and haven't been beaten.

Chantal's words flood back to me, and does sitting here, warm and clean, and drinking tea with Ilse mean I've broken my promise, already?

I've abandoned Pod Fifteen.

I'm a traitor, no different from Taylor.

The thought rattles through me and it makes me twitch in my seat.

'What are you thinking, Ned?'

It's a question I can't answer. Thoughts are smashing through my mind quicker than I can work them out. Taylor and Spencer were right. My Quadrant abandoned me, but did it? I was set up by my Warden, Andreas Lee, who is a sympathiser to the Powers-that-Be. He was an individual and I was in the wrong place at the wrong time. But what I'm really thinking about is the Holding Centre and Jack and the time he said to me that all our futures were a choice and not chance. It didn't make sense then, because I was about to be hung, but I wasn't hung, and I understand what he means now. Those words make total sense to me. I can pick who I want to be. It's what Chantal meant, I think. If I don't abandon Pod Fifteen in my mind then they are not abandoned. Even if I'm not there physically. It's a mental and emotional decision. It's a choice, and once I make that thought stick it happens. It becomes my life. It's what I'm doing with my innocence. I'm not a *Denounced*. I knew deep inside of me that it was an injustice before I discovered the truth of why, and somehow everything I've done has been to clear my name and set myself free.

'What do you want from me?' I ask Ilse.

'You know, Ned. In your heart, you know.'

I shake my head.

'I think I know, but I want you to tell me. So I can be sure.'

She stares at me.

Sips her tea.

Then she smiles, but the eyes don't smile and it makes me go cold inside.

'You have to agree to join us. Learn our ways and our customs so you understand the people who will eventually follow you. In time, you will see it is better than what you know and teachings of the Quadrants you are familiar with. Then we will give you more military training, training like you've never had. Then you'll lead, Ned. Lead part of the Army against your own and become the true Warrior and Leader you were destined to be. Your Secular World is consuming the planet. It's corrupt beyond anything we have ever witnessed. It does nothing, but take and destroy what we have. It's time to end it. It's time to make all the Quadrants fall under one rule. Our Rule. The Rule of the Power-that-Be. A system that has a Soul. Greatness, Ned. That's what we want from you. Greatness. But you have to want to step into it. We have to hear that you want it.'

'And what happens to the rest of Pod Fifteen?'

'We've discussed it already. Their fate is sealed.'

'If you let them go, I'll say yes.'

She stands and walks to the front of the balcony.

'Come and stand next to me, my child.'

I hesitate, but do as I'm told.

'Look out and what do you see?'

'Desert and mountains.'

'That's right… a vast area of land that has seen more blood and death than you could ever imagine. Freedom has its price. In life, you have to accept the things you can't change, and it's in that moment of acceptance you find your true strength. Pod Fifteen is gone. That time you knew is no more. Eat well and then sleep even better. Because tomorrow you have to decide what you want in your life. The Powers-that-Be will not ask again. Your destiny has arrived.'

24

Two women step into my room.

One is carrying a tray of food.

The other a tray of fresh water and more hot mint tea that I like so much.

Their faces are covered and all I can see is their dark brown eyes. Their gazes avoid me and I watch them put the trays on the table and then quietly leave the room.

It's almost like they weren't here.

I sit and take a mouthful of food, using my fingers as Omar had taught me. It's lamb with some kind of rice that I'm sure they call *couscous*. I like it, but I'm not hungry and after two mouthfuls I feel guilty toward the rest of my Pod as I gaze through my comfortable surroundings.

The best I have ever stayed in.

But I'm not fooled.

It's all part of the seduction that is happening to me. There is a betrayal sitting around the corner. I still don't understand why this life has happened to me, but the more everyone tells me what I should do, the more I'm compelled to do the opposite. I've always been like that. I wonder if it's why I've gotten into so much trouble for most of my life. Maybe the Powers-that-Be should ask me to do the opposite of what they want and by my own nature I will do what it is that they need me to do.

I doubt it somehow, smiling at my own thought.

I just don't want to be told what to do any more.

Is it that much to ask?

I push the plate away and stand and walk towards the bedroom. There's a jitteriness inside my stomach that makes it hard for me to sit still or even concentrate. I have this feeling that I'm supposed to put something right, but I'm not sure what it is and, anyway, even if I knew – I can't, because whether I like it or not this is not the beautiful apartment it is meant to be.

It's a prison.

And I'm still a prisoner.

As I have been for most of my life.

If I do join the Powers-that-Be, I'm effectively free if this Quadrant wins the War and I survive it. But what will happen to me afterwards? I will never be one of them and I might be all used up after that point. My usefulness gone. I'll be back a prisoner. One thing is for sure, Ilse won't ask me to join them again so at least I only have to see her one more time if I say no. She won't have hung the rest of Pod Fifteen yet, because she's going to use it as her final play if I still refuse her request. I see what she is now. An Agent between me and the Powers-that-Be and she doesn't want the failure, so I have some power left of my own, but not much, and how do I use it?

I climb onto the bed.

It's soft and the sheets smell of lavender.

And a honey scent breeze drifts in from the balcony.

More seduction.

More betrayal.

It's quiet until I close my eyes and the chaos of my life floods into my mind. I try to imagine what my father would say to calm me, but there's too much noise to hear his voice, too much upheaval going on inside my head to hear anything but Chantal's words of don't abandon Pod Fifteen.

But I have, I think and I hate myself for it.

I try to close my eyes and hope that sleep will relieve my pain. It doesn't and through the darkness, I see my sister and Rasa and Chantal, and they're fighting and Spencer is shouting and Ilse has a gun. The noise is loud and there are bangs and flashes of light. I can't see Diego and I'm calling his name as the fight and the noise move from the corners of my mind into a large bright room beyond.

I tense, opening my eyes.

Then I push up and sit on the end of the bed.

There's a strange silence, like something bad has happened and I'm in the pause before the next round.

I get up and gingerly peer into the main room.

I hear wood creak and then someone says.

'Ned. Where are you?'

It's Omar.

His deep, resonant voice is like no other I've ever heard.

Always calm.

Always in control.

'I'm here,' I say, stepping deeper into the room.

'Hello, my Friend. It's good to see you again. We have to move. Time never seems to our friend and especially tonight.'

I should hesitate, but I don't. I have hundreds of questions flood into my mind, but I don't ask any. I don't know why, but there's something familiar and I know in this moment that I trust him. Trust him like he was my father or Jack. The two men who never let me down.

I head for the door and see several of Omar's trusted men. They have killed the two Assault Soldiers who were guarding the room and are dragging them inside to hide their bodies.

Omar grabs my shoulders and looks me in the eyes.

'Do you trust me?'

I nod.

'Then stay close.'

I nod again.

He leads the way and before I know it we are running along the corridors. I see more dead Assault Soldiers and I wonder if Ilse is dead, too. I doubt it. She'll be harder to kill than a cockroach. We run on and I realise we are heading across and not down. I want to ask about the others, but we're moving too fast. We come to a window and Omar leaps out. We are on the roof of a building. I look down and see an ancient town, like the ones in our history books and the tapestries on the wall. It's quiet and the only people are the police and Assault Soldiers who fill the square below like ants in a nest.

Omar puts his finger to his lips for me to be quiet.

I nod.

He then points to the next building and I realise we are going to jump. The gap is big, but I'm not scared. I know I can do it. Omar runs and leaps across to the other side, his clothes catching the wind, like trails of smoke behind him. I run and leap and land on the other side with ease, rolling through my shoulders and bouncing to my feet. As I stand, I see his Faithfuls do the same. I count eight of them. Omar runs on and we repeat the process, turning right and jumping another building.

I get into the swing and a confidence swells through me.

We are silent and swift, and I like the feeling of the power as it churns inside of me.

Then I'm blinded by a shaft of light.

I trip and Omar grabs my shoulder and pulls me back, stopping me from tripping over the edge.

Voices echo from below and the swell of manic activity vibrates up.

Electronic bullets begin to spark around us and Omar's guards start to return fire, but we're backing off. Omar points back to the way we came and we re-jump the previous rooftop. An electronic arc explodes near my feet and I can feel its residue heat. Omar points down and we scramble from balcony to balcony making our way to the ground. It looks like a stupid move to me, but I see that one-side of the alley is blocked off and the Assault Soldiers can't get through. If we'd made it across the roof tops we would have avoided this route so in part it's still the way Omar wants to go.

It's then I hear a roar in the sky.

Two Assault planes circle into view, their spotlights so strong they wash out the night.

We run on, silent and focused. We turn left and right and then right and left, ducking into alley after alley, some so thin that I have to run sideways. Omar knows this route like a rat in a maze and my confidence returns as I see the lights of the planes move towards the back of the town as we head in the opposite direction.

We come to a dead end, but I know that it won't be.

Sure enough the floor opens and another one of Omar's Faithful guides us into a tunnel.

The hatch closes and a peace returns, the panting breaths of Omar's men the only sound.

The tunnel is damp and lit with fire torches.

I feel their heat on my face.

Omar smiles, sweat peppering his brow.

'Ned, I handed you in to protect my people and the many tribes who make the Great Deserts their home. I have seen many things and none worse that the Dome and the graves they produce. We want to protect our ways and our customers and the peace we have all been privileged, too.

You are our proof that the Powers-that-Be have changed course and we will start our own internal battle to get that changed. It's imperative you get home and tell your people of what is coming.'

One of Omar's Faithful hands him a small bag which he then passes to me.

'Inside is food and two maps. Through that small door there's a camel outside and it's trained to take you to the foot of a goat path. Once there, you follow the map until you come to the Port Town of Delf. You need to find Dock One and not Thirty-Four. It is where the *Denounced* are brought in. It's where you were brought in. The boat leaves exactly five hours after all the cargo has been unloaded and always at night. It will dock in eight nights from tomorrow. The ship is called *Shifting Horizons*. You have to find a way onto it and it will take you home. The second map takes you to your tribe. If you choose to rescue them you risk being caught. Ilse is a dangerous woman and is protected by the Powers-that-Be. As a Leader, I would tell you to go home and leave your tribe for the greater good. You could save, hundreds of thousands of lives both in our Quadrants and your own by sacrificing five lives. But I would tell you to find your family and do what you can to save them.'

I clutch the bag in my hands, uncertainty and confusion pounding through me.

'Only you can make that choice and I trust your judgement.'

'The Authorities and the people in my Quadrants won't listen to me. I'm a *Denounced* and I'm still not a man with his own digital credits.'

'You are more of a man than many who are three-times your age. Any man would be proud to have a son like you and I wish more than anything you could stay and we could spend quality time together. There is much we could teach each other, of that I'm convinced. However, that is not our destinies and something I have accepted. You need to find a way to make your people listen.'

'What about you?'

'Don't you concern yourself with me. As long as we clear this town before day-break we are safe.'

'But Spencer will turn you in. He will tell them what you did for us.'

'It is the word of a *Denounced* against an Elder of the Desert and in the Powers-that-Be's eyes I have already helped Ilse.'

He winks, a smile lighting up his face.

I nod.

Omar steps forward and pulls me into a hug, kisses me on both cheeks and then stares deep into my eyes. A sadness dances across his face and before I can say anything he turns, and he and his men run in the opposite direction. I watch them go, suddenly alone with a single flame, which is dying by the seconds.

I tug open the secret door.

A cold desert breeze swamps my face and I see the solitary camel kneeled and waiting for me to mount.

Indecision continues to seep through my blood and I can hear pounding footsteps and the noise of hovering planes and the vibration of people closing in.

I open the bag and pull out the two maps.

They are exactly as Omar said. One shows the path through a small mountainous range that will take me the City of Delf, its Port, Dock One, and ultimately home if I can board *Shifting Horizons*. The second is a guide through the labyrinth of corridors behind me that will take me to the cells where Pod Fifteen are held.

At the bottom of this map is written.

Destiny is choice not chance.

25

Confusion roots me to the spot and my head swims with a batch of fears about my future.

I take a deep breath and feel alone in a way I never have before.

I can leave and find my way to the City of Delf and its Port, and ultimately make it home, or I can stay and attempt to rescue the others with the risk of being caught and hung, the Powers-that-Be marching on uninterrupted to their Unification War.

Suddenly, the flame burns out and I'm thrown into darkness.

It exaggerates the fears dancing in my mind and the noises around me.

I fumble in the dark and find the handle to the secret door. I pull. The door is stiff and dusty and more like a portal than a door. It opens onto the desert and I look across the darkness and see a camel. It turns its head and seems to beckon me out, impatient. Nine or ten strides and I'm free. Once I mount, I'm sure the camel will gallop into the night as the Airborne Crews continue to focus on the City and nearby parameters.

I'll be free.

Finally.

The one thing I've wanted the most in my life.

But I won't be.

I will still be a *Denounced* and I will still have to prove my innocence.

And most of all, I will forever know what I did to be free, which was to leave the rest of my Pod behind to hang on Ilse's Gallows. Maybe Spencer would leave if he had the choice; even Rasa at a push. I'm only guessing at their actions, but I know I can't. It's not in me, no matter what I tell myself about being better on my own. I'm lying to myself. Pod Fifteen, for all their faults, are the closest I've ever had to a family since my parents died and my sister left me in the System.

Don't abandon us, Ned – you have to promise!

And I did.

I promised.

I close the secret door that would lead me to my freedom and hunt through the bag Omar gave me. Sure enough, I find what I'm looking for. A small torch. I turn it on by touching the back and grip it between my teeth as I examine the map in more detail. The concentration of the beam seems to calm my mind and I'm able to focus in on the noises around me, getting a sense of what is going on.

The heavy footsteps are not as menacing as I first imagined.

They are full of uncertainty and panic.

The Search Crews don't know where I am and I sense the fear of punishment over-hanging each member if they don't find me. It relaxes me some more and I return my attention to the map, occasionally shining the beam along the route Omar and his men ran.

I'm in a set of subterranean tunnels, and for now I'm safe. I can't work out if they are sewers or even tombs, but the feverish activity is all above my head and the closeness of the Assault Teams almost makes me laugh. I sit and study the map in more detail, wishing I had Kuro's skills. It takes me a few minutes to work out that these are streets and the once walls of the buildings have now become the foundations of Anbus above me.

It's the remnants of a City, another one now built on top. And what stretches out in front of me is a twisting mass of roads, streets and alleys, and even if Ilse's Assault Teams do enter, they still have to find me.

And will they even have a map?

I smile at Omar's deviousness.

The secret door I can escape through looks to be at the East of the City. This ancient sub city with its streets are mostly in the East side and slip across to the West Side, dissecting Anbus in two. I see now why we had to jump the roof tops and dart through the alleys above, which means I was kept in the South, because the balcony of the tower that was my cell faced The Land of the Valleys – the way we came out of the Great Desert so we've always been travelling North.

Omar has ringed a section off to the West and all I can think is it must be the Prison where the others are kept.

I cement the mental picture of Anbus in my mind, the City of Delf always to my North. My biggest danger from what I can see is rushing and getting my bearings confused, unable to work out which turn corresponds to the turns on the map.

I slow jog on.

The torch beam bouncing in front of me.

The noise of the Assault Teams above my head fades as I zig-zag my way West.

The streets I'm in are dusty and the bricks are mostly damp and soft to the touch, but the height is constant and it's enough for me to stand, just.

I wonder how many people know of this Secret World and how long it will take Ilse to work out I'm here, if she ever will.

It's then I stumble and almost fall.

I shine my light down to see what it was that nearly tripped me and gasp.

There are several skulls and bones and I can make out crushed rib cages. I wondered how these people died and if they were *Denounced*, like me, or are they from the Ancient World that these streets once belonged to.

Or maybe they just didn't have a map and it's a warning to me to pay attention to where I'm going.

I step around the bones and continue on.

A silence befalls me and it's like the Assault Teams have vanished and with it a calmness returns to my mind. I don't know what I'm going to do when I get to the Prison, but I have to trust Omar that there's some solution to my problem. I hope I'm smart enough to see what it is.

I come to a small step and sit and hunt through the bag. I find another torch and some water and dried fruit and biscuits. It's then I spot a knife. I take a large gulp from the leather drinking pouch and pull the knife clean from its scabbard. It's short and stubby and fits neatly into the bag, and is unlike any of the other knives I've seen Omar and his man carry before. I softly touch the blade and realise it is crystal sharp and could easily cut me to the bone.

I slip it back into the scabbard, deciding it's more an assassin's weapon than a utility knife, the thought leaving me cold.

Will I have to kill someone to ensure the rest of the Pod escape?

I take another sip of water; sling the bag over my shoulders and trek on.

My progress is slow but steady and without a map I'd have no chance of navigating my way anywhere. I turn right and then soft right again and come out of the streets into an open space of sorts. It looks like it was once a garden or even a small court yard. At the far end is a wall and it is where the map and the streets end. I'm in the last section of the West side and have finally moved from one end of Anbus to the other.

I shine the torch around me and can't see any door or hatch, or opening of any sorts.

I've come to a dead end.

A complete stop.

I fight against my rising panic, telling myself that Omar wouldn't have let me get this far without a way into the Prison. I sit on the floor and take a deep breath to calm my nerves and begin to work the light beam around the open space.

It's nothing but solid brick.

My chest tightens and that pit of despair that is my ever present partner builds inside my stomach.

I continue to let my eyes follow the beam, but I'm being too haphazard in looking for my answer when something cold hits my forehead and runs down my cheek. I touch it and it looks like blood. It's not. It's water and it's the colour of sand. Another drop hits my forehead and I move and shine the beam directly above my head. There's a small circle of damp brick and a solitary drip. Whatever it is has been there for a while and I see that I've sat in the one damp spot in the whole of the space.

I let the beam fall along the wall and it's then I see a protruding brick.

Then another.

And another.

I stand back and follow the line and see the protruding bricks are no accident.

It's a ladder, like a fake climbing wall in a fun park.

I shine the torch above, but there's no hatch or door, just the drip coming through the damp brick roof.

I put the torch between my teeth and use the protruding bricks to climb the wall. It's not that high, maybe twice my height, maybe a bit more. I can see that the water has eaten away at the cement or whatever it is that holds these bricks together. I work my fingers between the bricks and wriggle it lose. It falls with ease to the floor, dust and debris sprinkling onto my face, making me cough. I work out more bricks and like a house of cards several fall to the floor in a single thud, narrowly missing my head on the way down.

I freeze, scared that I've made too much noise.

I listen, but I can't hear anything except the silence of the night.

I shine the beam into the hole I've made and I seem to have come into another room or even some kind of wooden cupboard. It's a strange size. Tall, but narrow and long, like a corridor. It looks big enough for me to stand in and I pull some more bricks away so I can use the brick ladder to climb into the box with more ease.

I turn the torch off.

Then I sling my bag up and onto the floor, pulling myself up and into the new space.

I'm tempted to turn the torch back on but I sense I'm close to being outside and I don't want the beam to leak out and signal my whereabouts. I feel the sides and I'm right in that it's made of wood as a slight breeze cuts through the timber, so I was right again not to turn on my torch.

As my eyes continue to adjust to the inky light, I can't work out the space.

Instinctively, I look up and see a hatch and smile.

A way out.

Then my smile drops and my stomach wrenches into a knot.

Next to the hatch is another hatch and next to that is another.

I count six in total and it's then I know where I am.

I'm in the guts of a set of gallows.

The place the bodies fall when the Executioner pulls the lever.

And there are six hatches.

Enough for six people to be hanged together.

Enough for Pod Fifteen.

26

I'm sat on the floor breathing hard and I think I must have fallen, but I don't remember when or even if I fainted, or how much time has elapsed since I first realised where I am.

I do my best to get my panic under control, scared someone will hear my chopping breaths.

The wooden support that hides the hangman's drop is both solid at the main structural points, but also thin where its design is just to hide the dangling bodies from what I'm sure will be a large baying crowd, orchestrated by Ilse. I desperately want to turn on the torch so I can see better and try and work out what to do next.

I know I can't.

It's a stupid move, something Kuro would do because he's locked in his analytical world, common sense nowhere to be seen.

Think.

Think, I tell myself.

I suddenly remember the knife I have from Omar. It's short and stubby and surgically sharp. It's perfect for cutting rope and will slice through the hangman's knot in seconds.

I get it.

Pod Fifteen is all I have.

And this is the only place I can rescue them.

Think.

When they hang you, if you hit the floor then you don't die – it's what happened to me at the Holding Centre and it is why I'm still alive today.

I look up.

I need to stop the Pod from hitting the floor or I need something to stand on so I can cut the rope immediately.

But what if they drop all five of the Pod at once?

I can save one, maybe two, but three will die – I won't be able to move that fast.

Think.

Think.

I take another drink of water and it helps stop the spinning in my head. I'm not sure of the time but it looks dark enough outside to still be the middle of the night, and I sense I have time on my side if I can get an idea.

I just need an idea.

What would Omar do?

But he's not here.

I am.

I look back at the hatches, squinting through the darkness into the shadows above my head. They look to be spring loaded. I remember one of the boys at the Holding Centre telling me he knew a boy whose father made them. The hatch springs back so the Executioner doesn't fall through it. He can then move onto the next one and repeat the process. The hatch springing back also locks the rope in place which is better, apparently, but I'm not sure who for – the Executioner or the *Denounced* at the end of the rope.

Think.

Think.

I hear a tiny thud.

It makes me jump and for a split second I think I've been discovered.

I haven't.

A brick has worked its way lose and fallen into the entrance below. It reminds me to be careful of where I stand when near the hole I've created as the floor is weak and it's going to struggle to take my weight.

A fallen brick, I think.

The hole.

I scramble across and look through the opening and see the small pile of bricks and rubble that came from making the original opening. And I know from touching the walls along my journey that most are damp and soft and easy to pry loose. I lower myself back into the hole and work my way down the brick ladder, jumping the last section.

I turn on the torch, careful to keep the beam low as I inspect one of the bricks in more detail. They are small and crumbly, but light and easy to move. My attention is taken by the last wall in front of me. The one that ends the streets and leads into this once small court yard I'm standing in. One half of the wall goes all the way to the roof, but the second half staggers down in steps fading into the ground.

It's single banked.

Not double.

It's weak, I think.

I stare at it, picking my spot.

I move right two steps, then back three, rounding my shoulder into my neck.

I turn off the torch and hold it firmly in my hand, protecting the front. I then pull my head back to protect my skull and charge at the wall with all my strength.

Pain smashes into my shoulder and along my arm.

The wall bends as if it's made of rubber, and I feel my own force still propelling me forward, as I slow fall through the bricks and onto the floor the other side, mortar and dust enveloping me in one. I have to bury my head into my clothes and silent cough the dust from my throat and lungs. My eyes sting and I can't believe how much debris I've generated, but I think most of it has come from the floor and it's like a bowl of flour that has puffed out if you drop something into it.

I sit and wait for everything to settle, eventually turning the torch back on. The wall I ran into has crumbled to dust, but I've enough bricks to make my mounds. I don't know how well they'll work or how strong they'll be, but it should be enough to delay the drop while I cut each member of the Pod free.

Even if all five drop at once, it increases my chances of success.

I'm hit with an unexpected jolt of confidence as I realise that Ilse won't let the Executioner drop Pod Fifteen in one go. It'll spoil the entertainment for what I'm sure will be a record, sell-out crowd. Dropping everyone in one go would end the spectacle too quickly. No, Ilse will draw every ounce of effect she can from her display of power, and she'll drop each member of my Pod one at a time, with a pause in between.

I empty the bag that Omar gave me and start to fill it with bricks and head back to the top. I make my first small pile and although I'm more confident in my idea than I was a few moments ago, it's going to be slow hard work and I'll have to build six piles and not five, because I don't know which end the Executioner is going to start.

I don't know how long I work for other than my back and knees ache, like never before. My fingertips have become red raw and my hands are scratched beyond anything I can remember. I'm both pumped with adrenaline and tired in a way that leaves me feeling high.

I continue to work quick and hard and I finish my last pile, standing on the top to test my engineering. It could be more solid, but I don't have the time or the materials to keep working it. I can touch the underside of the hatch if I lift my hands. It's getting lighter outside, which means people will start to appear so I have no choice but to stop what I'm doing and to sit and wait.

I've come too far to risk getting heard and caught now.

I have to trust my work.

I always wanted to be an Engineer so here's my first real test.

My only concern is Chantal, as she is the smallest of us all and may not reach my mound of bricks, but if I'm quick enough I may be able to catch her.

She's the lightest and I'm sure I could do it.

I will do it, I tell myself.

I jump down and feed myself back into the hole and down into the hidden streets. I take a long slow drink of my water, more than I should and indulge myself a handful so I can wash my face and the dust from my eyes. It's a small comfort and I allow myself the feeling of relief it brings. I re-check the map and see the second street on my right is where we want to escape if my plan works. It's the longest run before a sharp left and should allow us a solid head-start if by any chance the Elites follow us down.

I place the bag on the ground to mark the spot.

I put the knife and torch in my pocket and head back to the guts of the gallows to make a final inspection of my work.

It's become light outside in my short time down in the streets and I'd forgotten how fast the mornings can rise in the desert.

It's dark one second then it's light in a blink of an eye.

I sit.

There's nothing I can do but keep my nerve and my emotions in check. It's going to be hard, maybe the hardest thing I've ever done. I wonder if I knew one of the prayers that I saw Omar's men do on the mats would help me. I dismiss the idea. It's a World I know nothing about. I'm not even sure if I have a Soul or even if I know what it means so how can I start with their prayers.

It's then I hear a man with heavy footsteps walk up the stairs at the far end and traverse from one side of the gallows to the next.

I know what he's going to do and I detest him for it.

Who would do such a job?

I step into the corner, hiding in the shadows of the wooden box and wait.

A hiss of air streaks out from the trapdoor mechanism at the far end of the gallows. Then the hatch snaps open, sending a shaft of light into the guts of this tomb before a bag falls on the end of a rope.

Thud.

The bag bounces once and swings in the air as the hatch door slams shut with a small part of the hatch peeled back to allow the rope to hang true.

The bag and the rope continue to swing in the confines of the space and if I was to dash out now I could cut the rope.

Then I smile.

The weighted bag has just given me another idea and it's the first time I warm with a real confidence since I've stepped into this box of death.

27

Since the Executioner finished rehearsing his death sequence, I've not moved from my corner spot.

The day has taken hold and most of the light I have filters in from the few cracks in the wooden platform above my head. There's enough light for me to see at the opposite end the makers of these gallows have not so much made a door, but more a panel which can be lifted out and gives access to remove the bodies once they're dead.

If I'd noticed what it was before, I would have tried to secure it shut to give us some extra time to escape, but I've left it too late. The noise is growing outside as more people enter the Square and I can't risk being heard. So I stay sat, transfixed on the hatches above my head, hoping that I'm wrong about where I am. I'm not, of course, and there's nothing I can do other than wait, which I'm beginning to realise is the hardest thing in life to do.

I pull the knife from its sheaf and stare at the blade. I'm not sure why, but it gives me a boost of confidence. I'm oddly confident, too, that I won't be discovered assuming I don't do something stupid enough to give myself away, which I'm not going to do.

I have the greatest weapon of them all on my side – surprise.

The trap doors have been tested and there's nothing else for them to do until it's time. I can only sense when that will be, but I feel it is a few hours away yet. At the Holding Centre, all Executions were carried out in the early mornings. I have no idea why that is other than maybe they have to get it done before breakfast, but I don't think that will happen today. In a few hours the sun's heat will be close to unbearable and it would make sense to wait until the cooler afternoon.

So I have to wait and I wonder if I should go into the hole and wait down there when the stairs creak. I tense as I stare up at the platform imagining the people above me. I count three and they are talking in the language of this Quadrant. I have no idea what is being said, but it strikes me that two of them are Court Official types, giving final instructions to the Executioner.

I get the impression this is a special event and it's important it all goes to plan. I hadn't thought of it before, but the Powers-that-Be must know that there are many people like Omar within these Quadrants who don't want to go to war. Perhaps this is another way of them demonstrating to their Quadrants who is in charge, and that the pending Unification War is coming whether a small minority want it or not.

In their own way, Omar, and supporters like him, are *Denounced*, the same as me.

I almost smile at the thought.

Omar the *Denounced*, but I get it.

Hanging Pod Fifteen is the same as hanging their own traitors.

The men above me move off the platform and I hear them walk down the wooden steps and then cut back and stride right by where I'm sat. It makes me hold my breath and I'm glad when they're gone. I stand and gently move to what is the front of the gallows. Through the semi-darkness, I carefully run my hands over the wooden front and find what I'm looking for.

I slip Omar's knife from its sheaf and delicately dig the wooden knot loose. It pops out and light drops in, and it's the first time I can see into the public Square, albeit at a side angle, as I'm almost laying flat on the floor. The Square is bigger than I realised and the floor dusty with orange coloured sand. The gallows have been ringed off so nobody can stand too close. I can see several Assault Teams keeping guard and the crowd is gathering, which I already knew from the increased noise.

I push up and gently move back to my corner rehearsing what I'm going to do in my mind.

My fear is really around Diego and Spencer. Both are big and strong, and my strength is nothing compared to Diego's. Their panic will make it harder for me to hold them and if surprise is on my side they are going to be surprised, too. They say a drowning man will always take you down, because his panic is more than yours. I hope that isn't true and I wonder if they'll be tied, and if they'll have hoods over their heads.

At the Holding Centre both were mandatory, but I don't know how it'll be here. Their hands will be tied, I'm sure of that, but I won't know until I know, so I decide there is nothing I can do but save my mental strength for the time that is surely coming soon.

I close my eyes and it brings an unexpected calmness. I recall the few hours before I thought I was going to die in the Holding Centre. After my meal of the burger and chocolate pudding, I was much calmer than I ever thought I would be. I don't know why. My father was always calm, and maybe it's something I inherited from him. I didn't think it was a trait that got passed down, but maybe it is – like intelligence and mental health, which can get passed from one generation to the next.

In the Holding Centre, Jack used to talk about the Stoics. People from the Old World who trained themselves to have no emotions. That seems strange to me because our emotions make us who we are, but I think it was more about what you can control and what you can't control. So, it's like, there's no point getting all worked up about something that is outside of your control. I think I get it, and it has nothing to do with suppressing your emotions, so maybe that's why I feel calm, because there's nothing I can do other than hope my plan works and whatever happens I will always know I came back for my Pod.

My proxy family.

That's more than my sister ever did for me.

Or Chantal's mother did for her.

The noise outside has grown and I shuffle across and look through the hole I made. The crowd is now locked shoulder-to-shoulder and Assault Guards have filled the inner ring. They are closer than I would like, but there's nothing I can do and my only relief is I don't see any of them wearing the thin green armbands so these are regular soldiers and not the Elites.

My heart then skips a beat as a sudden swell of tension penetrates through the crowd and into the box, hitting me like a punch in the face.

I can hear a solitary Assault Buggy approaching from behind me and I know what it is.

The prisoners are being brought to the gallows for their final moment.

The Buggy stops and the crowd seems to gasp and be excited all-in-one. It's hard for me to imagine what is happening and it's the cheer that chills me further. I don't know what is being said, but I'll recognise that voice until the day I die. Ilse has started to address the crowd in their own language. She's getting applause followed by cheers, each one louder than the last. Even though I don't know what she's saying, I've seen her address us within the Dome and there's a magnetism in the way she holds a crowd's attention.

It's a combination of fear and loathing.

I look at my mini-constructions and decide to move to the centre of this box. I don't know which side will go first, but I'm even more convinced that Ilse will not hang all of the Pod in one go. She'll want the maximum dramatic effect for her fans, but she'll also want to punish each of them individually by making them suffer that little bit more as they wait their turn to die.

I hate her.

I wish I could pull the lever on her and watch her fall through the hole.

Ilse stops talking and there's a change in the crowd's attitude.

The tension and excitement have changed to an intensity that pounds on the outside of the wooden gallows.

It's then I hear the first shuffle of feet.

It's Spencer.

I would recognise that lazy walk anywhere.

Next is Diego.

Rasa.

Kuro

And finally, Chantal.

I can't see them, but I follow them up the steps with my eyes, seeing each of their faces in my mind's eye as clear as if they were stopped in front of me.

Spencer walks above my head and stops on the hatch to my far left. I carefully shuffle across to prepare myself and it's only then that I notice the hole I've made to enter and leave could be our undoing and not our escape. To ensure we don't collapse into the streets below I need to catch Spencer from the front. It had been my intention to catch him from the back. I'm sure there would have been less resistance if I did. He would be easier to grip and his hands will be tied at the front, but our joint weight that close to hole is going to be an issue, so I have to catch him at the front.

I ease round and away from our escape hole.

The front it is.

My plan is simple enough.

They will drop and hit my mound.

I will hold them so they don't fall and break their necks, but I need to cut the rope and keep the tension, so the Executioner doesn't sense anything has gone wrong.

It's then all the different things that could go wrong begin to slam through my mind:

I don't catch Spencer in a clean way.

He fights too much.

He screams out my name.

I can't cut the rope.

I drop the knife

I can't keep the tension.

The Executioner sees what I'm doing.

My mounds are too short.

My structures crumble from the weight of two.

I lose my nerve.

The crowd goes quiet.

The tension ups.

Ilse begins to talk.

Her tone is quiet and solemn, but her voice is slowly rising and I know she is damning those who are about to die. Her voice grows louder and louder and it booms out through speakers that echo throughout Anbus. It's like she's become two people and she's everywhere at once.

Then she stops.

I hear the slow and deliberate walk of the Executioner come to stand above my head.

Spencer is going to be first.

I wait.

A drop of water seeps through the platform of the roof.

Spencer has peed himself.

It's okay to be scared, I think.

There's no shame and I wish I could tell him as Jack told me all those months ago.

Then I hear a *hiss* of air.

The trap door opens.

Light floods through.

And Spencer drops.

Feet first…

<h1 style="text-align:center">28</h1>

My plan blows up in my face.

I've underestimated the speed of Spencer's drop.

His panic and fight for life.

My own adrenaline.

And the sudden shaft of blinding light and the immediate darkness that followed.

He hits my mound with a force that I'm sure breaks both his legs.

He yelps, falling forward after the initial bounce, but I'm fast enough, aided by Omar's magically sharp knife, to both cut the rope above the hangman's knot and nudge him enough so he doesn't tumble backwards into our escape hole.

I grab hold of the cut rope and hang from it as if I was Spencer, slowly letting the rope come to a natural stop.

The rope creaks in that way dry hemp does.

I'm aided by Spencer's grunts and cries as his brain takes in what is happening. I was right about one thing that has helped us both. Ilse is cruel and vindictive enough that she's instructed the Executioner to not use masks.

The crowd has cheered and start to applaud as I allow the rope to stay taught but continue to swing gently as if the body is now dead.

Spencer gets himself together and stands, wide-eyed and in total disbelief.

I nod frantically to the knife that I've dropped, which is dangerously close to falling into the hole. He's smart enough to get what he needs to do and realises the hole is both our escape route and our current danger. He reaches out and picks up the knife and joins me on the crumbling mound that hasn't taken the impact well.

He hands me the knife and then reaches up to grab the rope to keep up the tension.

He says nothing as he knows what's coming and what I have to continue to do.

When it comes to the System and survival we have an understanding and are bonded forever.

I can hear Ilse start another speech.

It's beyond cruel to those waiting to die, but it's playing into my hands and I get a glimpse of how negative behaviour can come back to bite you.

Jack always said that's how life works.

I cut Spencer's ties from his wrists. In my rush to do it, I nick the pad of his left thumb and it slices open like newborn skin. Another reminder that without this knife Spencer would be dead.

I jump off the mound and stand by the next one.

I'm going to have to let whoever falls next hit the mound and then cut them free. It's beyond stupid to try and catch them and I have to hope their neck doesn't break before I get the chance to do my work.

At least I'm away from the escape hole and don't have to worry about its collapse.

Spencer starts to shake his head.

I'm not sure what he's saying, but he keeps nodding to the end trap.

They are not going in line.

It's one end and then the next.

Ilse's voice stops booming from the speakers and is replaced with an explosive tension that begins to seep poisonously into our box.

I move to the end and wait.

Hiss...

The trap door springs open and it's Chantal who falls through next.

She's oddly relaxed, like she's resigned to her end and she hits the mound with such a light touch that I've cut the rope and am pulling it tight before she even rolls to the floor. She misses banging into the edges of the box, but the cheer from the crowd would have masked the noise anyway.

I do the same pull on the rope and twist, allowing it to come to a stop as if Chantal was now dead.

I look down and even in the semi-darkness I can see Chantal is both crying and smiling.

It's like she knew I would be here and I'm more pleased to see her than I care to admit.

She jumps up and I cut her ties, careful not to slice her skin.

She climbs onto the mound and hangs from the rope, taking the tension.

Chantal nods to the centre one, nearest to Spencer as next to come.

She mouths Kuro, which I'm pleased about. He should be as easy to deal with as Chantal, and I'll get another practice before Rasa and Diego drop, both of whom I know will be difficult in their own ways.

Ilse finishes her rousing speech of damnation and the same silence befalls the crowd followed by the building tension that will soon be replaced by the hiss of the trap door and the cheer of relief.

I look up.

The Executioner's footfalls pound above my head.

Kuro is crying.

There's a pause, like they are waiting for more dramatic effect.

Then.

Hiss…

Kuro drops through the trap door and he's reaching for his own neck as if that is going to save him. I jump up and slice through the rope, barely missing his fingers as he reaches higher to grab past the knot. He's lucky because this knife would have cut his fingers clean off. I'm not sure how, but he flops to a sitting position as if a chair had been pulled out from under him. It makes me miss the rope and it goes too loose before I can grab it and I sense the Executioner taking a second look, but I manage to pull it tight and then swing, and the roar of the crowd seems to distract him enough for him not to check any more.

I imagine him taking a bow for his skill at hitting a button and murdering a *Denounced*.

Kuro looks up at me. His face is puffed with crying and he's looking around in a state of shock, but he sees what he has to do and reaches up for me to cut his ties before taking on the tension of the rope.

Three down.

Two to go.

I take a deep breath.

I hope it's Rasa next.

I move to the next mound in the middle of the six.

The sequence has started again.

Ilse's voice building through the speakers.

The crowd's tension building to boiling point.

The footsteps of the Executioner.

Silence.

Hiss…

The trap opens and Rasa falls next.

She's centre right, next to Kuro, and she's more forward than the others were.

She clips my mound at the front, which jerks her backwards, like a dog being pulled on the lead. Chantal gasps loudly. I leap forward and cut the rope, again thankful for this blade supplied by Omar. The rope slices in half and Rasa falls to the floor. She's choking loudly and I'm pulling on the rope doing my best to convince the Executioner his work is successful, but I sense him walk to the side of the trap. It's then he feels the rope and pulls it. The force is enough to lift me from my feet and he lets the rope drop and I bounce to a natural stop as if I've been hung.

It's a close call and I've dropped the knife again.

Rasa stands up and stifles her coughs, realising what is happening. If she's surprised at the rescue it doesn't show on her face, but that's Rasa. She bends down and picks up the knife, passing it across so I can cut her hands free. It's a balancing act between us, but once done, she reaches up and takes the hangman's rope from my hands and dangles as if she's dead. She's seen enough in her short life not to be surprised by much and I admire her ability to suppress her emotions and her pains and deal with what needs to be dealt with. She's a realist that way and there's so much pain held within her that I'm not sure we'll ever know her true story.

If we ever do get to safety, I imagine that we'll wake one day to see she's gone with just a note to say: *thank you.*

Spencer nods to the mound next to him, but Rasa shakes her head and nods to the one next to Chantal.

It's a fifty/ fifty but I trust Rasa more than Spencer.

I move to the mound next to Chantal and wait.

Spencer, Kuro, Chantal and Rasa are hanging from their ropes, feet off the ground. It makes them swing naturally and it's the smartest thing they could do.

I'm sure from above it looks a natural a hanging as you'll ever see.

The sequence begins its all too familiar round.

I'm sweating and pumped, but my mind is already on the next stage of our escape.

I look at the others and I point to the hole, indicating down and right. I'm unsure when we should move and how long the Pod can swing from the ropes. The second they let them go the tension will leave the hemp and signal that the bodies have gone. And I don't know how long they will wait before they come to cut the bodies down or the crowd will clear from the square.

It's a problem, I hadn't thought about.

Hiss...

The hatch next to Spencer opens and not the one I'm stood by.

Diego's comes crashing through.

They've not only tied his hands, but they've put straps around his arms and legs like he's a bound mummy. His strength was too much even for them.

He hits the mound with such force that it crumbles under his weight.

He's shouting and twisting and it's adding to the crowd's enjoyment.

I leap forward and miss the rope on the first swipe but catch it on my second attempt.

Diego falls forward and crashes into the wooden box.

It's loud and vibrates up.

Executioner footsteps edge round, which means he heard it too.

This time he's not distracted by the crowd and he pulls on the rope.

I'm too slow and he starts to reel it in.

'Go...' I scream at the others.

Chantal and Kuro jump through the hole. Myself, Spencer and Rasa bundle the twisting bull of Diego after them. He falls to the floor and hits the bottom hard enough to knock the wind out of him. He's seeing us, but he's not seeing us. He's fighting too much, and if I were to try and cut him free, I'm sure I would slice him to bits.

I grab the torch and shine it into the street the others need to run down.

Above us chaos is unfolding.

Spencer surprises me by jumping on Diego and pushing his face into the sand. It shouldn't work but it does. He calms. I bend and cut the ties from his wrist as Spencer helps Diego to his feet. I don't need to cut the ties that wrap around him as he rips them off like they were made of paper. He has no idea what is going on other than he knows he's alive and his friends are close.

We turn and run into the ancient streets as a Pod.

All six of us.

Whole.

Me leading the way.

Mayhem in our wake.

29

Even in the blackness, we sprint on.

The noises of an angry army are behind us. It's not close, or not yet. It seems more confused and surprised, and the advantage is all ours to lose.

I can almost hear Ilse's screams of frustration and anger at losing us once again.

I stop to catch my breath, turning to the others to check on them. The beam from the torch is weak and dying. I keep it low, more out of habit than I'm scared it'll spill into the nearby streets and give our location away. We've turned and entered too many different pathways to be followed without a map. I'm not convinced that Ilse and her Elites even knew of these ancient streets below Anbus until our escape a few moments ago – another advantage Omar has from living in these parts his entire life.

A combination of shock and expectant faces look back at me. It's the first time I notice everyone except myself are dressed in their purple *Denounced* tunics.

Ready for death.

They look gross and like red, it's a colour I will never use, if I ever get the chance to pick something for myself in this life again.

'Omar,' I say.

They nod, but they must have already known.

I look at Spencer.

Much of our troubles have been caused by him and Omar's warning still rings loud and clear in my ears.

I should expel him from our group, but I won't.

I can't, even though he believes I would have let Omar kill him and he's destroyed my chance of getting to know a great man, Spencer's been punished enough, and whether I like it or not – he's one of us and I have to stick by him.

We're all bonded by the System.

I hand the map and the torch to Kuro and point to where I think we are and where we need to be. I'm sure I'm right, but I know myself well enough that if I keep leading the way I'll get us lost and throw us right back into trouble. Kuro is a natural when it comes to directions and using maps. I beckon Rasa forward to join him. Together they will get us back to the spot where Omar left me. It looks a long way from where we currently are and we have to traverse back across Anbus, but I have faith in them both.

I don't know why, but I also want to be at the rear of the Pod.

It feels the right place for me to be.

Overlooking everyone, protecting the rear.

'Thank you,' Rasa says.

'It's okay. You would have done the same for us.'

She smiles, like it's not true, and she wouldn't have done it, but I don't believe her, or more to the point, I'm not going to believe it.

Diego closes his fist and I do the same and we knock knuckles – enough said.

Chantal gives me one of her pressing hugs, and it's the first time I don't feel embarrassed, but maybe because it's dark and it's hard to see my face.

Spencer steps in close, whispering into my ear. 'Please don't tell anyone, bro,' he says. 'You know.'

It takes me a few seconds to get what he means.

He peed his pants when he thought he was about to die. In the Holding Centre it is the ultimate sign of weakness. It means you were never going to be a man even if you had lived and survived the Hangman. The other boys would tease the weaker *Denounced* that they were cowards – born to pee their pants when their time came.

I nod.

It's okay, I think.

I wouldn't tell anyone anyway, and I don't agree with the boys from the Holding Centre.

Spencer is as brave as any of us – he's just lazy – and I hope that trait has gone from him forever after all that has happened.

'Thanks, bro… I always knew you'd come through.'

He says it in that sarcastic way he has that tells you he's your friend. I think it's the way they talk in his Quadrant, but it's okay with me. It means Spencer is back.

Spence

'We need to move and stay close,' I say.

Kuro leads off, Rasa close behind.

He moves slower than I would, but I know it's really faster and I trust that each turn is the correct one. There's no doubling back or confused frowns, other than the occasionally stop to confer with Rasa and once they agree, we move on.

The sound of chaos around us continues to come in and out of focus, but there's a distance to it. Our danger for now is if we get lost or our secret entrance is discovered.

I'm not sure how long we've walked, but it's when I trip on the skeletons and recognise the shape of the walls in this section that I know Kuro and Rasa have nearly navigated us to the spot I requested.

The power in the torch finally dies and I hand him the spare, realising I still have a small amount of water in the leather pouch.

We stop for the first time and take a breather.

I take a quick drink of water and then hand it to Chantal who does the same before passing it on to Rasa. It's then I notice the rope burn around her neck. It's raw and will probably scar. I remember the snap and how her head jerked back. She's holding it well, but she's in a lot of pain and she must have been closer to breaking her neck than I realised in the heat of the rescue.

'Four more streets and we'll be there,' Kuro says after finishing off the water.

'Then what?' Diego says.

'Omar gave me a second map that will lead us to the City of Delf. When it gets dark, Kuro continues the good work and gets us out of here. You good with that?' I say looking at Kuro.

He frowns all determined, and nods he's good.

I don't tell them before I had the choice of the camel and our next danger will be clearing Anbus's perimeters, but we've come this far, so I have to believe we can make it the rest of the way.

Chantal touches my arm to let me know we're moving on.

I smile back then fall in line, lost to my thoughts about the Unification War, Ilse, my sister, my life, and how I ended up being a *Denounced*.

I still don't know what was the single biggest mistake I made to end up in this mess.

Or is it a mess, I wonder.

What if it's the best thing that ever happened to me?

It's a strange thought to have and not one I've had before, as I usually obsess about what's happened and what is going to happen in the future.

Kuro turns another corner and shines the torch at the wall. It looks like a dead end, but it's not. If I stare hard enough, I can see the outline of the hidden door. Above our heads, the sound of the Assault Teams continues to echo. I sense they still don't know how to find us but my gut instinct is we should wait until the sound dies down before we venture out.

I tell everyone to sit and rest and I dish out a small portion of food from my bag, which is dry biscuits and the sweet dried fruit.

I wish we had some of that sweet mint tea, but I'm not complaining.

I'm happy to be alive.

We all are.

Rasa continues to rub at her sore neck.

Spencer and Diego rest their eyes, heads leaned back against the wall.

Chantal leans into Kuro.

It's then I hear it.

A distant bark.

It's a long way off, but it's still the unmistakable bark of a dog.

The Elites have finally worked out how to get to us.

Our smell will be our downfall.

I don't know how long it will take, but they'll find us, eventually.

I stand and lean into the door, pulling it open.

It creaks with age and lack of use, and the cool desert breeze sucks in.

It's a pleasant feeling compared to the dampness of these subterranean streets.

It's dark outside. The only light, the starry night flickering above.

I can't hear or see the Airborne Crews, but the dogs are getting louder.

Their barks closing like nets.

It's then I smile.

I'm sure this is Omar's last hand of help.

Before there was one camel.

Now I see six.

30

We sprint out towards the camels.

There's a unity that's returned even though we haven't spoken much since the escape from the gallows. I can sense a renewed urgency and it gives me a confidence to override the hundreds of fears and doubts that continue to spike my thoughts.

The camels turn their heads, impatient as if they've been waiting too long for us to show.

We all pick one and scramble into the saddles.

They grunt and stand in that awkward way I've never got used to, but once up they break into an immediate gallop. I was prepared, but I'm not sure the others were and I'm relieved to see no one has fallen.

Ahead, all I can see are the shadowy tops of sand dunes and beyond, in the far distance, a small mountainous range that is more a break in the terrain than anything serious we might have to navigate.

I'm sure it's our next destination.

I take a glance over my shoulder to check on the others, but my attentions immediately fall on the City of Anbus. It looks as if a fire has been started in the Square and light crashes out from the walled City in a defined V-shape merging with the starry night above. Around the edges, strong beams of light radiate from the sky and move zig-zagged along the parameters of the wall and nearby areas. I can't see the Airborne Crafts as they are the colour of night, but the light is their source and I count three.

I know in this moment, we've successfully escaped and it's as if the camels read my thoughts, because they slow into a fast trot that turns into a looping walk, which is easier and more comfortable to endure.

We've escaped.

For now.

I wonder how Omar trained these beasts to do what they've done, but nothing surprises me about the man. I hadn't thought about it before, but he is the opposite to Ilse in all his leadership qualities. He's fair and honest, and there's nothing vindictive or malicious in his actions, and I think he has the one thing that Ilse will never have, even if she lived a thousand years.

Respect.

From others.

And for himself.

I wonder, too, if I have it from my Pod or are they just grateful I saved their lives?

There's a difference, and I've learnt from the System that it's easy to bully and to be mean, and it takes a special person to step beyond that point.

I hope I can be that kind of person.

An Omar.

Because I'm not now.

I suddenly worry that I will never be that good, because of everything that's happened to me. I know I've used my size, strength and natural aggression in the past when maybe I shouldn't have.

Even with Pod Fifteen – my makeshift family.

I'm sorry for that. I will try and change, I tell myself.

The camel Rasa is riding begins to drift my way. It's dark and hard to make out anyone's features, but she keeps touching her neck, especially at the back where it was initially snapped back.

'Hurts?' I say.

'It'll be okay,' she says, in that defensive tone she uses when she's pretending not to be worried. It's the first time I notice her voice is hoarse and it's another reminder of how lucky she is to still be alive.

'What's going to happen when we get to the City of Delf?' she asks.

The others have drifted in and we're all in ear shot of one another.

'Nothing has changed,' I say. 'I'm going to find the Port then Dock One and figure out how to get on the ship so I can go home. From there, I don't know, but once we all get to Delf you can decide what you want to do.'

Silence.

The soft walk of the camels is all I can hear.

'I thought it was Dock Thirty-Four?' Kuro says.

'Omar lied to protect us and himself.'

'Oh…' Kuro says.

'Omar and his people have enough sympathisers who don't want a war. If you can find them it would be like living in a Doubter's Camp back in our Quadrant,' I say to Kuro.

I look across at Diego.

'You're going to try and get home with me, right?'

He nods his answer.

I turn to Spencer, but I'm really talking to Rasa, too.

'If you want to join the War, Ilse and the Powers-that-Be I won't stop you. But you're making a mistake. I think she will hang you on the spot and if she doesn't she will kill you even if these Quadrants win the Unification War, because she's going to get revenge on me one way or another.'

'I thought I could fight for the Powers-that-Be, but I can't,' Rasa says.

I wait for her to add something more, her reasons why, but it's not coming and probably never will.

'I'm not fighting for the Powers-that-Be even if they were to give me the chance,' Spencer says.

I wait for him to say something more but he doesn't, either.

'I'm staying with you, Ned. You know that,' Chantal adds.

I do. I look at Kuro, but I know his answer, too.

He nods a *yes*.

We're going home if we can get through the Port of Delf and onto *Shifting Horizons*. I'm not sure what we will do when we get home, because we are going to be in as much danger there as we are here.

That's why they hang *Denounced*, because you never have a home and you're better off dead.

Better off Dead is a chant from the Holding Centre and one I've sung myself on many occasions. Jack comes to my mind and it's then I notice that the soft sands of the desert have changed into the tougher, rockier terrain and the hills with the goat paths are nearly upon us, as is the light of the morning.

I don't know why, but I glance back over my shoulder.

The walled City of Anbus is long gone, and all I can think is Ilse must still be searching the subterranean streets, because even if she found the door we escaped from she won't think we've got this far.

For now, we've won and it gives me a warmth inside I don't often feel.

The camels begin to slow and then they suddenly stop.

Diego tries to make his move, but the camel grunts its displeasure and I tell him to stop.

It's then the camels begin to bend forward, collapsing into their sitting position.

I jump off first, stiff and sore from the night's ride, but filled with relief that we are finally here.

'Pass me the map,' Rasa says to Kuro.

He doesn't, instead nodding at two men who appear from behind the rocks. They are old and stooped with weather-beaten faces that make them look like they were carved from stone and not born. One of them is smoking a cigarette, a substance banned in our Secular World. Grey smoke falls from his nostrils, something I've never seen before and I'm momentarily fascinated by it. The more stooped of the two heads towards the camels, takes their reins and makes them stand before leading them away in a small herd. The second man, who is smoking the cigarette, walks towards us carrying six small pouches and a set of clothes. He doesn't smile or say a word, but hands each of us a pouch and then gives us new clothes.

He grunts and points to the rocks for us to get changed.

The girls go right, the boys left.

When we come out, we are all dressed the same in long robes and headscarves that can protect our faces from the sun and immediate identification.

We look like Tribe people.

The man takes the Denounced Tunics and starts a small fire and sets light to them. I gulp and am unexpectedly filled with a desire to cry, sorry that my own Denounced Tunic isn't in the mix. We watch in silence as the flames first blaze and then die, black smoke billowing out, our Tunics becoming nothing but ashes and dust.

I don't know why, but I'm watching a victory and it feels like the biggest step I've ever taken to freedom.

Something left me in those balls of black smoke and whatever it was I'm never going to let it infect me again.

The old man who gave us the clothes walks up to me and takes my arm and marches me forward a few steps, then points between two rocks.

It's then I see it.

The goat path.

The path to the City of Delf.

The path to freedom.

31

We walk on.

The goat path is only wide enough for one of us at a time and it winds a slow but steady climb through the rock-strewn hillside. The sun continues to blaze above our heads and I have no idea of the time other than it must be close to mid-afternoon. If we were out in the Great Desert we would have burnt to death by now, for sure. But this path hugs the rocks and seems to dart from one shaded spot to the next, like water taking the easiest route. These goats are smarter than us, I think, and I wonder how old this pathway really is. Like so many things about this Quadrant, I'm sure I'm experiencing an Ancient World I was taught had been long destroyed before my time.

And it isn't.

It's real with a grip of authenticity that is sometimes missing from the Digital World I know so well.

We continue on.

Silent.

The only sound walking feet on rough terrain.

Kuro leads the way and I notice we move a touch quicker when he has glasses. Up close, his eyesight is okay, but he's blind on distance without them. I admire that he's never once complained when his glasses have either been lost or taken from him.

He guides us to the next plateau, before our descent and subsequent climb ahead of the next sequence.

There are three more rotations according to the map before we'll see the Port Town of Delf, and the plateau is the first time we are able to spread out as a group.

I sit on a rock and reach into my bag for some water and a bite of food. The others follow and we naturally gather into a circle. Chantal doesn't like the figs as they are too sweet for her, so she trades them with Kuro for some olives and dried biscuits, which I like, too. Everyone looks shattered and thinner and we're all surviving on our reserve energy.

Spencer still doesn't look me in the eye, but it's more his embarrassment than anything malicious, and Rasa throws me the occasional half smile, which I guess is the closest I'll ever get to an apology. It's okay. I'm over their treachery and my jealousy, and I wonder if they're still a couple. Their friendship seems to have cooled, but a lot has happened in the last few days so it's hard to know for sure.

Kuro continues to study the map, burning the paths into his mind, but he needn't bother. The route we have to walk is obvious and once again I see that Omar has helped us as best he can. The time we traverse the other three hillsides, we'll be coming into the Port by early evening, so the dying light will be our friend once again.

From there, I don't know what's next.

But I'm relaxed about it, unsure why.

Maybe I'm beginning to trust myself again and we still have five nights to go of the eight before *Shifting Horizons* docks – time is with us for now. And there was something about the burning of the Denounced Tunics by the old man that washed out an ugliness I've held within. I still wish one of them had been mine, but seeing the other Tunics destroyed was good enough for me and it's an image that will last until the day I die.

I peel back the sleeve of my robe and look at my number tattooed into my wrist.

5-7-9-0-1-2-3.

It looks dull in this light, but when it gets darker it'll glow its luminous off-green. I want this removed from my wrist. That would mean changing how our Secular World puts you in the System and monitors you, and how you pay for your life, assuming you are free. It would be a massive change and I wonder if it can be done without a War.

Why not, I think.

Omar has made me see that the things you think are impossible, aren't always.

Like this place.

And the people.

And how it works.

We were told how cruel and evil those in the Non-Secular Quadrants can be.

But they're not.

Ilse and the Power-that-Be, maybe, but not Omar or his people. And it's the same in our Quadrant. The Lawyers and the Court Officials and the Wardens, yes, but not everyone.

There must be others who want their tattoos removed?

Others who want their freedom?

To live where they want and to believe in what they want to belive in?

'I'm sorry, but I'm still not sure I want to go back,' Spencer says, breaking my thoughts.

I look up to see him pushing the sand with the front of his boot, making a small mound. There's no conviction in his voice, but I'm going to take what he said at face value. Omar's words flash through my mind once again that one day I will have to kill Spencer for us to survive. I tense, concerned that this moment is about to arrive just when I thought we'd finally repaired our differences, and that we were all going to try and make it home.

'I'm coming,' Chantal says.

I know she will, but she's said it too quickly to try and stop any tension returning to our Pod.

It doesn't work.

'You're an idiot, Spencer, you know that,' Diego says. He looks at me and continues. 'I trust you to get us home. Just tell me what I have to do and I'll do it. Anything.'

'Me, too,' Kuro says.

He folds the map and carefully places it in his bag, like it's the last drop of water we have.

I stare at Rasa.

She shifts her weight and it's unusual to see her stuck on a decision, although I sense a shift of desire and she no longer wants to return home.

I'm not going to say anything, because I've said everything I want to say on the subject. My mind is made. I'm going home. To what, I don't know yet, but if we have a *Soul* and a *Destiny* and a *Fate* as Omar keeps telling me then mine is set to unfold in another place, at another time, in another set of circumstances.

Outside of Jack, Omar is the one man who's helped me the most and I'm going to do something I never do. I'm going to trust him all the way to the end and do what he says, which is to surrender to something bigger than myself.

Whatever that is.

I reach for my water and take a long gulp, pushing the lid back into the top.

I stand.

'If you want to stay in this Quadrant then you have to stay here for five days. After then the rest of us hopefully will be on *Shifting Horizons* and going home.' I toss my bag at Spencer's feet and continue. 'With your pack, you now have more than enough food and water for that time. After what I did for you, I trust you enough to wait here while we continue our escape. But you're making a mistake. That's the last time I'm going to say it.'

I look at Rasa.

I can't believe I thought I loved this woman. I don't hate her, not even Spencer, but she's not the person I imagined and it reminds me of the dynamic with my sister. Every woman who has ever been close to me has let me down. Even my mother dying was a kind of betrayal. It wasn't her fault, but she wasn't there when I needed her the most. I wish Omar was here so I could discuss it with him and try and understand it more but, like everything else in my life, I'm going to have to work it out for myself.

I will, of course.

It's time to move.

I turn and walk on, hearing the scuffle of feet and the rustle of bags.

I don't need to look back to know there are five others following.

Which means we're still a Pod – for now.

But I don't understand why Rasa or Spencer would want to stay? They must think they have more chance of survival. I don't see it. I just don't. Unless there's something I don't know. Something I don't understand, and never will.

We walk on.

My mind is tired from thinking about Rasa and Spencer and my confused emotions, and I'm glad when we start our ascent ready for the final hillside.

The sun has moved and although the heat of the day hasn't gone, the cool desert breeze has begun to kick in.

That means we'll see the Port Town of Delf before nightfall.

It's then I'm suddenly filled with jitters and I would run off if I could, but I won't.

I turn to check on the others and Chantal smiles and Kuro points ahead as he thinks I'm lost. Diego pulls up the rear and Rasa and Spencer have stayed with the group.

I turn back when it hits me.

I can smell the sea. It's the most familiar smell I have locked in my memory.

My father worked the Ports. He did something with computers and we had lots of digital credits and a good life according to my sister. Better than most, she would say. With holidays and a car and big house. I don't remember them, but I do remember my father talking about the boats and how he helped guide them in and out of busy shipping lanes. I always found it odd that he would die on a ferry, and had I not had my operation on my tonsils, I would have been on that boat with them.

Dead, too.

But I've been the walking dead for some time.

Drifting through this *Denounced* life, trying to fend off its curse.

Or that's how it feels.

So perhaps that smell isn't the smell of the sea at all, but the smell of my destiny, and what if Omar is right.

And that I do have a *Soul*, after all – something more inside of me than I ever thought I had.

What if we all do?

32

All the memories of my old life crash through my mind, making me feel dizzy.

Some I like.

Most I don't.

We're crouched in the shadows of the hillside looking down at the Port Town of Delf. Even though we're in the Non-Secular World, it's like I'm looking at a town from my own Quadrant.

It's a sprawling place with the buzz of business.

Watching on, I'm gripped with an unexpected memory of holding my father's hand, surrounded by the same intense energy.

Trucks and transport vehicles flow in-and-out of the main road. Dust from their tyres sits in the air like a constant cloud, unable to settle. I can spot shops and cafes and people walking around, and the smell of the sea is thick and rich in the evening air.

Assault Buggies dart in and out of the traffic.

The guards are heavily armed and there's a focus and intent in everything they do.

I look for Check Points or Sentries into the town, but I can't see any and, even better, I can't see any of the Elites with their unique green armbands

I relax some more seeing that most people are dressed like us – desert people. I spot a smarter black uniform, but it appears to be for Officials or those with more money, I guess. It's still a robe of sorts and some of the men carry smart leather cases, which are probably full of documents.

And they are only walking if they are stepping into a building or from a building back into their waiting vehicle. Women are walking around, too, but most have their faces covered, as do some of the men, which is all good news for us.

Kuro taps me on the shoulder and points off to my right.

A man is watching over thirty or so camels in a large fenced off pen, and it looks to me like a market where buyers and sellers can come together. There are makeshift food stalls nearby and although it's early evening the market doesn't look to have started yet. The gathering crowd are relaxed and chatty, and most are smoking, which still shocks me to see.

We continue to asses, the market slowly getting busier, as we grow more comfortable with the idea it's our place of entry into Delf, and that we should move soon if this is going to work.

'We shouldn't walk down together,' Rasa says.

I nod.

She's right, and I wasn't thinking, because I was going to do the exact opposite.

'Let's go down in three groups of two,' I say. 'We'll watch the Auction for a while and then slip into the heart of the town from there.'

There's a consensus nod from everyone.

'What if one group gets caught?' Kuro asks.

He's trying not to sound scared, but he doesn't like it when we're not together.

He feels isolated.

We all do, I guess, but we're not split, or not like we have been in the past.

'Rasa's right,' I say. 'Walking down in a single group of six runs the risk we'll get noticed. But this looks the type of town everyone is preoccupied with their own business. If we behave the same, we'll be safe, but it's better for us all in smaller groups.'

'I'm scared,' Kuro says, pushing his point more.

We all look at each other, nobody saying anything.

We are all scared, but it makes it worse to hear one of us say it so openly.

I step close to him.

'We've come this far and we can't stay crouched on this hillside in the shadows for ever. We only have four nights left after tonight. We enter the town then we find Dock One. From there we find a way onto the boat and then we get home. It's one thing at a time. If nothing else, we've learnt that much since we became a Pod.'

He nods.

'I'm sorry for being scared,' he says.

'It's okay. Go with Diego. Chantal come with me.'

I look at Rasa and Spencer.

'You coming or staying?'

'We're coming,' Rasa says.

I nod back, pleased.

'Come on,' Diego says, wrapping his head scarf around his face. He makes Kuro do the same and we watch them scramble down the hillside and casually tag on to a small group walking towards the Auction. Nobody even turns a head. I sigh a moment's relief. It couldn't have been easier and once they are nearly at the site, Spencer and Rasa lead out.

Rasa slips and stumbles. Spencer stops to help her to her feet. It's a moment of affection that makes me course with jealousy once again and I'm angry at myself that it still bothers me when I thought my feelings for Rasa had died.

'You still don't trust them, do you?' Chantal says.

I nod and shrug at the same time.

'It's not safe for us in these Quadrants and there are many dangers for us back home, but it's better we go back than stay here. I'm not convinced they believe that and it worries me. Maybe they know something we don't.'

'Why don't you ask them?'

'I'm not sure they would tell me.'

'But you don't know.'

She's both right and wrong.

'Let's go,' I say. 'And cover your face.'

I do the same and Chantal leads the way. The slope is steep and we skid down. Chantal is blessed with natural balance. Like a ballerina, I always think. Our only danger is if we gather too much speed and fall and tumble.

We don't.

We glide down and reach the tarmac road and wander towards the Auction.

Suddenly an Assault Buggy full of guards overtakes an oncoming truck and heads straight for us.

I'm gripped with fear and catch myself staring at the road by my feet. I'm doing the exact opposite of the advice I give everyone else – if you look guilty, then you are guilty, and you'll attract attention.

They drive on, dust from the Buggy's tyres blasting over me in a small cloud.

I blow out hard, Chantal turning to check on me.

I smile back and she returns the gesture.

I realise she's calmer than me and I steal some of her confidence.

As we get closer to the Auction, I'm hit with another worry. They are all speaking in the language of the Desert People and I don't understand them.

What if someone asks me a question?

I'll have to smile and nod and just walk on, and hope they don't react.

The others will have to do the same and we should have discussed it on the hillside before we came down.

I'm annoyed that we didn't as Chantal and I head towards the camel pen.

Diego and Kuro are off to my right and Rasa and Spencer have moved to the other side. They pretend to inspect one of the camels. I know they are trying to look like locals, but they are in danger of inviting a conversation from one of the Sellers. I up my speed and walk around the pen. My urgency gets their attention and I nod towards a dirt path that snakes past some poor quality housing and boys who are sat on a wall.

We walk on.

One of the boys shouts something to Rasa.

I look round and see that she's not covered her face properly. It's a poor mistake, because she's beyond beautiful, and not like the other women here, and the boys have noticed immediately. I remember Omar's warning and flecks of her blonde hair are wafting in the breeze, adding to the attention she is now getting. She clocks her mistake and pushes her exposed hair out of view, but the boys continue to shout and I'm scared Spencer is going to react.

He doesn't and we march on.

Once past the housing we hit a busy main road.

It's a bliss of chaos.

Cars and trucks.

Camels and donkeys.

Carts and Assault Teams all trying to navigate around each other, all surrounded by dust balls and piercing car horns.

I never thought I'd enjoy so much noise and if the boys are shouting at Rasa, we haven't a chance of hearing them.

There are road signs up ahead. I don't understand the language they are written in, but there's one with its own arrow and one word below it. I'm utterly convinced it's pointing to the Port. I follow its direction. Rasa and Spencer have crossed the road and are tracking us from the other side. Diego and Kuro have fallen back behind myself and Chantal, but we're moving as a unit. I sense we're getting more looks then we should. I check myself, and my face is covered as is Chantal's. I do a quick check on the others and I feel we are as camouflaged as we can be until I see it, or sense it more. Everyone else has more urgency about something they have to do. I'm back to not listening to my own advice and I think of the newbies in the Holding Centre. It's their uncertainty that gives them away and makes their life so miserable at the beginning.

I pick up the pace.

The others naturally follow and the change has an immediate impact.

We are suddenly in the same busy hustle as the other people.

Heads down, more of a march, and less of a nervous Out-of-Towner.

This isn't the place of tourists and the growing darkness has added an intensity that I didn't expect.

We walk on and it's the constant smell of the sea getting stronger that tells me we are going in the right direction. To my surprise, the road suddenly opens out and it's more like a main artery and it's then I see there's nobody walking but us. We've lost our camouflage of the crowd and I nod us back. I'm not sure how we've become so exposed, so quickly, and the road behind us doesn't look like the one we just walked down.

I'm confused and my nervousness is immediately transmitted to the others.

Maybe I missed a turning in the dying light.

I stop to take stock of where we are. The road we are on is full of trucks and nothing else, and the trucks appear to bottleneck into one single entry point that is heavily guarded by both Assault Guards and what I recognise as Port Authorities.

I surge with the heaviness of terror.

I can't see Ilse or the Elites but her presence is suddenly all around us.

A truck drives by and the driver stares at us like we're animals in a cage. It's a piercing, confused look and my instinct is we are in a place that people aren't allowed to walk.

A Forbidden Zone.

I look desperately around and see an alley up ahead.

I know it's a mistake, but I start to run as do the others. The clothes we are in are not great for sprinting and I nearly stumble as I stand on the front of my long robe.

It seems to take an age to get there and Diego is the last to duck in.

We run on, and it's not until we reach the end and turn right that I glimpse an Assault Buggy cruising slowly by looking for something.

Denounced.

Or at least why walkers were in a non-pedestrian section.

We all catch our breaths.

Nobody says anything, but I sense we've had a close call.

I'm not sure what to do next when Rasa wanders over to the end of the next street. I walk up behind her and see a large building that is under construction. It's still a skeleton and the construction workers have started to leave for the evening. It doesn't look the sort of place that has a night shift and there's a single sleepy looking Guard at the main gate, and a flimsy wire-fence, which surrounds the site itself.

Rasa looks at me and smiles.

We have a place to stay for the evening and, more importantly, we have a bird's eye view of the Port Town of Delf.

<h1 style="text-align:center">33</h1>

The construction crews continue to leave in groups.

Most climb into the back of waiting trucks, some cars and the others wander off in the opposite direction from where we are stood. It further confirms to me that we did venture into a non-pedestrian zone, and in my desire to get home and out of this place, I was over-keen to find Dock One. It's a mistake that could have cost us everything and I tell myself that patience has always been my friend, even when I haven't wanted to befriend it, so don't abandon it now.

The dust from the last truck skidding out settles, and an unexpected silence falls and with it an anxiety I can't define. I sense we've all absorbed it in our own way and that we've temporarily retreated to another place of safety within ourselves.

We are so close to getting out of here, yet so far, too.

I notice that Chantal has moved closer to me as Rasa has to Spencer.

I continue to fight with my moments of jealousy and I'll be glad when they finally pass. I have enough to worry about without getting myself caught in the middle of Spencer and Rasa's love.

I nod Kuro over.

'What do you think?' I ask.

He glimpses into the sky.

'It'll be dark soon and there's only one Guard.'

This I know, but I'm hoping he'll confirm something else.

He continues. 'The fence isn't really a fence to keep people in or out. I would say it's more a boundary, like this is the space we work in. Nothing more.'

I smile to myself. It's what I wanted him to confirm.

'There's barbed wire that runs the top,' I say.

Kuro shrugs, like he's indifferent to its potential danger.

'It's old and not sharp and it lacks any tension. It looks leftover to me. Like someone's second thought. Better use it than throw it away.'

'It'll still cut us as we climb over,' Spencer adds.

Spencer's comment tells me we are all thinking the same, which is good. We're going in and probably over the fence. It's just a matter of how and when and at which point.

Chantal sits on the dusty ground, removes her boots and rubs at her tired feet. We take her lead and sit and stretch out, resting our backs against the wall of the building. We've found a temporary safe-spot and we all take a drink and eat a dried biscuit.

The sun has finally dropped from the sky and the tangerine orange that will forever fascinate me drifts to blackness. The desert chill that always accompanies the change kisses my skin and I enjoy its touch.

It's the closest I'm going to get to a shower.

I turn my attention back to the Construction Site Guard. He reminds me of Jack at the Holding Centre. He has the same kind of round, happy face, and he's overweight and limps slightly from his swollen ankles. He looks like a nice man. Someone who would listen to your troubles and give you good advice, or at least try.

Kuro's right.

He's not here to protect anything, more just to watch and raise an alarm if he hears anything, which he won't.

Or not from us – on some things, Ilse's training taught us well.

He steps into the Guard House and I suddenly realise what he's about to do and it's our opportunity to move.

I jump to my feet and the others follow, the tension to move immediate, Chantal scrambling to tie her boots.

I watch him and I'm right. He's doing what we saw at the Tribe of the Nomads.

He starting to pray.

And I can't help but think he's a *Denounced*, but he's not.

He's doing what is right for him.

In his Quadrant.

And I wonder if he has a *Soul*, too.

Rasa points something out to me. It's off to the left as the fence runs parallel with the skeleton building. She's pointing at a cover made of heavy material that is part of a rubbish mound, which is waiting to be cleared. The material looks strong enough to throw across the barbed wire and protect us from getting cut.

I nudge Kuro and point it out. He smiles and nods his agreement.

I don't have to say anything to the others and these moments in the Pod always give me a boost of hope.

We all know what we have to do without saying a word.

I should thank Marcellus for his training, but I won't.

He's dead because of me and I have no regrets.

It was him or me.

I won, he didn't.

We dash out and run to the cover that is made from a waxy sort of material I've never seen before. It's heavier than it looks. I take one side as Spencer takes the other. We step forward and on the silent count of three, we sling it up and onto the barbed wire. The fence sags under its weight, only helping us more.

I lean against the fence, Spencer opposite.

We cup hands.

Chantal takes a few steps back and then runs at the fence, planting her foot into the centre of our cupped hands and springs up and onto the top. She slips to the other side with ease. Next is Rasa. She's so athletic, I'm sure she could have leapt the fence without our help. I barely feel her weight in our cupped hands. She doesn't drop to the other side, but perches herself on the top and waits for Diego.

Strength and power are his skills, but not athletic ability that requires spring.

He hits the centre of our cupped hands and I feel the muscles in my wrist twist with pain under his downward force. Rasa grabs his arms and helps him scramble over. The sag in the fence works against him, because there's not enough tension for him to get a solid foothold, but he clambers over and drops to the other side, panting hard.

But he's made it, and that's all that matters.

Rasa stays on top.

Kuro doesn't even take a step back. He places his foot into our cupped hands and springs up and over in one fluid motion. A life running from trouble has given him natural speed and agility. I lean back against the fence and cup my hands in front of me. Spencer does the same as Kuro and plants his right foot into my hands. He bounces gently on a count of three and then pushes up. Rasa grabs his arms and they share what I'm sure is a lover's joke as he flips up and over.

I try to ignore it, but I can't.

Stabbing pains sprinkle my stomach.

I turn and look up.

Rasa is staring at me.

Hands out waiting to pull me up.

We look into each other's eyes and I see something else.

Regret, I think.

A pain, I don't understand.

I wonder what she sees in me – nothing, maybe.

An empty *Soul*.

I'm still not sure what went wrong between us and I think of my sister, Liz. She is one of those people that if you get too close they push you away. I'm like that, I know. It's a defence mechanism I learnt once I became an orphan. It's something that one day I will have to address.

Rasa has it in her, too.

It's all about trust, I think, and it's a terrible disease when you lack trust for those you are supposed to love.

'Come on,' she whispers.

It's laced with a friendly tone I don't expect.

I nod, jam one foot into the fence and spring up, grabbing her hands.

They are soft and familiar and warm.

She guides me over the fence and I drop to the other side, knowing two things in that instant.

Rasa will never love me.

Spencer will always be jealous of me and it's more to do with Rasa than it ever was with being Head of Pod Fifteen.

Again, I force Omar's prediction from my mind. He's been right on everything he's said so far, but I want him to be wrong on this one, and that I won't have to kill Spencer in order to survive being a *Denounced*.

Diego pulls the waxy material off the fence and it springs back up and looks exactly the same as it did before we broke another law and entered this place. The only give away is the waxy material is back inside the compound where a minute ago it was outside. I'm not worried. The Guard of this site will never notice.

We run into the skeleton of the building and head for the central stairwell, galloping the steps to the top.

I count twenty floors, but Kuro corrects me and says it twenty-five.

I don't care if it's thirty-five or forty.

The view is perfect.

We can see out and nobody can see us if we stay behind the central pillars for what I think will be another few floors still to be added to the building.

I look down into the Docks of Delf.

Beyond the main security gate there are large numbers painted into the floor.

On the far right I can see Dock One.

On the far left, I can see Dock Fifty.

The whole thing stretches for miles and is the biggest Port I've even seen.

I turn my attention back to Dock One.

The space is vacant.

Waiting…

34

We drink and eat from the rations that Omar's men provided and watch in silence as the black of night finally arrives.

Our new vantage point and the changing light provides two unexpected favours – it's not only brought more protection from being spotted, but the street lights are flickering on and the Port is slowly being swathed in a neon light, which allows us a better understanding of the layout and what we have to contend with.

Kuro blows out a short whistle, more to himself than any one of us in particular.

He's right, and my first thought again in this new light is how vast the Town of Delf is. It could be the Capital of this Quadrant, or even the Capital of the Non-Secular World.

I stand and walk to the end of the floor and look down. I'm directly above the top of the Guard House. The light inside has dimmed and I imagine the man who reminds me of Jack fast asleep – I'm sure Jack would be, too, if he was on such an easy watch.

I hope that one of the few men who showed me kindness is still alive and helping *Denounced* in the Holding Centre as best he knows how.

I take a shallow breath as an unexpected thought catches me in a panic.

What if Jack knew all along about the Powers-that-Be and he's one of the many sympathisers they have in our Quadrant?

It's why he kept telling me to be strong.

It's why he kept telling me it would be okay.

He always secretly knew the outcome and that I was going to live for a little bit longer.

The thought builds in my mind and I start to feel resentment towards him, hoping more than anything else that I'm wrong. If he isn't the man I thought he was I'm not sure I could ever trust anyone again. His continued acts of selflessness and kindness always gave me hope.

I turn to face away from the Docks, a heaviness lingering in my body as I push Jack to the back of my mind.

The Port Town of Delf is on a gentle slope that flattens out before it reaches the vicinity of the Docks. I can't see exactly where we entered the Town, but there's a hard stop where the street lights end and the wilderness of the desert begins. Trucks are still entering and leaving the Town, and their lights weave out along the main road going to somewhere I don't know, and don't care to ever know. Apart from the road, it's a mass of no-man's land and I can see the ghost like outline of the hills we cut through via the goat path. Although I can only see it in my mind's eye, I get a picture of the Great Desert and then Anbus and beyond that Omar's World and the Mountains and the Mine until the pictures in my mind stop at Ilse's Dome.

Her *City of Hope*.

Her *City of Death*.

Apart from us and Taylor, I can't help but think no-one else survived.

The thought darkens my mood.

I turn back and face the Docks. We're at the foot of another no-man's land, but one that is man-made and looks to be under development. There are more skeleton buildings like this one and they are starting to encroach upon the Docks. The Port itself and the Docks are beyond what I had imagined when Omar described them to me. He didn't want to scare me and deliberately played the size of this place down.

He was right to do so, because the truth may have broken my resolve to get home.

Which is being tested now.

There's only one road into the Docks. Each truck passes through a heavily guarded double gate. It's the same set-up that we had in the Holding Centre – one door closes behind you, before the next one opens. The fence that divides the Docks from the rest of Delf is double banked and fierce dogs roam freely in the dead space. Armed Assault Guards sit in towers evenly spaced. It's the first time I've seen security cameras that pan in gentle circles from long dedicated poles. The fence doesn't have a sag point and we're never going to be able to throw a heavy wax cover over the barbed wire, which I'm sure hums with the sound of electricity.

It must be twenty metres high, if not more.

What would my father do if he was me?

He would leave, no question, but I can't do that because I have nowhere else to go.

I'm a prisoner of sorts.

I wonder what Jack would do?

Nothing, other than talk and say that something will work itself out – but it won't, not this time.

And Omar?

But that's a pointless question, because he would have had a plan before he got to this point.

Or would he?

He always told me I would know what to do, which means he didn't.

But I don't.

My final test is here and I'm about to fail.

So what shall I do?

It's then I see my thinking is all wrong.

The real question is what would *Ilse* do?

If anyone could escalate the stakes to a new level to find a solution, it's her.

What can she still teach me, I think, as I sense her presence and look back at the Assault Guards manning the Security Gates.

She knows I'm here.

And she won't give up until we're all dead.

I work my eyes back to Dock One.

It's still empty.

Waiting for *Shifting Horizons* to arrive.

Full of *Denounced*.

I hadn't really thought of it before, but that's how we came here. In our boxes, loaded onto one of those trucks and then driven out of the Docks, through Delf and along the road that winds through the Great Desert, eventually reaching the Dome. I almost laugh at Kuro, Diego and Spencer's first escape attempt. Had they got out of the Dome where would they have gone – nowhere. They would have been caught within minutes and we'd all be dead now.

Rasa was right to try and stop them.

I was wrong to let them go.

But I was a different person then to what I am today.

Better, I hope.

Or, maybe not.

I don't know any more.

How do I judge?

I look back at the Port Security Fence and let my eyes go first left and then right. I'm not sure what I'm looking for because there's no way through. I see some smaller Check Points, but they look to be for Special Personnel, or even the Assault Guards or Port Staff. I have a fantasy that we could pretend to be one of them as we did with the Hunter Packs when we escaped the Dome, but it's not going to work here because I can see we are going to need special passes with face recognition and fingerprints and uniforms, all of which we have no chance of obtaining.

The depth of despair weighs in my stomach – no, my *Soul*.

I check back at the gate for the Assault Guards and an Assault Buggy that is leaving the Docks catches my attention. It has one driver and two people in the back. There's something about the outline of the people that draws my interest even more. I squint through the darkness, but I don't have to.

The lights around the fences are powerful enough.

I should be surprised at what I see.

I should be shocked and worried.

But I'm none of these things.

Instead, I have an odd sense of relief – a calmness, I didn't expect.

In the back seats are Taylor and Suki.

At least she made it out and she's alive.

I watch the Assault Buggy pass through the Security Check and continue along the main road, but then it slows and stops at the alley we ran down.

My heart starts to pound.

I turn to the others, but they've all fallen asleep.

I turn back to Taylor and Suki.

They are easy to follow, because a beam of light from two torches bounces in front of them, like a hopping rabbit.

Taylor is tracking our path, like he knows it was us who entered the non-pedestrian zone.

They turn into the final stretch and come out in front of the construction site.

I step away from the edge of the floor and move to the hidden safety of the central pillar.

Taylor wakes the Guard in the Guard House. I hear shouting and I'm shocked that Taylor can already speak their language. The Guard clearly shouldn't have been asleep and I bet Taylor is hitting and pushing the old man around.

Taylor exits the Guard House and stops outside, examining the fence. He walks a few metres left and then shines the torch along the parameter. His beam stops on where we leapt over. He looks at the pile of debris and then the waxy cover that is now on the other side. He knows there's something not right about the set-up, but he's not smart enough to put it all together.

He may be able to speak two languages, but he can't think in either of them.

He walks right and shines the beam along the fence, checking for gaps.

Nothing takes his attention.

He turns the torch off and snaps round and looks up.

Smart... kind of.

I knew it was coming as it's an old trick the Guards use in the Holding Centre to catch for moving shadows.

He's looking straight at me, but he can't see me because of the pillar and the inky night and the fact that I didn't flinch.

I can't see his eyes.

But his hatred radiates out.

And he knows something that I know, too.

We are here.

He just doesn't realise how close.

35

I sit alone and watch the night slip away and with it the activity in-and-around the Port increases.

Even though this is not my Quadrant, or even my World – there is something familiar about the landscape and the smell of the sea, which makes me think of happier times. And for all the dangers ahead of us – some I know and many I don't – I've spent so much of my life in Institutions that whatever happens in the next four days I'm going to hold this moment of peace within.

Omar would be proud of me, I'm sure.

I hear a gentle shuffle of feet and Chantal comes to join me on the ledge of the floor. She dangles her feet over the edge, the same as myself. There's something deeply familiar about Chantal, like I've known her all my life, and it reminds me once again of her importance to our Pod.

She's our emotional glue.

Her presence keeps us connected in a way I can't always describe or even understand – but I'm thankful for it, that much I do know.

'Isn't it dangerous this exposed?' she asks.

I nod.

'It is, and we should move. I'm sure the whole of Delf will start to wake-up soon. Anyway, the construction crews will be here shortly. They'll want to start work before it gets too hot.'

We have to move but I wait a beat, taking in the scene for one more time, slowly tapping into the energy I know I'm going to need for what is sure to be one of the most difficult days of my life.

'I thought the desert was beautiful,' Chantal says, her voice catching me off-guard. I nod my agreement, as she continues. 'Harsh but beautiful. In some ways I could live in Omar's Tribe. I mean ... I know I'm not one of them and all that, and he'd have to invite me, of course, because I don't want to be an uninvited guest. But that wandering life is something I understand. In a strange way, it can be relaxing to be on the move all the time. Is that wrong?'

She smiles at me and I hadn't thought of it before, but in our own way our Pod is mostly made up of individual wanderers, especially myself and Spencer who've wandered from one Community Home to another. That red trunk they gave me when I was seven years old has never totally been unpacked. It's just followed me around until I ended up being convicted of being a *Denounced* and then was finally destroyed.

The one positive from this madness, I think with a smile.

'They're not our people,' I say. 'And in time when the novelty wears off, we'd be in as much trouble as we were in the Dome – always outsiders hoping for approval.'

'I know,' she says, pointing in front of us. 'The trucks into the Port never stop, do they? Is that what you've been studying?'

I didn't think of it in those terms but that's exactly what I've been doing. The trucks never stop going in and out of the gates. Different intensities at different parts of the day and night, and it's slowly building to its frenzied height, but it's a constant stream of traffic past the high-end security gates that I can't fathom how we're going to penetrate. Before Chantal joined me, I had this crazy idea that we could somehow swim into the Port. We would go north of the Town, past the borders of Delf and wait for the night to descend and then use the tide and the dead of night to float back in. I temporarily forgot that Chantal can't swim when I was playing with the idea, but anyway, if the front of the Port is this well guarded then the rear is going to be the same.

It was a stupid idea and a waste of valuable energy and mental time.

'You can do it, Ned. I know you can.'

'You sound like Omar.'

'I'm sorry,' she says, catching the annoyance in my voice.

'It's like trying to break-out of the Holding Centre,' I say. 'But worse, because if we can break-in, we then have to pretend to be someone from the Port. And that means clothes and IDs and stuff we can't get. I wish that I did have an idea, but I don't – that's the truth. My mind is a blank and now we have the dangers of staying out-of-sight while we try and get an idea. In four nights from today, *Shifting Horizons* will dock and leave again on the same night and we have to be on it, or it's over for us.'

She nods and smiles and looks unworried.

'We've never had anywhere to go so I wouldn't worry about that bit,' she says, giving me a gentle nudge in the ribs.

I smile.

She has a point.

I'm tempted to tell her we were visited by Taylor and Suki last night, but I decide against it. It will only add to the undercurrent of tension she's trying to pretend isn't with us. I glance back at the others. They are still asleep. Curled up, using hands as pillows and a restlessness in their bodies that never leaves them. I can't remember the last time I slept well, and that is part of my problem. My mind is so tired, I'm sure it's starting to shut down and work against me.

'Omar lied to me about one thing.'

Chantal turns and looks at me waiting for me to continue – the kindness in her eyes never seeming to dull.

'He lied to me about the size of this place. For all his powers, they come to a stop at that goat path we crossed. His World is back there, which is why he couldn't help us here.'

Chantal nods.

There's something thoughtful about it.

Compassionate, I suddenly realise. It's a word that rarely comes to my mind and on the odd times it does it leaves me uncomfortable, like now, because I'm not that compassionate to those around me.

Or even myself.

'But that's a good thing,' she says. 'It means he knows his limitations.'

I feel the crease of a frown forming.

I shrug and she continues.

'That means, he knew where your powers begin and his stops. Your survival skills and instincts are built for places like this and not in open spaces like the desert. You haven't worked out how to get into the Port, because you're not thinking like Ned. You're thinking like someone else, maybe Omar. You're looking for a magic solution and there isn't one. Even I know that. What is Ned good at, and what he's good at is what will get us past the gates and home.'

'I'm not good at anything,' I say.

'That's not true. You are good at lots of things. Like gauging distances for one. Tell me how far it is to the Main Security Gate from here?'

'It's two-and-half kilometres.'

'See. I didn't know that and I bet you're right.'

'But how does it help us… it doesn't.'

'It doesn't now, but it might later. And never forget that people trust you, Ned. They want to follow you. They want to be you.'

'I'm not sure about that.'

'You're wrong. They are jealous of you.'

'Even you?'

'Sometimes, yes. You don't need anyone to survive. I do. It's not fair.'

'How do you know that I don't need anyone?'

'Some people just don't and you are one of those people. If you can connect with that thing inside of you that you're truly good at then you'll get us home. I know that. Omar knew it. It's why he risked everything to help you.'

'To help us.'

'No, Ned. He only helped you. We were an addition that he had to help if he wanted to keep your trust. It's another reason why Spencer hates you right now.'

I want to talk more, but the noise vibrating back from the awakening city tells me it's time to move.

But where do we go?

My own question gives me an instant headache.

I turn to see the others begin to stir and stretch. Their own defence mechanisms kicking in with the increase in noise. Beyond them, off to my right, and past the fencing we climbed, I see the dust trail of two trucks and sense they are full of construction workers heading our way.

Their day about to start.

Ours, too.

'Ned…' Spencer says. I turn to see him coming up the central staircase. 'Check this out.'

I spin my feet around and stand, helping Chantal up. Rasa is already stood and is brushing the dust from her clothes, rubbing at her sore neck. Kuro is rolling the stiff ache out of his shoulder from the night on the concrete floor, and Diego still looks half asleep although he's stood, a slow yawn creeping across his face. Spencer, beckons us to join him on the stairs. We do and he skips down two levels and we come to a small section that the walls have already been put in place and within it the construction workers have made a temporary canteen and rest area.

Spencer's already heated some water and made us fresh mint tea. It's an unexpected and pleasant surprise. He points to a large container and I see it's full of fresh water. I tell the others to fill up their water pouches and Spencer starts to empty some dried biscuits and fruit he's found in one of the cupboards into his bag, passing it onto the others to do the same.

If I'm supposed to feel guilty for stealing this food.

I don't.

I take another sip of my tea when I ping with a sense of anxiety. It's my internal alarm sounding and I'm aware of myself enough to never ignore it. I'm about to tell the others to finish up when I spot sets of grey trousers and tunic tops hanging on pegs from the wall. They are not dissimilar to our *Denounced* uniforms. They are the construction workers change of clothes. We are still dressed as desert people, which was good to get us into Delf and is okay for walking on the edges of this Port Town, but here, closer to the Port itself another change is necessary.

I walk over and grab a set and throw it across to Chantal and then Kuro. Spencer and Diego get it immediately. I get one for myself and put it into by bag as Spencer hands one to Rasa.

It's the first time I don't twitch with jealousy, but I have bigger worries on my mind – I still don't know how to get us into the Port, never mind onto *Shifting Horizons* and home.

'It's time to go,' I say.

We step out of the makeshift canteen-cum-rest quarters. It would have been a better place to have stayed last night had we found it but the view of the trucks and the Port is non-existent from here so we did the right thing by staying high.

'We walk out, as they walk in. Just act normal and keep going as if we do this every day. If someone speaks, smile but don't stop. We'll head back to the alley.'

'Then what?' Spencer asks.

It's just a question.

There's nothing challenging in his tone, which gives me added confidence.

'One step at a time. The streets around here seem fairly deserted so I think we'll be safe. Maybe, we have to come back here again for one more night. At least we know there's a comfortable spot and a good view of the Port.'

They all nod and we head for the central staircase and I suddenly tell the others to wait while I run back up to the roof.

I'm not sure why I do it, other than an internal nag and a desire to have one more check on the trucks.

It's then I see two Assault Buggies heading back this way.

The speed they are moving is kicking up a dust bowl, masking the occupants, but I don't need to see them to know Taylor couldn't sleep last night, either.

He's had that niggle I know so well.

The one I had a few seconds ago.

'Run,' I say heading back down the stairs. 'RUN!'

36

I'm a beat too slow.

Rasa slips and then tumbles in front of me and I try to block her fall, but can't.

It's then I hear something crack as she barrel-rolls the last quarter of the dusty cement steps.

The heavy impact followed by the motionlessness of her body stops us all in our tracks.

She's dead – is my immediate thought. And with it, the air is being sucked from around me and I'm being pulled backwards into a never-ending vacuum.

I can't think where I am.

Who I am.

What is it I'm supposed to do next.

Rasa is dead.

A moment before we were six and a split second later we're now five.

It's the feral cry from Spencer yelling her name that brings me back to reality. Chantal is already at her side, softly calling Rasa's name, trying to coax some life from her.

She is motionless, no sign of a response, and Taylor's presence along with his back-up Assault Team is playing though my mind.

My shock finally passes and I run down the few flights of steps and snatch Chantal out of the way and bend in close to Rasa. Blood fills her mouth, and her eyes are rolled up into her head. She's breathing, but it's choppy and short, and there's no strength in any of her breaths.

I'm no doctor, but it's not good, and she's badly unconscious at best.

I glare at Diego and shout, 'Taylor! He's on his way!'

I don't have to say it twice. Diego hands his food-bag and water pouch to Spencer, bends down and lifts Rasa across his shoulders in a Fireman's Lift.

He shuffles her into position like she's a few kilos and not the sixty plus of warrior muscle that she probably is.

We run on, down ten more flights and head towards the main gate and security hut. The Site Guard has already opened the entrance and is stood outside drinking mint-tea and smoking a cigarette and doing nothing but letting time tick by.

He sees us and looks all confused, but is momentarily distracted as one of the construction workers entering stops to get a light for his cigarette. The Guard does as he's asked, but doesn't take his eyes off us as he shouts something at me in their language.

I find myself nodding.

It's Kuro who runs forward and starts pointing to a small parked pick-up outside of the gate. I get it. Kuro is saying it's all under control and we're taking her to the hospital and there's nothing to worry about. I point to the vehicle, like it's ours, and everything is taken care of. It's then I see the small marks on the Guard's face and I know for sure that Taylor pushed him around last night, so why isn't he making the connection to us?

Maybe it's our clothes or the suddenness of the unexpected, or the fact we are going out and not coming in, but he isn't the type to interfere and nods us forward, like he's somehow organised the whole thing. We hurry past him and we're helped by the mass of morning workers flooding into the site who aren't taking much notice of us rushing out, like they've seen it all before.

Diego is keeping pace and we clear the construction site and the parked pick-up and head into the alley.

'Keep going,' I shout.

The others are holding back, staying behind Diego, which I understand. We come to the spot where we stopped and observed the construction site the night before and we halt like it's our end point.

It's not.

I take in our surroundings again, hoping for some inspiration.

We can't go left as it'll take us straight into the no-go-zone for pedestrians and the on-coming Taylor and his Assault support. Right is too exposed and puts us back in sight of the construction crews and Site Guard, so we have no choice but to go straight on.

And it's a long road with nowhere to veer off.

My insides become tight with anxiety that we won't clear the road before Taylor enters the alley and it's then I hear the Assault Buggies skid to a stop.

'They are too wide to enter the alley,' Spencer says.

He's right and I turn to Diego.

'Can you run faster?'

He looks at me panicked and then nods.

'Spencer, Kuro, Chantal… go… go… go.'

They hesitate for a split second, but they know it's the right thing to do.

They sprint off.

I stay with Diego, pacing him and then upping it a fraction like I did when we ran in the Dome and in the Great Desert. It works and he's moving faster than I ever could carrying the dead-weight of Rasa. He's sweating and he's panting hard, but his concentration is laser like and focused on the end of this long lane, like his life depends on it.

And it does.

All of ours.

I look up to see Spencer, Kuro and Chantal make the end and turn right, dropping out of view.

Three clear.

Three to go.

I look back and I can't hear anyone coming, but I sense Taylor is close to entering this section of the alley, but at the far end. If he looks right first towards the construction site it might be the split second difference we need.

If he looks left – it's over.

We're done.

'You've got to up the pace,' I say to Diego. 'You have to find something else within. Something…'

He grunts and groans and his face is puffed and he's crying, but he does what I ask and he finds that extra. That something which is more than fear, more than just wanting to get home.

It's about us.

It's about the Pod.

It's about fighting for something that is more than just your own wants and needs.

We hit the bend and fall out of view, Diego gasping for breath, like I've never heard a person do before.

We were milli-seconds from being caught, of that I have no doubt.

Kuro comes running towards me and beckons me on as Chantal and Spencer tend to Rasa and Diego. I stand and run to him and we head to the next bend. Up ahead is set of derelict buildings that look set to be pulled down for the next round of regeneration.

But it's not the buildings I'm supposed to be looking at.

Off to my right is an open grate into the ground and a rusty metal ladder is bolted to the inside wall. As I near, the smell is fetid and I can hear the loud buzz of flies. The others join us, Diego carrying Rasa. Chantal stands at my side and peers into the hole. She has her headscarf wrapped around her mouth and nose, and is pushing down hard with her hand to hold it in place. I do the same, but I still have to stop myself from gagging. I hunt for my torch and bounce the light into the space below. At the far end is an open sewer that appears semi-blocked. The pool of water is green and black and there's something about the black that isn't right until I realise it's the flies.

Millions of them.

Making a moving river.

'We're going in,' I say.

'WHAT?' Spencer gasps.

'Are you crazy?' Chantal says.

'Would you go down there if you didn't have to?'

She shakes her head.

'Diego's done,' Kuro says. 'He can't run any more.'

'I'll take her,' Spencer says. 'We can run on.'

'We need to hide and hide now,' I say. 'We're going down.'

Chantal scurries down first without being asked again. Spencer follows with the same hardened resolve. Kuro helps me lift Rasa from Diego's shoulders and lower her into the cesspit. Spencer takes her weight and shuffles Rasa onto his shoulders in a Fireman's Lift.

It's then I see all the blood on Diego's clothes from Rasa mouth.

He spots it too and I'm sure I have the same shocked expression across my face.

It's like she's been shot and has bled out.

Bled to death.

'Down,' I tell him.

He enters the pit, followed by Kuro and then myself.

The second we hit the inside, we're attacked by a swarm of flies – the noise a constant scream. We wrap our headscarves tighter around our faces, leaving nothing but our eyes exposed, but even these the flies want to eat.

They're relentless.

The noise cascading up and down in a volume beyond my imagination.

I shine my torch beam into the space, brushing at my face like my hands are wiper blades on a car. There's a gentle slope of concrete that leads to the main cesspool, but there must have been a surge of water at various periods, because we're all stood in a shallow slush of putrid mud-like-water.

I point for everyone to move back towards the walls into the darker parts of the cesspit. It's pointless shouting my instructions, because nobody is going to hear me over the buzz of the flies, plus I'm scared that if I open my mouth they'll rush in and choke me to death.

I switch off the beam and the only light coming into the cesspit is from the vertical shaft that spills from the grate we entered.

The flies continue to hiss around me.

I'm swiping at my eyes, so I can have some vision.

It makes them more angry and more determined to eat my pupils and send me blind.

The others have pulled their head scarfs completely around their faces and the blood on Diego's tunic has become a feasting ground. It's then I notice that we've gone from white robes to black. Our clothes are covered in hundreds of thousands of black flies. I hate every second of this, but they've camouflaged us in a way I could never imagine.

Suddenly, the shaft of light that enters through the grate is broken by a shadow. In the spilt second before I have to close my eyes, I see Taylor peer into the cesspit, his nose and mouth covered by his hand. It's nothing but a cursory glance before he moves on and for now we're as safe as we're ever going to be in this Quadrant.

I cover my eyes with the rest of my headscarf.

We wait.

The flies seem to settle and their buzz is replaced by the distant noise of car horns.

And trucks.

And Taylor's voice issuing angry commands.

And I move my hand and it sends the flies into another frenzied round of buzzing, which adds to the chaos since Rasa's fall.

Chaos.

Chaos, I think.

It's then I have my answer to Chantal's question.

What am I good at? she asked.

I'm good at creating *chaos*.

I always have been.

In fact, I'm an expert at it.

It's how I've survived this long.

37

I'm not sure how long it's been since I saw Taylor's shadow, but I can't stay in this cesspit any more.

As I'm sure the others can't either – it'll kill us long before Ilse ever will.

I move and hundreds of thousands of flies hiss as they moan at being disturbed from my clothes.

It starts a chain reaction and within seconds the cesspit is alive with hissing flies.

I wade through the sludge to the others and touch them individually on the arms to indicate it's time to get out. Spencer is in pain from having held Rasa across his shoulders for so long, but there's nothing he can do except endure it for a fraction longer and I know he's willing to take that extra hit for her.

We wade through the sludge and flies towards the rusty ladder and climb out into the bright light, blinking hard as we do. The relief at being outside is almost the same as escaping the Dome.

The heat of the day is starting to bite, so I figure we've been in the cesspit for a good hour, as we ran from the construction site with the morning sun finding its feet.

Diego takes Rasa from Spencer and puts her into a Fireman's Lift. There's a lifelessness to her that nobody wants to comment on, including myself.

Kuro walks over to me expectant and I tell him to scout out left and I'll go right.

Chantal volunteers her services, but I tell her to stay with Rasa.

Diego and Spencer move over to the cooler shades of the wall while myself and Kuro head out, Spencer rolling the numbness out of his shoulders and needing the extra rest.

I warn Kuro to be careful and if he spots Taylor to move fast to warn the others. We're not going to like it, but the cesspit is the best hiding spot we have, and if we have to go back in, then we have to go back in.

End of story.

I turn right and then cut immediately left and soon find my bearings. I can see the construction site we stayed in last night and we've not moved down as far as I had thought or would have liked. I don't see Taylor or his back-up Assault Team, but more importantly, I don't sense their presence.

Hard right and in the near distance, I spot a small crop of disused apartments with no windows and broken walls, the roof caved in on one side. It reminds me of the *City of Hope,* but at least this one is made of bricks and not resin, and isn't part of Ilse's Dome.

It's also surrounded by a broken fence, which will be easy to scramble under or even pull down.

I re-check around me to make sure I haven't missed anything.

I don't think I have.

I'd rather be further away from the alley and construction site, but at least in the disused apartment block we can rest, change our clothes and try and work out how bad Rasa is injured. Continuing to carry her and trying to find a good place to rest is going to be impossible and will draw too much attention if we're spotted. I hate to think it, but her injury has already hindered us and I'm worried of the ongoing consequences. I block that thought, deciding that the building is tall enough to get another view of the Port, and if it's a choice between the cesspit and the apartment block – the block wins every time.

I jog back to the others and see Kuro a beat behind me. He's seen the same buildings as myself, coming to the same conclusions about the apartment block.

I want to ask after Rasa but seeing her on the ground while Chantal strokes her hair tells me all that I need to know.

It's not good and it's not getting better.

Diego lifts her onto his shoulders and I ask him if he'll be okay for another ten minutes at most. He nods that he will and with that we track back to the building I saw, staying in the shadows of this disused part of Delf.

Once the apartment block is in sight, I ask Kuro to do a quick scout to make sure the place is empty.

We wait, nobody saying a word, as I occasionally glance at Rasa and then Spencer then back to Rasa. I recognise something in Spencer's eyes that I once saw in my own. It's that moment you know you've lost everyone important in your life and that you're now on your own. It's both a vacant and wild expression as your mind desperately tries to find another person you can bring into your life, but you know there's no-one out there for you.

And never will be.

He's in love with Rasa and I've missed the depths of his feelings towards her.

Kuro comes back and gives the all clear.

Cautiously, we move out to the fence. The wire is slack and old, and I find us a good entry point. Spencer helps me bend part of the wire back on itself, enough for us to duck under. I go first, followed by Spencer and then Chantal. We fish Rasa underneath and it's the first time I notice her skin has gone the sickly white of death. I help lift her onto

Spencer's shoulders as Kuro and Diego duck through to our side.

We jog to the main door and it's been nailed closed, but with no real conviction. I shoulder it open with ease. As I do, a dog begins to growl. I see it, along with two more, in the corner, towards the back of the apartments. The other two join in. They are big and aggressive and scabby looking, but we outnumber them, and their growls are more stay away than attack, which is fine by me.

There is a set of stairs to our right and we head up.

I'm sure this was once a set of residential apartments.

Maybe not expensive as the rooms are small, but it's hard to tell as now it's just concrete and dust and wire and bare steel beams.

We head to the top and I count eight floors as we go.

Spencer lays Rasa down on the floor and Chantal immediately starts to wash her face and hands. I want to tell her to go easy on the water, but I decide against it. It'll make me sound like I don't care and it couldn't be further from the truth. Watching Chantal wash Rasa makes me see how filthy we've all become and I can still smell the cesspit on myself. I tell the others to change into the grey construction worker's clothes we stole and to dump our desert robes in a room far enough away that the stench on them won't bother us.

We change and then all use a bit of our water to wash our hands and face.

I'm not sure it fixes the smell, but it cleans my mind of the flies if nothing else.

I go to the window and am joined by Kuro who hands me one of his dried biscuits.

I'm not hungry, but I take it and throw him a smile.

'Do me a favour,' I say.

He nods, concerned.

'Go to the next window and check out the Port and Docks. I'm going to do the same and then we'll compare notes.'

'What am I looking for?'

'A way in.'

'Oh…' he says, walking off, head down, expressing my own worry in his stooped shuffle.

I do my best to forget about Rasa and its implications to us, as I concentrate on my task. I wish I had a more elevated view, but I do have a different angle, which will give me a different perspective, and it's enough to still see the Port and Dock One and the Trucks and the Main Security Gate.

I let my eyes wander and keep my thoughts open.

I don't know what I'm looking for, but I know that I can't keep staring at the Security Gate hoping it's going to disappear or magically open its gates to six *Denounced* from a foreign Quadrant.

My eyes fall on the waters past the docks. I'm a strong swimmer and I think again if we can come in via the water, but I'm even more convinced it'll have as much security that side as it does on the traffic side.

Even the thick-skulled Taylor could work that out.

My eyes and mind come back to the Docks and I stare at Dock One. Since leaving the construction site and coming to this derelict building there's been a change. They've moved in one of the freight cranes and there's a truck nearby waiting for a load, and two men are hauling ropes to the water's edge. According to Omar's information we should still have four nights before *Shifting Horizons* docks and leaves on the same night.

It's not.

It's coming home tonight with its fresh cargo of *Denounced*.

I know it deep within.

My heart sinks and that hollow gap within me widens.

Time is ticking against us.

Kuro rejoins me. He has that questioning look he carries when he's not sure of his ideas. I never understand why, because we'd be long dead without them and he should trust himself more. Or maybe he shouldn't. Maybe it's his lack of trust, which makes him so good.

He checks and rechecks and checks again.

Spencer could do with more of Kuro's uncertainty – it would do him some good.

'What's up?'

'Have you noticed the square trucks. They're odd.'

'Show me.'

He points one out and I'd seen them before, but hadn't overly clocked them. A truck is a truck to me and I wouldn't call them odd, but they're not exactly aerodynamic, either. We watch them together and I slowly see what I think Kuro has noticed. There're more of these style trucks than I realised at first, and they seem to peel off and go through a different entry point that I hadn't noticed or seen from the construction site.

And once the trucks are inside the Port they all head to one large warehouse.

Dedicated to those trucks.

I look back at their Security Entrance and it's definitely just for them – nothing else is going through it.

They are still being checked, but it's more casual. Not as stringent as the Main Gate.

I stare back at their end point. It's a hub. A City within a City within a City. And the people that work there put on orange bibs and load the goods from the trucks into the warehouse, while other teams also wearing orange bibs, take the boxes from the warehouse into buggies and head for individual Docks.

Docks with boats already anchored.

And then I get it as Kuro says.

'I think it's the catering?'

I look back and watch the whole separate work force and routine go about its business. It's like being a *Denounced* in our Quadrant. You run a parallel life to the other people in your World. And that's what these catering trucks and crews are doing. It's a parallel work flow to the main transport trucks and the business of unloading and loading the boats.

But not as guarded.

Not a regulated.

But not easier, either.

I'd be fool to think it was.

'You had a bad fall,' I hear Chantal say in that gentle way of hers.

I turn to see Spencer standing over Rasa, smiling; doing his best to hold back his tears of joy.

Rasa is sat up, her eyes open. She's sipping water and looking dazed like she's no idea of where she is or what's happened to her for the last ten years of her life.

I smile all reassuring, but can't help but think she looks terrible. At least I don't have to worry about how we sneak a dead weight into the Port or worse – have to face the conversation of leaving her here. For now, we're six again, as I turn back to the Docks and watch another round of catering trucks go about their routine.

It's simple.

Well organised.

And most of all it has people.

So it's not going to notice six new faces, especially if we can get six orange bibs.

38

We watch Kuro walk over to the parked trucks, our lives balanced in the palms of his hands – something I would never have dreamt was possible a few months ago.

For someone as nervous as Kuro, he's looking ice-cool and focused, and Ilse would be proud of her training if she could witness his transformation now.

I would, too, if I wasn't shaking so much inside.

All the Port-bound trucks are filtered into one long queue that ultimately leads to the Main Security Gate, which becomes a no-go-pedestrian-zone.

Assault Guards and Port Police swarm the area worse than the flies in the cesspit.

Or not quite.

It was Spencer who spotted it when he came to join us at the windows – and it was a good spot for someone who's distracted by love. There's a place where the drivers can meet and rest, that's what we're looking at. They are stood in groups chatting and smoking and drinking their mint-teas, and I can see some of them praying or is it talking to their *Souls* – I don't know and not sure I ever will. But none of their trucks are locked and some of the drivers have even left their engines running and their cabin doors slightly ajar. Probably to keep the cabin cool or just to let some fresh air recycle. This is another hub within a hub, and it gently slopes towards the Main Security Fence and all the mass of security that is waiting down there for those who would dare to risk breaking the law.

Denounced.

I check back on Rasa. She has recovered some more from her fall, but she's still unsteady on her feet, and I'm sure she slurred her words a moment ago when she was whispering to Chantal. Or maybe I'm wrong and she didn't slur. It's loud and noisy this close to the main road, and there's an energy coming back from the Port and nearby streets that makes it hard to think, never mind hear someone speak quietly even if they are close to you.

I turn my attention back to Kuro.

I remember how cool he looked when he stole the watch from the Trainer in the Dome. Living all that time in a Doubter's Camp, mixed with his natural nervousness, makes him the perfect pick-pocket.

He's invisible when he wants to be.

And he is now as he wanders over to a parked truck.

Its engine running.

He checks left and right, casual as you can, before he pries open the cabin door and climbs in.

There's nothing rushed.

Natural.

Like he owns the truck, and in this moment he does.

He closes the cabin door and with it I hold my breath.

I can't see him any more, but he should be easing off the handbrake, putting the engine in gear and about to lay the weight across the accelerator, before jumping back out and locking the door on his way.

The truck starts to move.

Slow at first.

But not for long.

Come on, I think.

Then the cabin door opens and he jumps out as the truck heads for the security fence, picking up speed.

I want to run out and high-five Kuro.

But he doesn't turn back to us instead he heads for another parked truck.

NO, I scream in my mind…*NO!*

Our plan was one only and we spent a long time picking the truck and the place of entry and how we should play it.

That's all gone out of the window now.

Men start to shout as they see the truck moving, some running after it.

But it's too late to intercept Kuro and drag him back as he repeats the process, aided by the building mayhem the first truck is causing.

Truck two, gently follows the path of the first, building speed.

And if chaos had a sound of hope – it starts.

The guards by the fence start to wave at the first oncoming truck for it to stop. Their pleading waves slowly turn into frantic ones followed by the drawing of their weapons.

The pursuing drivers turn back and duck for cover.

The guards open fire.

Blue arcs explode like fireworks and the first truck's windscreen blows out, as do some of the tires, but it's not enough to stop the momentum of a forty-tonne truck.

It smashes into the fence.

The wire crumbles around it like cheap cling-film.

White sparks jettison from the fence and into the cabin.

I always knew the fence was electrified. Dogs attack, trying to jump into the driver's side of the cabin, like they've been trained to react that way. The first fence is breached but not the second. Then the guards' attention turns to the second oncoming truck and it's the same reaction but more intense.

They know they are under attack.

Assault Teams and Assault Planes come into view.

Hundreds of guards and soldiers appearing from nowhere, coming out of the ground, as Kuro casually rejoins us.

I want to shout at him for taking the risk of the second truck, but it's worked in our favour and we step out of the shadows of the alley and head for the catering truck we marked out. The driver, like most of the others, has stepped out of his cabin to check on the pandemonium.

And it is pandemonium.

Everything that we asked for in our dreams is playing out in front of us.

Between the cabin and the main body of the catering trucks are two panels – one on either side. It's more a protective shield between the two parts of the truck than anything else. There's a small slit in the side panel with a handle inside. I insert my hand and twist the handle and the panel opens. For all the sweat of worrying how we were going to get inside the Port this couldn't be easier if it works and I'm worried at the stroll we are taking.

Chaos working for us.

My heart rate is as close to normal as I can imagine.

I feel calm in a way I can't explain.

Chaos my weapon of choice.

We step into the dead-space between the cabin and the main body of the truck.

Six of us is a tight fit and we have to stand over wires and pipes and caps and the axel that bends the body of the truck from the cabin when the driver turns. I think the main body must be refrigerated as there's an air-con unit stuck onto the side, which hums and makes the standing space even tighter.

And hotter.

But we're in.

I click the panel shut and there's nothing to do but wait.

And it could be a long one from the noise vibrating back from outside.

And it is.

My legs ache and we are sweating and in some ways it is worse than being in the Great Desert, because the sun above our heads seems focused on us more in this tight space. But the noise slowly returns to something I would call normal and the Assault Planes quit their pass-overs. It's then the cabin door opens and the driver climbs back in. It's another long wait, but he starts the truck and we nudge forward, slowly at first, finally picking up speed. The movement makes the air-con unit hum and it finally blows out a cooler stream of air. We all let the relief wash over us and it's then I know we've been moved into the second lane.

The Catering Lane.

We come to a stop, but not for long, and it's a slow crawl to what is surely the second Security Gate.

I tense.

It's coming.

The Driver begins to talk to what must be the Sentry at the Gate. The Driver gets out of his truck and slams his door shut. Together, they walk to the end and I hear the rear doors being opened. There's only one of three ways they'll find us and that is if they open the panel, jump on the roof and look down, or an Assault Plane passes over.

We stare at each other.

I know what we're all thinking, because the same thought is jammed into my own mind.

We've come this far.

Give us that piece of luck we never had – the one we didn't get when our names were thrown into the hat and were pulled out *Denounced*.

The Driver closes the rear doors and walks back with the Sentry, stopping by the panel. I don't speak their language, but I understand tone and I want to smile and jump with joy, because the Driver is getting back into his cabin and we've been waved through. The truck jolts forward and we are rocked back-and-forth, before the Driver moves into a steady pace.

We're in.

Inside the Port.

The fence that has kept us out is now the fence that will keep us in.

It's like being in the Holding Centre all over again, but different.

The truck slows to a stop and another form of chaos takes over. A better one, if there's such a thing. I listen, but I know what it is. It's the crews that unpack the trucks and the other drivers and the noise of the hub that is this catering centre of the Port.

It's industrious.

Persistent.

Twenty-four-seven.

The Driver stops the engine and he opens the cabin door and steps out. It's then I notice my hands are shaking and I have flick it out and force myself to concentrate. I nod to Chantal and she climbs into Diego's cupped hands and he lifts her up, slow and steady. She peers over the top and nods the all-clear to Kuro. I open the panel door and Kuro steps out and casually wanders over to the wall where hundreds of orange bibs are hung on pegs. He grabs six and comes back as we filter out of our hiding space, slipping on the bibs.

Casual.

A crew comes out and starts to unload the truck we came in on.

Nobody pays much attention to us as dozens of crews come and go, and the most important thing, I think, is to keep moving.

So we walk.

Not as a Pod but as a *Crew*.

I'm not sure where we are going, but standing still will get us caught of that I'm sure. And all I can see is a hive of activity, and trucks and doors into the giant warehouse, and boxes and crates and containers. Buggies are coming and going. Some with crews and some with lone drivers. We head for the left of the warehouse – the part that seems to be where the catering supplies leave the warehouse to go to the boats, and it's then I see what I realise I was subconsciously looking for.

In Ports like these, containers are either full or empty, which means they are being loaded or unloaded and when they're empty they get stored for collection, and sure enough there're hundreds of them just waiting to be collected.

These ones are big enough to hide a herd of camels.

We slip between them and breathe a sigh of relief.

We have nothing else to do but wait.

Wait for the dark.

Wait for *Shifting Horizons* to arrive.

Wait for Taylor and Ilse, because they're coming.

Like me... they understand the music of chaos.

And I played them their tune.

39

The others have managed to grab some sleep, albeit troubled.

I envy their ability to switch off or maybe they're so exhausted their bodies are starting to protest and sleep is a way to escape the pain of being a *Denounced*.

I wish my body would protest some more.

I need the rest.

I need the escape.

I nudge Spencer's legs with my feet and he opens his eyes. I nod him up and his movement triggers the others to stir from their snatched slumber.

I don't have to say anything as I lean against one of the giant containers and stare at Dock One.

We are all silent as we watch our history unfold.

Shifting Horizons is docking.

Denounced are arriving.

The Experiments for the Unification War continue.

There's a hive of activity as ropes are being attached from the boat to the dock and the loading crane is slowly easing into its final position. I watch the gangplank being lowered from the ship and there's an eerie squeak which vibrates out as it slowly connects with the dock.

'I don't know why but I always thought the boat would be smaller?' Diego says, surprise lacing his voice.

'Must have come a long way,' Spencer adds.

'Interesting that it can get through the Quadrant Blockades with ease,' Kuro says.

'Omar told me that the Powers-that-Be have powerful friends in our Secular World.'

'When will it leave again?' Rasa asks.

No mistake this time… she's slurred her words, but I ignore it. She's up and moving and we have bigger issues to worry about.

'Tonight. This boat only operates in the cover of darkness. It's a ghost,' I say.

The others nod, because we all know we have one chance to get onboard and right now it's not obvious how we're going to do it.

I watch the dock-crane slow and begin to unload containers from the Hold and place them directly onto the trucks that have moved into position. I count only ten rotations from Hold to Trucks before the crane edges down and lifts another container from the forward Hold.

Another truck has pulled in but the container being lifted can't be attached to the back of this vehicle as it already has its own built-on store unit. The Driver gets out and watches the container being lowered to the dock before he walks to the back of his truck and opens the loading doors.

I'm leaned hard against the container I'm stood next to wanting to morph more in the shadows. The others do the same and we watch Taylor and Suki arrive in an Assault Buggy, followed by a back-up crew of six Elites in a second Buggy. They stop at a short distance from the parked truck and watch the container continue to be lowered to the ground.

Six more people arrive in two Assault Buggies and it takes me a second to realise they are Trainers from the Dome. One is the woman with the snake tattoo and pulled-back hair who monitored us for a while, and was one of the tougher Trainers we had.

The container bounces gently on the dock floor and the Trainers run out and release the crane clamps as one of them opens the container door.

Chantal has her hand to her mouth and tears are rolling down her cheeks.

Rasa is shaking her head and Diego has his fists clenched.

Spencer and Kuro look on impassive.

A numbness has enveloped me but I'm understanding Omar's words more-and-more.

My mission is to get back home and to help others in the future and not these *Denounced*.

They are on their own and I carry their sadness within me.

We continue to watch our history unfold as coffin-like-boxes are loaded from the shipping container into the truck. When we were taken to the Dome there was ninety of us, making fifteen Pods. I've counted over two-hundred coffin-boxes so far and the Trainers are still loading so that could be forty Pods or more. The Powers-that-Be must have upped their game, and all I can think is they are finishing off their studies for the final push before the Unification War begins.

Ilse a key component of the experiments and feeding information back into their war effort.

'Get ready,' I say. 'It's now or never.'

There's a second wave of activity I nearly missed fixated on the arriving *Denounced*. A smaller gangplank has telescoped from the front of the ship and catering buggies full of supplies have begun to caravan from the catering hub. Dock One is close enough to the Hub that some of the workers are walking out, about to pass us.

'Now.'

We edge out in our orange bibs and slot into the catering crew that has opted to walk. The lateness of the night and the sudden hive of activity works in our favour. I dare a glance at Taylor, but he's deeply preoccupied with inspecting the coffin-boxes and monitoring the loading.

Suki watches on like she's Queen Bee and I guess she is.

We are within her watching radar and a minuscule mistake on our part will cost us dear.

The men in front of us pick up boxes from the catering buggies and head to the forward gangplank. There's a delay over a broken box and we queue, waiting our turn. The delay is normal, but not moving froths anxiety within me. One of the catering crew leaders shouts at me. I have no idea what he wants and I freeze, staring at him. He shouts again, his frustration obvious. All those fears of being centre of attention and how I got picked out by Marcellus at the Dome flood back.

Move, I tell myself, but I can't.

I'm stuck.

Then Chantal taps me on the arm and points to a box and I step forward, snatching it in my arms and head for the forward gangplank of the ship.

I had a panic attack and I know why. I had our Quadrant and our pending success in the front of my mind and I lost sight of what I need to do to finish this off.

I was thinking we were there and we're not.

Not even close.

I want to check on the others, but I can't.

I can feel Suki and even Taylor's eyes burning into me or am I being paranoid – I don't know.

I step onto the gangplank and eventually duck into the ship and with it a relief washes over me like I've never felt before.

I stay in line and weave through the tight metal corridors that takes me to the kitchen storerooms.

I put my box down next to the one the person placed in front of me and head back. I'm not going out again, ever, and I step out of line and pretend to have an issue with my shoe. As the others step from the storehouse we all linger until Rasa is clear then we head back as if we're going out. A break in the line appears from the oncoming loading crews and we duck right at speed and drop into another corridor, Rasa shutting the heavy metal door behind us.

The gantry is dark, lit by dimmed lights.

I'm panting hard and so are the others.

We can hear the catering crew continue their work just beyond the door. I rip off my bib and throw it the floor. The others do, too. The orange glow moves to my feet and I scoop them up and shove them behind a fire extinguisher.

Think.

Kuro goes to say something but I put my finger to my lips as the noise behind the door increases.

He nods.

Think.

The food storehouse is behind us. That means the main food hall won't be far and the crews' quarters, again close. Above us will probably be the main control room of the ship and the Captain's cabin won't be far, either. That means we need to get to a quieter part of the ship and quick.

We're now stowaways.

Better than *Denounced*.

But not by much – especially in this Quadrant.

Kuro steps in close and whispers in my ear.

'The replacement crew will be coming soon. Our safest place will be in the Hold. They'll be empty for the journey back.'

I nod.

I was coming to the same conclusion.

There should be a door into the Hold from the depths of the ship so going high is not an option.

We head away from the door we came through and follow the dim lights. I have a moment's relief when I see a set of steel stairs heading down.

I don't care where they go as long as they are away from where we came in.

We drop down two flights and there's a porthole up ahead and beyond that another set of stairs leading down.

We continue on and I stop by the porthole to get my bearings from the Docks. The Driver of the truck is closing the back doors and some of the Trainers are climbing into the large driver's cabin ready for the long trek back to the Dome. The catering crews are still loading, but the crane has moved on to another Dock.

From what I can tell, we've moved about a third of the way along from the front of the boat, so we should be coming to the first Hold soon if we can get lower and don't encounter any locked doors or crew members.

Good, I tell myself.

This is good.

The Assault Buggy with the Elites begins to move. It does a large half-circle pulling in front of the truck – an escort out. I can't see the Buggy with Taylor, so it might have gone.

I allow myself a smile but it's a moment of pride I can't afford.

From the corner of my eye I catch him walking the main gangplank into the ship.

I want to believe it's part of his job.

But it's not.

He's coming aboard for the same reason he returned to the construction site.

There's nag inside of him, which he can't scratch.

And he's right, because that tune of chaos I sang is still playing in his mind.

40

When it comes to killing, Taylor's instincts are as good as any assassins.

He's heading for the Hold and I can hear his purposeful footsteps on the floors above me, descending, coming for us.

He knows we are here.

He just does.

Listening to him, I can't decide why he has come alone other than he may have embarrassed himself at the construction site by saying Pod Fifteen was present, so he doesn't want to pull the Elites in again to find himself in the exact same position. I remind myself he's still new to the Powers-that-Be and he needs his prize, a defining moment that sets him out as one of the elite – the Chosen.

He needs *me*.

Ned 5-7-9-0-1-2-3.

'He's coming. He knows we're here,' I say to the others in a low whisper.

'How?' Spencer asks.

'Because he's been brought up through the System,' I say. The others nod.

They know what I mean.

'What do you want to do?' Diego asks.

'It's six against one,' Spencer says.

'Five,' I say, looking at Rasa.

She doesn't say anything back.

There's something wrong and she's damaged herself badly, and we all know it. In some ways, it scares us more than Taylor and the Powers-that-Be. The idea that we could be five and not six breaks something we may never be able to fix.

Ever.

Footsteps on a steel ladder echoe close by.

It gives me an idea. Like in a Fun House I once went to with mirrors, but this game is going to be echoes.

'Let's spread out,' I say. 'And then run in different directions. Like rats in a maze. Make a noise with your feet, but not much. Enough to sound scared. But we're not, remember. We're in charge.'

'But he'll hear us?' Kuro says. The crease of concern in his forehead the deepest I've ever seen.

My answer is the broadest smile I've probably ever given in my whole life.

It's infectious and the others get it, smiling back.

'Stay in the shadows,' I say to Rasa.

She nods.

Just stay with us is what I really want to say, but I won't, because it'll voice how scared we all are for her.

We spread out.

Spencer goes up a deck.

Diego stays with me.

Chantal goes one way.

Kuro goes down a deck.

Then it starts.

Our game of running, echo and pause.

Repeated:

> Running.
>
> Echo.
>
> Pause.

We're at our best in moments like this. Even though we can't see each other, we instinctively know when to move and when it's time to be still.

I soon get to grips with the echoes, which are ours and the echoes that belong to Taylor.

His are more urgent.

Desperate, even.

He senses a victory – he's going to be the Super Star he wants to be within this Quadrant, within the Powers-that-Be.

Or not if I have my way.

More of the same.

Running.

Echo.

Pause.

Then it comes – a door slams and I hear someone lock it.

But the two aren't connected.

Taylor slammed.

Chantal locked.

I run along the dimly lit corridor and shudder to a stop.

In front of me is my nemesis.

Or so he thinks.

He's smiling, rolling his shoulders for the fight he's sure he's going to win and, if I'm being truthful with myself, he maybe could.

He's tough.

I've never denied it.

Am I scared of him?

For sure, I'd be stupid not to be.

But…

Diego steps out of the shadows.

Then Spencer.

Then Kuro and Chantal

Followed by Rasa.

Taylor's smile doesn't flicker as he slips his handgun from his holster and aims it at me.

'Good to see you again,' he says.

'Likewise,' I say.

He scans the Pod.

'Still one-on-one from what I can tell,' he says.

'You think?'

'I know,' he says, nodding at the weapon in his hand.

'You're worse than Ilse, you know that,' I say.

'And how do you figure that?'

'Because you're one of us and you sold out.'

'When was ever looking after Number One selling out?'

'The second you shook hands with Ilse.'

'You're more stupid than my drunk father and that takes some beating.'

I smile and nod as it happens from nowhere.

Chaos.

Kuro sprays the contents of the fire extinguisher at Taylor.

Sub-zero foam covers him in seconds and he drops the gun, but his feral instincts honed by the System take over. He steps out of the spray and moves forward, fists clenched and he's moving fast.

Very.

It's enough to catch six people off guard.

He hits me and I don't see it coming in the dimmed light. Searing pain crashes into my jaw and splits into my neck and head. I stumble backwards and I'm thankful for the wall that I'm able to use to push off otherwise I would have hit the deck. I'm not going to fight him because in the madness of the moment I have another idea.

I grab him around the head and start to pull him down.

I want him on the floor.

Surrendered.

Diego's now joined in the fight and so has Spencer. I know Rasa would join in if she could, but she can't.

Taylor's throwing punching and grunting and there's an inner power I can't explain.

He's a champion, really.

An alpha specimen that they should put in a science lab and study.

And he's grunting and throwing punches and Diego loses his mighty grip.

I hit Taylor with a hard right hook.

It's a great punch.

Anyone else it would have floored, game over.

Not him.

I'm not sure it even registered.

He's coming at me again and Spencer is throwing punches and Diego has him around the waist, but it's making no difference.

I grab him around the neck and this time I'm not letting him go.

We've got to pull him to the floor but we're losing and for the first time I start to look for the gun and wonder why Rasa hasn't stepped in.

But she's sick.

'Kuro,' I shout. 'THE GUN.'

Then Taylor drops like he's been shot.

And he has in a way.

Kuro has crashed a fire extinguisher into his back with such force it's taken the wind straight out of Taylor.

It's better than a shot and it's enough to give us the pause we needed. Diego sits on him and rams his Assault jacket down so it traps Taylor's arms and Spencer jumps on his legs.

If they're not broken, he's dead-legged him for sure.

It's then I see the handcuffs in Taylor's utility belt.

I slip them from the fast release holder and cuff him.

Game over.

We step off him and watch him on the floor. He gets his breath back and he's smiling and I'm going to give him that.

He's a warrior.

I just wish he was on our side.

One of us.

But he never will be.

Loyalty and tribe and family are words he will never understand.

'You're still going to lose,' he says.

It's then I kick him in the face.

I regret doing it, because it's a moment of cowardice from me, but it shuts him up while he deals with the pain and the blood in his mouth and the tooth that is now loose.

'When we were running around I found the Hold we came in on... or the Denounced Hold... or whatever you want to call it,' Kuro says.

'Where?' I say.

'Down one, second door along.'

'Show me.'

Kuro and I run on and I didn't realise how close we were. We are in the depths of the ship, below the water line. I open the door and step into what is a gaping hole in the centre of the ship. It's dark and echoes our footsteps and has long steel walls, and there's something deeply depressing about it and I can't believe we were transported to this World in this very place.

In front of me are several empty coffin-like-boxes.

I look at Kuro and smile.

He smiles back.

We run back to the others and Taylor is still semi-dazed, but he's going to live.

It'll take more than a coward's kick to finish him off.

'Strip him,' I say. 'Kuro you know what to do.'

Spencer and Diego undress Taylor and I put on the uniform.

'How do I look,' I say to Rasa.

'Awful,' she says with a smile.

'Good.'

'I need you. Chantal is too small for what I need. Are you okay?'

She thinks for a second.

'I can't fight.'

'I don't want you to.'

'Then I'm okay.'

'Diego come with me. Spencer can you carry Taylor into the Hold?'

'I'll help him,' say Kuro.

'Me, too,' say Chantal.

Spencer nods.

'Rasa, Diego… come with me.'

We move as fast as we can to the top of the ship. I hate being on the open deck, but I have no choice for what I want to do. Ilse and the Powers-that-Be must never suspect we're on *Shifting Horizons* or our game is up.

This boat can be turned around at any time.

I look over the edge, dressed as Taylor and start to wave at Suki. It takes a few moments, but she sees me and waves back. I sense she was beginning to get worried by the relief in her wave and the smile on her face. It's then I beckon her in. She jumps out of the Assault Buggy and heads for the main gangplank.

I check on the catering crews. They are still loading, but it's coming to an end, so our time is about to run out.

We head down to greet Suki.

I stay in the shadows.

She comes up, smiling and as I step out into the light, Diego rushes her. The surprise is all ours. She wants to scream, but I force my hand over her mouth as I wrestle the gun from her hand and Diego forces her to the ground. She's strong, but no match for Diego and the struggle is over in seconds.

'You call out and I'll shoot you. It's that simple. Get it?'

It takes a moment but she nods.

'Strip,' I say.

It takes another moment for her to realise I'm serious.

She nods again and Diego lets her stand.

She strips from her uniform and Rasa slips it on.

Rasa's skin tone and build are different to Suki's, but it's night and from a distance she still looks female and we'll be two, which is the key element.

I take the handcuffs from Suki's utility belt and cuff her.

'Take her to the Hold,' I say to Diego.

I look back at Rasa.

'You okay?'

She shakes her head.

'I have a headache, like I can't explain.'

'All I need you to do is sit in the Assault Buggy and be Suki?'

'Okay, I can do that.'

41

We walk down the main gangplank and it bounces under our feet like a trampoline.

I step onto the docks first and head for Taylor's Assault Buggy. It's then I realise that every time I've seen Taylor in the Buggy with just Suki, it's been Suki who's been driving.

We need to keep the consistency for any chance of this to work.

'Can you drive?' I ask Rasa.

Her own thoughts stop her in her tracks and she stares at me long and hard then finally indicates that she can. I breath out a sigh of relief as I climb into the passenger side.

The key is still in the ignition.

'But not fast,' she adds, leaning forward to start the vehicle.

'Steady is all we need.'

I check back to see the catering crews are finishing off. Their front gangplank into the ship will soon be retracted. More men are walking towards us and there's no doubt in my mind this is the replacement crew heading for work. I'm unsure about how much time we have left before *Shifting Horizons* sets sail, but the morning light is nipping at the creases of the dark sky.

'Where are we heading?' Rasa asks.

The truck with the new *Denounced* arrivals has cleared the Main Security Gate and the Driver appears to be doing some last-minute checks before the long journey to the Dome. To our left is the Assault Teams, Police and Port Authorities' separate entrance. Beyond is the main Watch Tower and what I'm sure is the Security's Epicentre for the Port. Off to my right and in the middle distance, a work crew is busily repairing the security parameter, and the two trucks Kuro released to start this mini war have long been towed away. I glance back at the Watch Tower and see the unmistakable silhouette of Ilse standing on the outside observation deck looking directly at me. My instinct is to run, or even drop my head, but I can't.

I'm Taylor, remember.

I'm sure the pause is too long, but I acknowledge her presence with a single wave and then give her the OK sign, telling Rasa to head for the Security's separate entrance.

Our desert headscarves, which is standard dress for all the Assault Teams, even the Elites, has been our saviour – more than Omar in many ways.

'Remember, to keep it steady,' I say to Rasa.

The Buggy jerks forward and for a second I'm sure Rasa is going to lose control. I cringe inside at the mistake and I can't tell if Ilse saw it or not, or if she is watching the Denounced Truck finally head out of Town.

We slow as we approach the Security Gate and Ilse is still watching on. I glance across at the Denounced Truck and it's picking up speed. The second Assault Buggy has its lights on and is sounding its horn so other trucks and vehicles will move out of its way. Rasa starts to slow our Buggy as the Guard at the first gate raises his hand for us to stop. He has one arm relaxed across his assault rifle that is strapped high in front of his chest.

We stop.

He says something to me.

I haven't a clue what it is, but his hand is out so he's asking for our papers or passes or whatever it is I need to get out.

I stare at him.

My mind is closing down.

My breath is getting short and sharp.

My panic attack is rising.

Ilse is still looking on.

I tap my top pocket and look inside.

I'm not sure exactly what I'm looking for but there's nothing that resembles a pass or documentation.

I go to search the next pocket, but I suddenly have a flash of being in the Holding Centre.

Once I start to search my pockets, I lose my credibility and give my power away.

I'll look guilty and it's the biggest crime I can commit against myself.

He says something else and I stare at Rasa and see the growing pain that she's doing her best to conceal and I'm suddenly scared she's going to pass out on me.

I flick my attention back to my Guard and grunt something out. Jabbing at my Elites' Armband and then at the Security Barrier and then at the Denounced Truck that is nearly out of sight. He takes a half step back as he didn't expect the out-burst and it's only then I see he's not wearing an Elites' Armband, so I have the upper hand. I jab my finger at him again, and flip my hand up as for him to open the barrier – NOW.

I point for Rasa to drive on.

She looks at me as the first barrier is still closed, but she does as I ask.

We edge forward and I'll know in a split second whether our game is over or not.

I snatch another look at Ilse on the observation deck.

I can't tell if she's watching or not, but it's imperative she see us leave and I'm sure she's clocked us heading out.

Then the barrier opens.

Slow and reluctant, like the Guard knows he's been duped.

We drive on to the second one, which begins to open without us stopping or another Guard insisting on seeing our passes.

I'm cold and my legs have started to tremble.

I see the gate guards staring at us, but I keep my focus hard forward like I'm above their procedures and the Denounced Truck is our priority. The road we're on snakes up and joins the main truck route in-and-out of the Port. But it branches left, too, and would head, from what I can tell back towards the construction site we originally hid in.

I take another glance up and see that Ilse has stepped off the Observation Deck and has gone inside.

'Go left,' I say as calm as I can.

Rasa does and we drive out of the glare of the main lights.

She slows and pulls into a dark alley, killing the lights on the Buggy.

I drop my head forward and take several deep breaths.

We now have to go back in and hope that Ilse will either stay inside the Watch Tower long enough for us to pass or that she is already on her way out.

She can't ever see us return.

Or it's over.

'I don't think I'm going to make it, Ned,' is all I hear in the dark of the night. 'Tell Spencer, I'm sorry.'

Her voice grips me in a moment's selfishness and I'm twisted into jealousy and anger and pains I've not felt for years.

It's another loss.

And they never get any easier, no matter what they tell you.

'Do you love him?' I ask.

She doesn't say anything, but I see the shadowy nod of confirmation.

The hot stabs of jealousy twist deeper and deeper.

'Then we need to get you back,' I say.

'I've got this bad headache, Ned, and everything is a blur. What if I'm bleeding on the inside? You know in the head? It means I'm dead, right?'

'What if you've got terrible concussion, nothing more? It was a bad fall.'

She attempts a smile, but it's all worry.

'I've had concussion before and it's not like this. This is something else. It's bad, Ned. I know it is.'

'I have a secret,' I say.

'What?'

'I can't drive.'

She starts to laugh.

'I'm serious. We have to go back in or we'll miss the ship.'

'I'm not sure I can do it. You can walk in.'

'I can't and you know I can't.'

'I can barely see you never mind drive this thing any more. I'm sorry, Ned. I let you down. And I'm sorry, I never loved you. I thought maybe that I could, but I can't. Spencer and I are the same. We are broken and we understand each other. You're a good, man. You can be arrogant and mean at times, but there's a good person in there waiting to come out. You are better than me in many ways, and you'll always make me feel insecure because of it. There's something bad inside of me and I'm not meaning this injury. I'm rotten. In a different time and in a different way I could be like Ilse. I get her, you know.'

I don't know what to say because we all have that thing in us to be like Ilse. Even Chantal. That's because we've had to endure the System and it corrupts your mind and then I guess, your *Soul*, and then there's no way back. But I think of Omar's words: *our destiny is our choice, not chance*. And as each day passes, I'm beginning to see the truth in what he has tried to ram home to me.

'This is your injury talking. We have to go.'

'I can't, Ned. I'm done.'

I snatch round and grab the front of her uniform and pull her forward.

'We've come this far. You, me, all of us. You've got to do it. If not for the Pod. For Spencer. You owe him that. If you're that bad and you love him that much. Die in his arms. Give him that.'

'I can't see.'

'I'll guide you.'

She starts to laugh, but tears are cascading down her face in a way I've never seen before.

The invincible Rasa finally broken, by a stupid slip on some concrete steps.

'You can do it,' I whisper. 'And you're not like Ilse. Not even close. And I'm not better than you. I'm different as we all are, but not better.'

We stare at each other and she slowly nods and wipes her eyes before starting the Buggy.

We pull out and I tell her to turn right, before telling her to increase the speed and then to veer more to the left as she drifts into the centre of the road. I tell her that she needs to start to slow as we approach the Security Barriers. I glance up and see Ilse has gone from the Watch Tower or certainly the Observation Point.

If she's watching us from inside there's nothing I can do and we're done.

The guards at the gate see us and I lean forward in the moving Buggy and indicate for them to raise the barrier.

We're not slowing.

It's the longest pause in my life that I can recall as I remind Rasa to keep her steady pace and that we need to edge a touch more to the left.

As she adjusts the vehicle's direction the Security Barrier begins to raise.

We pass through and as we clear the second barrier, I tell Rasa to increase the speed and to take an easy right. She doesn't know it, but it's taking us towards the containers we hid amongst by the catering hub. I tell her to slow as we approach them from the rear. I can just make out *Shifting Horizons* and my instinct is it's almost ready to set sail.

I tell Rasa to stop and I jump out and run to the first container and open the doors.

It's empty.

I guide Rasa forward and she drives the Buggy inside the container.

I help her out and I close the doors.

If luck is on our side this Buggy won't be found for weeks or might even end up taking a long distant trip in one of the ships to a Quadrant far from this Port.

I take Rasa's hand and guide her though the containers and we come out to where we joined the catering crews earlier this evening. I don't want to run as it'll draw attention, but we need to move fast, as the final preparations are being done and if I'm not mistaken the Captain is entering the ship as the catering crew finish up.

I give it a beat until I see the Captain disappear inside and then we march as fast as we can. I have Rasa by the sleeve and I guide her forward. The maintenance crew by the main gangplank look surprised to see us, but they don't say anything and I'm reminded by the bow of their heads of the power of the arm band I'm wearing.

I wave them on as if they should continue with their work as we head for the forward gangplank. It bounces under our weight and once we duck under the entrance into the ship I could collapse on the floor with exhaustion and relief.

I get my bearings and tell Rasa to wait here.

I get a broken smile as I head off to the kitchen store room. I've come in a slightly different way and end up walking into the main mess hall. It's full with the new crew getting some pre-departure food.

The second they see me they go silent and all raise to their feet.

I'm not sure who is more surprised them or me, but it seems to me they think they are in trouble.

I stare at them like they are and their heads drop.

I walk on and into the store room and pick up a box of food and the largest container of water I can carry.

I come out.

A man looks at me confused, but I stare him out and he lets his eyes drop to the floor.

I walk on out and almost laugh from nerves as I hear the gangplanks being retracted.

Shifting Horizons is set to sail.

We're free... almost.

42

I find Rasa leant against the wall of the metal corridor, eyes closed as if she's fallen asleep on her feet.

Even in the dark I know her words in the Buggy could come true.

This is more than concussion.

I touch her gently on the arm and she wakes, but not from a slumber, from somewhere else – like she's been dancing with the dead.

'Do you want me take one of those?' she asks.

'It's okay… I'm good.'

'You need my help, Ned. I can carry things, I just can't fight.'

With the box and the water I'm carrying, I can barely move, and it's been a struggle to get this far, so I nod and smile and say. 'The water if you can?'

She leans in and takes it from my hands, and it's the first time I see her right eye is so badly bloodshot that I can't see any white.

We don't speak as we make our way along the dimly lit steel corridor to a set of alloy stairs.

Each deck we descend, I feel a touch safer.

A touch more removed from Ilse and the Powers-that-Be.

I open the Hold door and step through.

Chantal and Kuro rush to greet us and Diego is a beat behind them. He takes the box from me and Spencer lifts the water container from Rasa, as Chantal immediately inspects her face and eyes. Chantal throws me a concerned look, and we both know Rasa is in more trouble than she was before we left the boat and returned. I don't know what to say. We're not doctors and we've no chance of access to one.

Chantal guides Rasa to the corner and sits her down.

I look up to see the ship's crew have closed the roof of the Hold and we're now in a giant metal silo with ugly welded lines that define the panels that make up the space.

It smells of diesel.

Diego and Spencer have laid Taylor in one of the coffin-like-boxes we all arrived in.

He's heard me return and it triggers his grunts and groans, as he takes up his fight again and attempts to break free.

In my own way, I admire his spirit.

His protests echo out as he shouts my name, and he's sure to be heard at some point if we don't shut him up.

Diego and Spencer look at me and I nod them away as I walk over to Taylor.

He spits at me as I approach him.

'Kick a man when he's handcuffed... you're gutless... you're a coward... I'm gonna enjoy hanging you myself... I'll fix the knot so it chokes you long and hard before you die,' he snarls.

'I seem to remember you head-butting me when my hands were tied.'

If he's registered what I've said it doesn't show as he continues to struggle to break free, his wrists straining at the metal handcuffs.

It's a pointless struggle, but that's Taylor – he's never giving up.

'Shut up,' I say.

'Make me. Get me OUT. HELLO,' he screeches at the top of his voice.

I pull a knife from my utility belt and cut a corner off from my headscarf, and then lean over and shove it into

Taylor's mouth. He twists and turns his head, rage pumping through his veins, but he can't spit it out and it dulls his cries for help.

I lean in close.

'If you're not careful we'll nail the lid shut.'

I'm not sure if he hears me past his rage, so I move across to the wall and lift the lid of the box. Spencer comes to help me and together we secure it in place. His muffled grunts continue, but for now the only people who are going to hear him is us. He has to run out steam at some point, I think. Even Taylor needs a rest from his rage.

I walk over to the next box and see Suki.

She's laying quiet, but there's a fear in her eyes that I don't associate with her.

'What are you going to do with me?' she asks.

'That depends on how much trouble you intend to give us,' I say.

'You'll get no trouble from me,' she says. 'I had to join the Powers-that-Be or they would have hung me. I had no choice. Don't punish me for wanting to live. It's my right and my choice.'

'You're right on one thing… we all have a choice,' I say, turning away.

Kuro has opened the box of food and is breaking it out. It's an assortment of cakes and dried meats and foods I don't recognise.

'If we eat light, we maybe have ten days, twelve if we're lucky,' he says. He nods at the water container. 'Five at most,' he adds. 'But none of us are going to be able to wash. We're gonna smell worse than we do already.'

The sudden rattle of the anchor being hauled vibrates loud through the bottom of the ship and we all look at each other.

We made it.

For now.

Then there's a slight sway and a few moments later *Shifting Horizons* pulls out of Dock One.

The engines pump.

The propellers turn.

We've set sail.

We're going home.

To what, I have no idea.

But the Powers-that-Be and their four Quadrants are no longer our homes.

They never were.

It was always a temporary camping spot, one that we were supposed to die in and now we are trading one set of dangers for another.

I slip out of my Elites' uniform and dump it on the floor, kicking it away. I change back into the grey construction clothes we pinched from the site. I sit and lean my back against the metal wall and take one of the dried biscuits that I still have left from Omar's supply.

I wonder what he's doing now and if he knows we made it out or not.

Or even if he's still alive.

But I think he is.

'How is she?' I say to Chantal.

'Asleep, but she needs a doctor.'

I know that, but she's not going to get one so we have a problem that even I can't fix for now.'

'What shall we do with these two?' Kuro asks.

'Throw them over the side,' Spencer says. 'They'd do it to us.'

I say nothing, but we're not murderers so it's not going to happen and I don't believe Spencer would do it, either. Or not now, not after everything that has happened.

'If we make it home, they're *Denounced* again,' I say with a smile.

'So are we,' Spencer adds. It feels like a sudden challenge, but I let it go.

We're all tired and there's a strange atmosphere that's descended, like when we first got to the Dome and didn't know each other.

This should be a victory, but it's not… it's something else, something I can't describe. Even though we're heading home, we are heading for the unknown and oddly we've left somewhere that we were beginning to understand.

'What if the ship's crew finds us?' Kuro asks.

I shake my head.

'They won't unless we make a noise. I've seen them. It's a skeleton shift. They have no need to come down here. Their job is to slip this boat back to our Quadrant and past the Blockades. As long as we're like mice, we're ghosts, for now.'

I stretch out and contemplate how long this place is going to be our home. We have enough food for ten days and I find it hard to believe we were originally drugged for that long on our journey here.

Boredom is our next danger, followed by how we are going to get off this ship.

Taylor has given up his groans and protests – for now, anyway. It makes me hope he can become an ally, because I've changed his future whether he likes it or not. He now has to face the same dangers as us when we return home, and for all my hatred towards him I know I'd rather have him on my side than against me.

We are six.

Why not be eight?

Suki will do what Taylor decides.

The others all sit and settle and get as comfortable as they can on this cold steel floor.

I sense *Shifting Horizons* has cleared the Port and is picking up knots as it heads out to sea.

We have a pause in our troubles.

I glance back at Rasa.

The rope burn across her neck is looking more pronounced.

A warning that she's danced with death once too many times and it's finally caught up with her.

Chantal continues to stroke her hair and Rasa looks at peace in a way I've never seen and don't like. I'm still jealous of Spencer, but I shouldn't be. You can't make someone love you, and you shouldn't try, and it's something I'm going to have to accept.

I close my eyes and Jack springs into my mind, followed by Omar and my sister and the Courts and my Parents and the Dome, but most of all I can see my Red Trunk.

I detest the colour, as I let myself drift into sleep, dwelling on the one thought that never leaves my mind.

For all that's happened…

I'm still a *Denounced*.

To be continued…

READ AN EXTRACT OF BOOK 3

CREAKING DAWN

Pod Fifteen finally navigate their way home, but have they made the biggest mistake of their lives? They are still convicted Denounced. Hunted by a System desperate to hang them. Ned and the rest of the Pod need a place to bide their time and think, finding refuge in a Doubter's Camp. But is their safe haven really that safe, or just another deadly trap waiting to spring? With the Unification War looming and nobody willing to listen, Ned is torn between saving his Pod and the love of his life, or saving a Secular World that wants him dead.

Creaking Dawn concludes the Denounced Series.

1

I've been lucky today.

I've slept.

And it's a rare treat, like the scent of clean air or not having to watch my back for the Powers-that-Be.

It's Taylor who's woken me with his relentless picking at the handcuffs that trap him into our world. It's a task he's committed himself to for every waking moment since we captured him. It's part to annoy us as a Pod and part to keep us all on our toes in case he manages to miraculously pry them off.

I can't see him doing the second part, but you never know with him.

The annoying part he exceeds at and it's kept us all on our toes, just in case.

I continue to watch him with a bubbling admiration that I would never let him or the other Pod members know about.

He's a beast of a person, really.

He's strong and determined and aggressive, like I've never seen in anyone before. And he's right in his own assessment that he's hard to kill.

They say if the world was ever destroyed the only thing that would survive are cockroaches.

I think they're wrong.

It would be cockroaches and Taylor, and the thought makes me wish once again that he was one of us, or at least fighting on our side.

I stare at the others – Spencer, Kuro, Diego, Rasa and Chantal. Apart from Rasa, who continues to come in and out of unconsciousness, the others sleep, unaware that Taylor is plotting to kill them given a snippet of a chance. He's desperate to go back to Quadrants 5-to-8 and be one of Ilse's Elite Soldiers for the Powers-that-Be. I can see it in his eyes that if he can somehow escape and warn the crew of Shifting Horizons he'd be a hero and get the kudos he so desperately wants.

He'd have won.

He suddenly smiles, more to himself, before he stops picking at the mechanism of the handcuffs, letting his eyes come up to rest on mine.

We stare at each other and I feel a weary unease begin to take hold.

He's fighting to get into my Soul, somehow picking at it like he is the handcuffs. I'm not sure what he sees, or even if he understands what he's looking at. I'm aware that I'm glimpsing parts of him I've not seen before and I see a dark, troubled interior that is waiting to revenge the wrongs which have been inflicted upon him.

I get it.

I've been there myself.

I want to tell him I get it too.

But it'll be wasting my time, because he's no different from the Wardens and the Court Officials and the Judges and the Lawyers and Ilse, and all those who have done their best to try and destroy my life. They have listened to the propaganda around them and have made up their minds long before they had looked at the truth that so blatantly stares them in the face. Taylor can't even see that he has the option to think and behave differently.

To take a different view to what he is thinking now, even for a few minutes.

Omar taught me that you can do it, you can change your thoughts and opinions.

It's not always easy.

It's tough.

But it can be done.

And Taylor is locked on course, like Shifting Horizons is locked on course to dock in our Quadrant, and there's nothing I can do or say to alter anything.

So I won't.

I'll accept it.

I have, too.

Taylor steps back and leans against the steel walls of the Hold, which has been our home for the last ten days and ten nights, and slowly slides to the floor, keeping his eyes locked on mine.

His smile has changed and it's somewhere between a sneer and a laugh, but more edged towards the sneer.

I think about closing my eyes and ignoring him as I have for most of the journey, but I don't this time.

I keep staring.

Waiting.

Wondering.

Worrying, even.

'You're a cruel, person, Ned. The cruellest I've ever encountered.'

'How so?' I say.

'You know how so.'

I do, but I disagree with him. He's given us all no choice.

We've kept the handcuffs on him twenty-four-seven. He's been cuffed to the wall via a rope as thick as my ankle, or cuffed to Diego and Spencer when he's been allowed his hour's walk around the Hold. And he's slept in the transport box out of protest, but we've kept him cuffed in there, his cuffed arm always at an uncomfortable angle, the rope, pulled tight for his night's sleep.

It's cruel and to add to his anger and isolation, we released Suki from her handcuffs after two days.

She's been the model prisoner. Keeping quiet and doing as we asked but, more importantly, she's kept her distance from Taylor, siding with us in attitude if not in voice.

Something has changed within her and I don't know what it is, but I sense she'd rather take her chances as a Denounced in our Quadrant than a free Elite Soldier in the World of the Powers-that-Be.

As we all know, it's a tough choice, but she's made the right one, or that's what I think.

But not Taylor.

She's now someone else to add to his hate list, which I'm sure is long.

He continues, his voice a whisper but somehow penetrating.

'You've treated me like a wild dog and I'm gonna make you pay for what you've done to me.'

'And how are you going to do that?'

'I don't know. But I'll get my time again. You'll see.'

'I might throw you off the boat. Watch you sink to the ocean floor. Then we'll have a party afterwards to celebrate.'

'Fake words from a fake man.'

'Don't tempt me.'

'You would have done it by now if you were going to do it. It's not in you, Ned. You have strange ideas about what is going to happen to you, and what is right and wrong. But I'll tell you what is going to happen to you. You're going to land back home and they'll catch you in a heartbeat, and then they'll laugh at you for being the most stupid Denounced of all time. Then while they're still laughing at you, they're going to put a rope around your neck and then pull the lever and watch you fall through the trap door, and the last thing you'll hear before your neck snaps is their howls of laughter.'

'Is that right,' I say.

I know I'm forcing my smile and trying to pretend I'm cool, but there's a sprinkling of truth in what Taylor is saying to me.

More than a sprinkling, really.

He's scaring me and he knows that he is.

His smile is more confident than mine and I wish I was a better actor than I am.

'You had it all, Ned. Ilse wanted you to be her protege. You were her Star Pupil and she was lining you up to be an Elite within the Powers-that-Be. We could have all ridden your wave. We could have all been Stars under you. You could have protected us all like you so desperately want to, but just in a different way. You could have had your own power-base. People would have pretended to follow the Powers-that-Be, but they would really be followers of Ned. Then after we had won the Unification War, you could have had it all. The Power. The Control. The Fame. The Digital Credits. You could have saved as many Denounced as you wanted. But more than all that. You could have had your Freedom. FREE… DOM. And you threw it away to prove your innocence. Something that's never going to happen. EV… ER. Watch my lips, Ned. EV… ER.'

'Shut up. You don't know what you're talking about.'

'Whatsup? You scared? You should be. The laughing, Ned. That's all you're going to hear. Laughter at your stupidity. The Denounced who was free and who returned to be hung.'

I start to sweat with anger and fear and hate.

I want my freedom, but I want it on my terms. I'm not a Denounced and I'm not Ilse's puppet or the Powers-that-Be or even Omar's.

I own myself and that's how it will always be.

'Listen to me, Ned.' Taylor's voice dropping to a guttural whisper. 'All you have to do is release me from these cuffs. Then we shake hands. Be partners. You and me. Then we go upstairs together and tell the crew to turn this boat around. The Powers-that-Be won't punish them for missing the next pick-up if it's you who returns. We'll be heroes, Ned. True Elites.'

'Forget it.'

He smiles.

'I tell you what. Why don't you wake the others and put it to the vote?'

'Their minds are made up. We're going home.'

'Your mind is made up. Spencer still wants revenge on our Quadrant, if I'm right. And I am. He's a real, man. You're the weak one, Ned. You think you're strong, but going back to our Quadrant is a sign of weakness not strength.'

Taylor raises his hands and presents them to me.

The rope we used to attach him to the steel ring in the wall goes taught.

He tugs at it hard and fast.

Anger and frustration fuelling his sneering smile.

'Come on, Ned. Let's put it to the vote? Or, even better, you can be a real leader and make a decision by letting me go. After you do, we'll head upstairs and do this thing they call destiny.'

I stand, slow and deliberate.

Taylor matches me.

He's hyped. He's been practicing his speech for days and now he's said his bit, he wants his answer.

I walk towards him.

There's a metre between us, less.

I can smell the hatred on his breath.

It's hot.

I can see it in his eyes.

It burns bright.

'The only person who is laughing is me… at you. I'm laughing, because you don't get it and never will. You should join us. We'd be stronger with you, I can't deny it.'

'I'm not going back.'

'You have no choice. Change is coming. Peaceful change. The System is going to fall and it's not going to be via a Unification War. No more hangings. No more Denounced. No more Doubters. We're all going to be free to choose our own lives.'

Taylor yanks at the rope, his anger boiling over.

'I'm going to kill you, Ned. And I'm going to enjoy doing it. Piece by piece.'

'We'll see about that,' I say, walking towards the Hold door.

'You're a coward. You always were and you always will be. I want you to come back and kick me in the teeth again. Kick me while I'm tied up.'

He yanks so hard at the rope it makes me turn back. I watch him kneel and he juts out his chin towards me.

'Come on. Do it. I know you want to. It'll make you feel good. It'll make you feel like a real man. Something you will never be. I'm giving you the chance to be an adult, even for a few split seconds.'

He starts to laugh at me.

It's low at first, but gets louder by the second and I think he looks more like a wild dog than any wild dog I've ever seen.

I turn again from him and put my hand on the handle of the Hold door.

'Ned?' He says.

There's something in his voice that makes me stop and turn back once more.

'What?' I say.

'Rasa.'

'What about her?'

'She's going to die and I'm going to bury you next to her.'

'Is that right,' I say, turning and stepping out of the Hold, closing the door behind me.

'Yeah, that's right,' he shouts, his voice echoing behind me.

ACKNOWLEDGEMENTS

At the risk of repeating the Acknowledgments from Book 1, *A Grey Sun*, I will be forever grateful for those who gave me their support so I could strive to be the writer I want to be. This book is for you, my new readers, and for the many friends I've accumulated along the way. I can't thank you enough.

However, in getting *Shifting Horizons* published, I would personally like to thank the following people:

Sara Starbuck who not only edited the book, but pushed me to improve it at every corner. Leila and Ali Dewji at *I AM Self-Publishing* who once again finalised the process and then joyfully helped me pull the trigger: www.iamselfpublishing.com. Binatang at 99-Designs for his artwork and book-cover design, and his continued patience with all my minor changes. Sheniz Dervish for encouraging me on.

And finally, to Aline Julia O'Dea – aka – my mum. She unfortunately passed away during the writing of this book and never saw the finished version. I want to thank her for so much and for so many things, but none more than the gift of life. Rest in Peace. I love you.

THE AUTHOR

If you have got this far then thank you for spending your precious time with my work. If you would like to know more about myself and my books then please visit: <u>www.sjsherwood.com</u>

Otherwise, feel free to contact me via my Contacts Page and I will personally answer any questions.

If you enjoyed *Shifting Horizons* or the first book *A Grey Sun*, I would appreciate your comments on my Amazon Review. They do really help!

And finally, I look forward to meeting you soon for the concluding and thrilling finale of The Denounced with *Creaking Dawn*.

SJ Sherwood.